A BREATH OF AIR...

in which the innocent savage
meets the savage civilized, and
love throws a sheltered beauty
into the arms of a questionable
hero—proves once again that
Miss Godden is a practiced con-
jurer of a high and powerful
order.

"In her characteristic way the
author unravels a fantastic but
believable story with great skill
and beauty." Library Journal

"This story of Miss Godden's casts a pretty spell;
it lulls the imagination with its picture of languorous living where every pleasure is available..."
Edward Weeks, The Atlantic

"Confected with admirable skill."
J. H. Jackson, San Francisco Chronicle

"Here is an idyllic tale ... with her imaginative
quality, the skilled craftsmanship and originality
of her style, the artistry of her storytelling ...
Rumer Godden has woven into (A Breath of Air)
much of her own magic." Virginia Kirkus

Other SIGNET Novels You Will Enjoy

ISLANDIA *by Austin Tappan Wright*
A young American goes to live in a 20th century Utopian society where the people are technologically primitive, but highly sophisticated in their understanding of life's meaning. "One of the most remarkable examples of ingenuity in the history of literary invention."—Clifton Fadiman. (#Y2870—$1.25)

THE STRODE VENTURER *by Hammond Innes*
This highly acclaimed adventure novel is the story of an idealistic young Englishman who flees his family's cynical financial dealings and goes to live and work among the oppressed natives of the Maldive Islands. (#P3029—60¢)

THE TEAHOUSE OF THE AUGUST MOON
by Vern Sneider
The hilarious chronicle of what happened when the American Army tried to "democratize" an Okinawan village. (#T3284—75¢)

THE THREE SIRENS *by Irving Wallace*
What happens to a varied group of American men and women when they encounter the sexual freedoms of an unspoiled South Sea island. (#T2523—75¢)

A
BREATH OF AIR

Rumer Godden

A SIGNET BOOK

Published by The New American Library

SIGNET TRADEMARK REG. U.S. PAT. OFF. AND FOREIGN COUNTRIES
REGISTERED TRADEMARK—MARCA REGISTRADA
HECHO EN CHICAGO, U.S.A.

SIGNET BOOKS are published by
The New American Library, Inc.,
1301 Avenue of the Americas, New York, New York 10019

PRINTED IN THE UNITED STATES OF AMERICA

*And, sowing the kernels of it in the sea,
bring forth more islands.*

—THE TEMPEST

*(from which I have also taken
the story of the book.* R. G.*)*

CHAPTER I

THE noise that the Water Star made as she came down out to sea sounded on the island like the humming of an insect, but it was in the very early morning when most insects are asleep. A few islanders, out early, looked up at the sky; they knew of aeroplanes but, seeing nothing, they went on with their daily business. The men out with the fishing boats were more puzzled, but none of them was as far out to sea as the Hat, and no one saw her settle with a first splash on the water. They shrugged their shoulders and went back to their fishing.

The island was the island Mānoa, now called Terraqueous, in the Indian Pacific, long. 123.15E, lat. 11.40S.

CHAPTER II

IF A magician's stick had been waved and the island had appeared out of the sea, Valentine could not have been more surprised to see it.

"Did your father make a spell?" he asked Charis afterwards. He laughed as he asked it, but then it had been no laughing matter. They had been far out, over the sea, when the engine gave its first cough. "Christ!" said McGinty, but Valentine did not turn back; instead he flew on. "What made me fly on then?" he asked afterwards. "It was damn stupidity. Perhaps I was light-headed."

McGinty thought so. "You're flaming crazy!" cried McGinty. "If we come down on that sea we'll break up. And even if we don't break up, they'll never find us. Skipper! Val! For Christ's sake!"

"Shut up!" said Valentine.

He looked at the altimeter which had at last come to rest. It showed five thousand and dropping. The engine coughed again, and he looked down into the twilight gulf.

"For Christ's sake," McGinty began again.

"Look," said Valentine.

A mark lay like a slur on the horizon. Valentine had not seen it himself until that moment. The engine spluttered and, in a minute or two, ceased. "Can you make it?" McGinty's voice was a whisper. His face was white.

Valentine did not answer. He was listening. As the engines ceased the plane became all sound, the sound of flying; out of the air, muted, except for her own sound, the Water Star glided down on the island that seemed to rise, as island in a transformation scene, out of the sea to meet her, assuming height and contours. Now Valentine saw it was too far away, but nearer was its satellite, a small rock island rising from a cream edge of lather, and as they circled, coming down on it, it was the shape of a hat, its brim the lather of breaking waves, its crown a hill of greyish rock from which floated a trail of smoke like a feather. "Volcanic," said Valentine.

The other island was now impossibly far away, a long shape, blue with distance, rising into a mountain. "We can't reach it," said Valentine, and presently, gently, he brought the Water Star down in the bay of the hat island. The water came up round the Water Star, deluging her, and then sank away, leaving them rocking on a dark swell where the rollers might have been whalebacks rising and falling.

"Where the hell are we?" asked McGinty. He was not ungrateful for the island, but his fright had made his voice shrill and angry. He released the pin of his harness and shook it off and climbed out on the float.

Here, on the surface of the sea, it was barely light. The Water Star heaved and rose drunkenly on the swell, wing

8

up, wing down, but her life and impetus were gone. Mc-Ginty chafed at her helplessness but to Valentine there came an extraordinary sense of rest. "We might be any-place!" said McGinty, looking at the bare rocks, the surf, and the twilight sea; even to him his voice sounded small in the emptiness. "We're lost," said McGinty.

Valentine shook his head.

"What else are we?" asked McGinty aggressively.

"Safe," said Valentine and shut his eyes.

He did not want to be disturbed; the sounds of that first sea morning beat softly on the air, sounds empty of life except for the sounds of birds and of waves. To Valentine it felt like the first morning of a new world. Was that because I had thought we should not see morning again? he thought. He was reluctant to speak or move; he felt he must begin to live and stir slowly, gently, as embryo life stirred, letting time uncoil itself. He rested, lulled by the sound of the surf, but beside him McGinty fidgeted. Valentine knew that if he did not speak first McGinty would; reluctantly he half opened his eyes. The first sunlight had come down on the sea, and it struck his eyes with brightness, dazzling him; he felt it on his lids. "And there was light," said Valentine and shut his eyes again.

McGinty took no notice. He was used to Valentine. He had been with him since Valentine bought his Proctor, the Water Star, and they had done a good few hundreds of hours together. "Clever chap but talks punk!" McGinty would have said of Valentine.

Valentine would talk in poetry for an hour or more, and McGinty had long ago learned not to listen, though bits, words, and phrases had seeped into his mind and sometimes came up unexpectedly among his own limited stock of words.

"I wonder where we are," said McGinty restlessly again. "There's nothing here but rocks. We must get to that other island. I wonder what it is." Valentine sighed and opened his eyes. There was nothing to give them a clue; there was only this small conical island and the bigger island that lay behind it. "What island could it be?" asked McGinty.

His young pink face was strained with tiredness, his

9

eyes looked sore. Valentine knew he must be bruised and chilled and stiff and hungry, as he was himself, but McGinty was McGinty still. "I am I," McGinty said to all the world. "You are you," and unless people were the same as he and things were accustomed, he had no way of participating in them. Nothing that impinged on McGinty was allowed to alter him. To Valentine that had seemed a virtue; now, suddenly, he found it irritating. He ought to be shocked at the very least, thought Valentine. He ought to be shaken out of himself after a night like that.

Valentine yawned and stretched as much as he was able in his seat; he was reluctant to move, but he knew he must do something: he looked at the journey log, looked at his watch, added in the landing time. "That last leg was eleven hours, nineteen minutes," he told McGinty. "With the winds in that weather, God knows how many miles we are out of course."

"And I wonder where that storm hatched itself out from?" said McGinty resentfully. "There shouldn't have been a storm. The met had nothing to say when we left."

All trace of storm had vanished from the light though there was an extra coolness in the wind and darker colours in the sea; the morning was cool, clear, and as indifferent as a child. "But don't be deceived," said Valentine. "Indifferent, yes, but not a child," and he remembered the first moment in the darkening light when the Water Star seemed to have been lifted and dropped, with the force of a lift down a shaft, into a void of darkness in which she was not flown but blown by the wind, lifted and dropped and hurled and twanged. Sometimes we must have gone down a sheer five hundred feet or more and come up with a big enough jolt to make you think we had hit the sea, thought Valentine. He remembered how McGinty's eyes had rolled round to look at him and at the St. Elmo's fire that ran in two vague balls on the wing tips and made a halo in the arc of the propeller. McGinty had not seen a storm like this.

"If we had hit a big cu-nimb," said Valentine to McGinty now, "it would have broken us up like a matchbox!"

McGinty nodded. "And the bloody radio going dead!"

said McGinty. Everything that McGinty relied upon had failed him.

Valentine had been afraid to use up petrol in an attempt to climb up above the weather, and he could not use the sextant. The rain on the windshield was so heavy that they might have been under the sea, except for the violent bucketing and dropping of the plane. They were shaken and chilled to the bone. They did not have time or a smooth enough moment for coffee.

Valentine still felt, now, as if he were in the plane, his hands still gripping the wheel, his body pulling back as he tried to lift it, feeling each gulf and abyss of air; his head was still spinning and seemed at first large, and then to shrink away to a pin-head. At last there had come a curious suffusing of light round the plane, a paleness in the blackness, paleness without light, creeping. McGinty touched Valentine's arm; far off, high up on the port wing tip, was a crack of light. It swung below their feet as the Water Star tilted; as they dropped it rose, and dropped as they came up, and, gradually, the blackness dimmed and grew pale, and Valentine saw McGinty's lips shape "Dawn," and he nodded. He remembered now how his neck had hurt as he nodded. Five minutes later they had broken out of the storm and were in a clear sky.

They had looked down and found they were flying over a faintly glimmering sea scattered with islands. Beyond them a wide sea stretched like a gulf. "Flying west a half-north," Valentine had said. "We must be hundreds of miles out of our way."

"Bet we'll be running pretty low on juice, Skipper," said McGinty. "Why not come down here?" And it was then that Valentine had shaken his head.

"For God's sake," said McGinty, "you're not going to take her out over that sea! If we come down there we've had it!" But Valentine flew straight on.

~~~~~~~~It is said, when a ship moves, she loses her hull. The rubber dinghy had no hull, but she came on airily towards the larger island, buoyant on the swell, two

11

streams of bubbles in her wake and small inundations shining where the paddles had pitted the sea.

From far off the larger island had seemed itself to be floating in the air, a pale blue cumulus miraged above scintillating water; but, as they paddled nearer, in the increasing light it began to detach itself from its background and stand out clearly, with a cloud to cap its mountain; it gave the mountain a look of being capped with snow and drawn up into infinity. "It always seemed larger than it was," said Valentine afterwards. He might have said it seemed like the whole world.

The island was familiar to Valentine, and he knew why. Everyone, at some time or another, has visited an island or had an island of his own, a coral island, a desert island, a treasure or Swiss Family Robinson island, an island of the mind. To Valentine this one was so familiar that it was stereotyped. It opened on a crescent bay that had a settlement of native huts and trees at the far end.

"There are people here," said McGinty with satisfaction.

Valentine felt it was almost a pity. "Yes. There's a town," he said and sighed.

McGinty sighed too; if that were all the town it was serious for them.

Flying fish went past them, sprinkling them with light drops and pocking the waves. The sun had grown stronger, and where they dipped their paddles the water broke into infinitesimal rainbows, small arcs and prisms of colour. The rainbows seemed significant to Valentine and he remembered that, no matter how stereotyped his islands had been, they were always magical to him. He lifted his head to look at the sweep of white sand along the margin of the bay, at the green above it and the hill with its white cloud, and in that moment he had from the island a sense of music, invisible music that crept by him on the water. All music is invisible, argued Valentine, or is it called invisible when its source can't be seen? This, if it were music, which his sense denied though his ears heard it, was intrinsic in the island itself; if it were anything, it was wind and water music, and he could see the waves, even the wind that suddenly wrinkled the sea.

Nonsense! said Valentine severely to himself. It isn't music at all. But still the music persisted.

Valentine was, by habit, cool and sure; he refused to be anything else. "I want my head in the clouds but my feet on the ground," said Valentine. He was sometimes asked, "Mr. Doubleday, what is the secret of your great success?" "Only that I haven't a secret," Valentine answered, and he always said, "I work."

That was true. He had worked passionately. To the outside world his rise had been surprising; to Valentine it had been logically slow. "I started at ten," he might have said. "I was ten when I went into *Pelican Pie*. It has been twenty years. Twenty years is a long time, and mine have been twice as long because I worked twice as hard." He was well named Doubleday, because he fitted in twice as much as most people into each day. "I don't remember much of the first ten years," said Valentine, "but you can double my twenty." He found, to his surprise, that made him fifty years old. "That is nearer my age," said Valentine. He felt at least fifty; he was tired. Bone tired, thought Valentine. Perhaps I am tired out.

He did not know. He felt worse than tired. He felt unutterably stale. For the past few weeks—months? years? thought Valentine, he had had a distaste for life; lately he had not been able to sleep and it was difficult to talk or eat or work. "I can't *work!*" the words burst from him in a frenzy of worry. The more he worried, the worse he worked. I used to work easily; now I can't work at all. What has happened to me? thought Valentine. Why can't I get back to what I was before? Now he rested his paddle on his knees and the music sounded in his ear, the music that he said was nonsense.

"It's not a town," McGinty was saying in disgust. "It's hardly a village, just some huts." He was looking through Valentine's glasses. "I don't see a road," said McGinty, turning the glasses, "or anything that you could call a building. There doesn't seem to be any life about."

"If there are huts there must be islanders," said Valentine.

"It looks a one-horse place to me," said McGinty.

"I don't see even one horse," said Valentine. He was wrong. There was one horse.

13

Their arms and backs and shoulders and legs were aching; they seemed to have been paddling this clumsy dinghy for an æon; when an eddy of current caught it, it sometimes spun round or moved like a crab sideways. Valentine's neck hurt and his head at the temples felt stretched. His feet were cold and his whole body felt chilled though he was sweating; he was clammy with sweat.

"What a goddam place to get landed in," said Mc-Ginty, looking morosely towards the island.

"For God's sake!" snapped Valentine. "Can't you wait till we have landed before you start to crab it?"

"I only said—" McGinty's voice was surly.

"Yes, I know," said Valentine.

"It's you who want to get back," said McGinty. "It's your play we're tearing back for, not mine."

"Yes, I know," said Valentine wearily again. He looked at the dispatch case between his feet. He had automatically picked it up when they left the Water Star. Now he came to think of it, he wondered why they had not taken anything else, not as much as a razor. Well, I suppose we shall come back, he thought, but the thought seemed to have no certainty in his mind. Everything seemed drifting, cut loose. The dinghy wallowed and turned round clumsily; they seemed to be making no headway at all. The sun was getting higher. We must have been all of two hours, thought Valentine.

"We have to get petrol, don't we?" McGinty was asking aggrieved. He looked again towards the shore, at the trees and dots of huts. "How the hell will there be any petrol there?"

"There won't," said Valentine.

"Well then?" asked McGinty aggressively.

"Well then?" said Valentine. He was almost too tired to care.

Imperceptibly they were coming nearer the island. The current brought them nearer, and they rounded a promontory that up till then they had not seen; it ran out, making a headland above the sea. A house came into view, standing in trees, a house like the native houses, thatched and brown-walled, but a large house. Valentine took the glasses from McGinty and, looking through

14

them, saw flowering trees above lawns and steps leading down to the beach, where boats lay at anchor and a jetty was built out into the water on wooden poles; it looked empty, rapt. Then he saw that smoke was going up from the back and a flag was flying from a flagpole and fluttering on the breeze, a flag of blue and white. Valentine looked at the flag, the house, the smooth lawns and plumes of blossoming trees. "Someone discovered this island before we did," he said.

"It must be someone white," said McGinty. "No wog would keep a garden like that."

"What about the garden of Eden," said Valentine. "Adam was a wog."

"He wasn't!" McGinty was beginning indignantly when the dinghy came up with a bump against something that was floating in the sea.

At first it looked like two pig-bodies floating, swollen in death; then they saw that they were two canvas bags, fastened to a floating cork that was dragging an end of chain and must have broken loose from a buoy. The bags were padlocked and sealed and labelled. "Mail," said Valentine. Gingerly leaning over, he dragged them to the side of the dinghy.

"Careful! You'll have us over!" said McGinty.

Valentine read the labels. "J. van Loomis" and a date. The date was eighteen months old. "You were right," he told McGinty. "It's a white man," and he looked towards the house. "Castle van Loomis, I think," he said. "We had better put in there."

"Better go down to the village," said McGinty. "Can't call it a town. The current is taking us there, and it would be a job to paddle against it, back to the house. They will have seen us, won't they? If there is any petrol, it will more likely be in the town than in a house. Let's get on." He looked at the mail bags as Valentine held them floating at the side of the dinghy. "Better take those in."

McGinty pulled them round and tied them behind the dinghy. "We shall want this van Loomis to help us," he said. "May as well start off on the right foot. You would think *someone* would have found them," said McGinty, looking round. There were dots of boats far out to sea to the right of them. "Fishing boats," said McGinty. "They

15

should have come across them, but all natives are damn lazy. We can tow them." Pulled down by the weight of the bags, they kept a straighter course, and the current took them more quickly now towards the little town.

The sun had begun to warm Valentine; he felt it soaking into him, and his body was comforted. Drowsiness began to fill his head, and more and more he felt as if he were dreaming. He half shut his eyes, leaving their direction to McGinty, letting his paddle steer slightly against the side of the dinghy, letting the current take them.

"Wake up, Skip!" said McGinty sharply. Valentine jerked into half-wakefulness. "I said that six times!" said McGinty. His young face was severe.

"Why say it at all?" said Valentine. "Why . . . bother to wake up?"

CHAPTER III

IT WAS before breakfast that same morning that Charis van Loomis had caught the houseboy Filipino kissing one of the housemaids, Flora Annie.

There was nothing in that; on the island boys and girls were always kissing, and a kiss was particularly nothing to Filipino; he kissed as lightly as a swallow flies. It was not only the kiss; it was that the storm had given Charis a wakeful night and had seemed to bring to a head all her other wakeful nights, her restlessness and tossing; she was restless because she was continually stabbed by tiresome, painful thoughts. Now she had a further bitter little stab: it was that she was four years older than Flora Annie and never had been kissed; she never would be kissed, never could be, because there was no one to kiss her. On the island Charis was alone of her kind; for her there were no Filipinos, no moment, for her, as this was for Flora Annie, who had flicked away round the corner with a

16

burst of giggling laughter and a flutter of red and white cloth. It was this that made Charis rude to her father, Mr. van Loomis, at breakfast.

The breakfast table was laid on the veranda by a balustrade where orange bignonia creeper grew and swung and hid it from the sea; but, through its tendrils and keys of flowers, Charis could look at the sky and across lawns and flowers and pink and white cassia trees to a cascade of morning glory, the great royal blue convolvulus that grew looped on bamboo arches above the flight of steps. Grass and trees and bushes were still dripping from the storm; the lawn was strewn with leaves and scattered blossom, and the garden boys with wet naked legs were picking up branches and twigs and sweeping the paths, while the grave young gardener. Resurrection, was walking by the beds, looking at what the night had done to his flowers. Squirrels ran up and down the trees; on the trunk of one of them a woodpecker moved his gaudy head as he tapped. It was not warm enough yet for the butterflies, but the lizards were out on the walls or on any stones that had caught the sun.

The table was laid with silky grass mats, thin china, silver, and a bowl of flowers. There was coffee, the pot of island pottery, the coffee from bushes that Mr. van Loomis had cultivated. There was brown bread and white bread and oatcake and the island thin unleavened bread cakes. There was honey and butter and wild orange marmalade. There was grilled fish and home-cured ham and eggs, and melons and oranges, pomegranates and grapes. None of this pleased Charis. She looked across the table with stormy eyes and said, "I'm sorry I was rude, Father, but I want to know."

"Why now?" said Mr. van Loomis with a sigh. "You have never asked before. Why now? Why?"

"Why? Go and ask a bird why it flies," Charis might have said. "Or an ant why it makes a little heap or a turtle why it comes up the beach to lay its eggs in the sand; ask a moth about the lamp that burns its wings or a foal why it turns into a horse, or even grass inanimate—or is it animate?—why it grows. Because the time is come," Charis might have said, but she only looked more stormy and said again, "I want to know."

17

"What could you possibly want to know that I haven't taught you?" asked Mr. van Loomis. "I have taught you everything."

"Not those sort of things," said Charis. "I want to know real things," and she cried miserably, "I don't know *anything!*"

"You are very ungrateful," said Mr. van Loomis, helping himself to fish and toast and butter. The cook's eleven-year-old son, Webster, made the toast, squatting down with his back to them in front of a small brazier so that Mr. van Loomis should have it piping hot. "You have been taught as scarcely any girls are taught," said Mr. van Loomis severely, buttering his toast. "You have had my undivided attention since you were a year old, or almost undivided," said Mr. van Loomis. "I have had . . . er . . . other things to see to," he said more severely. "Things you wouldn't understand. You were only a little girl."

"I'm not a little girl now," said Charis. "I am nearly twenty-one." She knew what Mr. van Loomis meant by other things. There were relations that were called part-brothers and sisters on the island. Charis found herself wondering, suddenly, if she had part-brothers and sisters; she remembered a house on another part of the island where she had once ridden, and her father and Pheasant who were never angry had been angry; there was a child there, Charis remembered, that had blue eyes; perhaps more than one child. Charis fixed her own eyes on her father and said, "Have you ever seen an island man with blue eyes?" and then blushed herself as she realized that he was blushing.

Charis, thought Mr. van Loomis, is not as lovable as she was as a child. Instead of listening when he talked to her, now she seemed to have thoughts of her own. It seemed to Mr. van Loomis that she was trying to trap him, but Charis was not thinking of Mr. van Loomis, she was thinking of herself. Yes, I am nearly twenty-one, thought Charis.

Mr. van Loomis was eating fish caught offshore by his second boat boy that morning; it had been grilled on pointed sticks over a wood fire, as he had taught his cook Serendipity to cook it; it was delicious but he scarcely noticed it; he was disturbed. Charis was eating nothing; she played with a piece of toast and looked at the table with eyes that were resentful and, Mr. van Loomis feared, inclined to be tearful; he could not bear tears, particularly Charis's tears. Charis cried so seldom that there must be something really wrong. Flora Annie had run full tilt into him round the corner that morning; he had an inkling of what it was; it left him helpless.

"Shall I call Pheasant?" he said.

"*Pheasant!*" said Charis scornfully.

Pheasant had been Charis's nurse, but lately, mysteriously, they had changed places and Pheasant was now the child, Charis the grown-up one. Pheasant was too fat, too comfortable, to recognize these tremblings and stirrings that had grown almost to an agony in Charis. Pheasant was simple; she would call them growing pains. "Pheasant!" said Charis as if she spoke down her nostrils not through her lips.

"Very well, I won't call her," said Mr. van Loomis meekly.

While he and Charis were safely at breakfast the servants and their relations and friends gathered in the courtyard outside the kitchen for gossip and tea. They squatted down on their hams, contentedly playing the island game of knacker, a kind of draughts, or smoking their abominably smelling green cigars, or eating slices of Mr. van Loomis's melons. They were all there under the lichee tree that grew in the centre of the court.

Round Niu, the head man, there was a little space of respect. Niu was old, dried to an extraordinary lightness and thinness; he was small and black (the islanders said "black" or "fair" for the dark or pale brown of their skins); Niu's skin was not wrinkled but stretched to a papery thinness so that he had the look of a monkey skull; his grey switch of hair was combed back from his large forehead, his eyes were big and mournful and reserved. He was dressed in the island "cloth," a length of cloth, white or dyed with vegetable dyes, and worn round the waist, hanging to above the ankles and pleated in folds from the waist knot in front; all the islanders wore cloths, but Niu wore what they did not, flat grass slippers with flapping heels that let them hear him everywhere he went. Once upon a time Niu had been chief on the island; Mr. van Loomis kept Niu at his right hand so that he always knew where he was, and the slippers told the islanders. For all that, Niu remained unfathomable and secret.

Next to him in honourable place came Pheasant. Mr. van Loomis had brought her as a young Negress from Puerto when he himself came, and she had stayed on the island ever since. It was he who had named her Pheasant because her plumpness, especially her plump neck, and her glossy colours reminded him of pheasants. As if starting from that, Pheasant had become the island namer. She had named all the island babies born round the house and in the villages near since she came. Pheasant's names were distinguished and various. She could read but not with understanding, and she took them for their sound from the outsides of Mr. van Loomis's books, sometimes the title, sometimes the author's name, sometimes the publisher's, but it had a way of being the right name. She had successfully named such different people as the big cowman Hutchinson, Niu's young twin grandson, the grave young gardener Resurrection, and Orange Flower's curly-headed baby Golden Treasury.

Pheasant was not plump now, she was fat; with good eating and soft living she had grown immense, but she was still spotless, still capable, still busy; Mr. van Loomis would not have kept her else. She was too fat to sit on the ground, and she sat now on a low stool with her sewing. Pheasant was the only woman on the island who sewed; she had taught Charis, but Charis was enough of an islander to go without it.

Near Pheasant in the shade of the lichee tree was Serendipity the cook, the head gardener, and the first boatman Luck. This was the place of honour. Near them again were the two young housemaids, Orange Flower and Flora Annie, the gardeners, the boatmen, and the young groom. Farther off were the wash girls, the spinning and weaving girls, the cook boys, the garden boys, and the sweeping boys. It took a great many island servants to do a little work, but that made it more enjoyable; they enjoyed being with one another, and the house and garden sounded with a happy hum of voices and laughter. The maids giggled as they ran steaming cloths two by two

20

along the wood floors of the corridors and verandas, polished now to a dark, mirrored smoothness; three gardeners pruned one bush, two cook boys rubbed soup through a muslin, two men stained one small boat.

Niu kept separate, his slippers flapping their signal as he went, and there was another being who kept separate, and that was Niu's elder grandson, the houseboy who had kissed Flora Annie, the young man Filipino.

Filipino was an uneasy being; he upset all the other young men. Niu had kept him in hand, but, more and more, it was becoming impossible to keep a hand on Filipino.

Pheasant had named him Filipino, an exception to her usual names, because he was a twin. He was born the year they came to the island. Twins were rare there. When Pheasant was sent for to come with a name, she arrived with a name for a boy, Ressurrection, but there was another, unexpected baby. "Well, name him, name him," said the islanders, crowding into the hut. It was a bad moment for Pheasant; she valued her prestige and Mr. van Loomis's library was far away. She licked her lips and stood uneasily. "Give him a name." She looked down at the pale brown morsels of babies and suddenly she had a vision of two small kernels in a nut—and she called him Filipino.

Filipino was not noisy; he was airy. He would not sit in the servants' sprawling quarters round the kitchen; he would not sleep in his grandfather's house, though, nominally, he was supposed to live there. He had built himself a small open hut on the shore under a palm tree, by some chema bushes that grew there in the sand; there he lay, when he could, on his string bed, not sleeping but propped on his elbows, his chin on his hands, gazing far out to sea. "What did he see?" the islanders asked him. There was nothing to see, but Filipino saw marvellous things. It made the islanders uneasy; nothing Filipino did would have astonished them; if he had been seen on a bat's back they would not have been surprised.

Even Charis could not always follow where his mind went; she knew he had a range that she had not. She had thought much of Filipino, admired him, confided in him; they had been companions. Now Charis saw him kissing

21

Flora Annie and shut her eyes in pain. Lately things had changed with Filipino; she had thought it was she who had changed, but if Filipino were going after girls, that left her finally behind. To Filipino, Charis was a cloud, a standard, something white and high above him, who led him and was told his dreams. It had not occurred to anyone that Charis too was an island girl.

To island eyes, Charis was very plain, and she, naturally, had island eyes. As she had never seen a white woman she could judge herself only from the faces she saw round her; she could compare herself, for instance, only with Flora Annie. Flora Annie was acknowledged to be a beauty; she had a golden skin flushed with health, ripe red lips, and pearly little teeth like a child's that showed when she smiled; her eyes were iridescent, and she had long rippling blue-black hair that she wore twisted up in a knot with a flower; she wore shells or flowers in her ears that showed every time she moved her pretty neck; her neck ran down in softness to her breasts that came up pointed and swelling from the scarf she wore or did not wear tied loosely round them. Charis wore short-sleeved blouses sewn by Pheasant and held in by a wide sash tied round her waist over her cloth; she was the only young woman on the island whose breasts were never seen. The difference was like her white skin, and though her breasts were hidden, they were strangely conspicuous; it gave her a sense of being pilloried. She felt colourless beside the other girls; even their toenails were deep pink while hers were pale, and there was no nail polish on the island. Charis had not heard of nail polish; she used to rub her nails to make them glow, but the glow soon faded.

Charis looked at herself in an old mirror that had been her mother's and that Mr. van Loomis had brought to the island from the home he would not talk of, the home where Charis was born. It was strange to think her mother's face had looked into the same mirror; Charis wondered if hers had been as pale? As ugly, thought Charis, as mine? Her face was not ugly; she had her father's forehead that was distinctly noble, and hers was an improvement on his in that she had none of the obstinancy that he showed in heaviness round his eyes and in the set

22

of his ears; Charis's ears, though unadorned with shells (another of the differences her father had ordained), were set exceedingly well; her nose was straight and so were her eyebrows, straight and uncompromising; her eyes were unmistakably fine, and she had a pleasing fall of mouse-brown hair. It was true that her teeth were not like pearls—she had the usual European teeth—and beside the island girls her body was small and light and immature, and that made her feel inferior again; it was strange that Charis, the island queen, should often feel inferior but . . . Orange Flower is no older than I am, thought Charis, and she has had a baby and is expecting another. I suppose I could have a baby too, thought Charis. I could have had three or four by now . . . but she did not really believe it. She seemed too small, and she sighed again. She was convinced she was hideous. She had never heard of the word "facile," so that she could not apply it to the island girls; she had no way of measuring what she was that they were not; she knew only that she was not what they were.

Charis's lot on the island was queenly, but it was not enviable; if she were near-royalty, she was very lonely. She heard the laughter and banter from the servants' quarters, she saw the groups of boys and girls on the beach, playing in the surf and wandering off into the woods and along the shore for picnics. Picnics reached their peak each spring in the courtship month that waxed in excitement as the moon grew full. It was the courtship month now. Charis sighed.

"Why can't I go for a picnic?" she had asked last year.

"You can't," Mr. van Loomis had answered shortly. He would say no more than that.

"But I want to go for a picnic," she said to Pheasant.

Pheasant too had said, "You can't do dat." Pheasant sounded scandalized.

"I shall," said Charis.

"Not while Ah got breaf!" said Pheasant.

"Why can't I?"

"You kin come foh a picnic with yo' ole Pheasant, mah lamb. Jest you an' me."

"That wouldn't be a picnic," said Charis, and Pheasant

was shocked. "Ah sho' gwine speak ter yo' Pa 'bout you," said Pheasant.

For Charis the island was almost as unpeopled as if the islanders had been spirits and only her father and she had been alive on it. Tears pricked her eyelids as she sat behind the coffee pot, but, at Mr. van Loomis's look, she blinked them away.

Yet, up to a little while ago, she had been perfectly happy; hers had been a halcyon childhood; she had her beautiful, orderly, well-regulated home, her father's and Pheasant's love and care; she had the adulation or, at least, the respect of the servants and islanders; and she had the whole island of sun and beauty and balmy content. Nothing ugly or rough or frightening had ever come near the small Charis. She had her pets, her birds and dogs and her white pony, Dominion, the only pony on the island; the pony was called Dominion because, her father said, it gave her dominion over palm and pine; on Dominion she rode from end to end of the island and from the shore to the pines on the mountaintop. She had her garden and books and toys; she had her lessons with her father, and, if they were stern and hard and trying, she was enough of a scholar to like to be tried; she had the physical pleasures of intense well-being, of swimming in the warm-surfed sea, of sunbathing, of walking and riding, of fishing with her father and the boatmen. She had all these things still, but all of them were spoilt. "Why spoil them?" Charis asked Charis. "Why let this rise up and spoil it all?" The answer was that she could not help it. It had begun with Mario.

She remembered, when she was reading *The Cherry Orchard,* she had found Anya's cry, *"What have you done to me, Petya, that I no longer love the cherry orchard?"* It was not only Petya's talk, it was also Petya himself who had done that to Anya. Charis had thought so much of Anya and other girls she read of that they had become real to her: Rosalind and Emma, Becky, Dora, and Anna Karenina; she used to pretend they were her sisters; now they were no use as sisters. They were only ink and paper, all that happened to them was there in black and white. Charis did not know what had happened to her except that, for her, it was not Petya; it was Mario.

She saw that clearly now. Sitting at the breakfast table, she could have cried, "What have you done to me, Mario, that I no longer love the island?"

Mr. van Loomis and Charis and Pheasant were not the only aliens on the island. When they had come there they had found Mario's mother installed. She was a Spanish woman, married to a minor island chief, but she had kept her own name, and Mario was called Mario Fernandes. She had been a strange, coarse, cruel, wrathful woman, who had made her imprint on the whole island and ousted its chief, Niu's father, from his right.

On the island, if anyone chose to oust you, you did not oppose them, but, if unspeakably oppressed, without argument you put an end to the oppressor. You did not quarrel or argue: you killed. Mario's mother lived, and it was this simple fact that told the islanders she was a witch; nothing could be done against her. It was rumoured that she had killed her own husband because he protested against her taking other people's chickens, but, when Mr. van Loomis came, he seemed to have no fear of witches. He kept Mario's mother in her house, stopped all her traffic with the people, and, though she was violently angry, presently it was she who died. Then the people knew that Mr. van Loomis was a magician.

He did everything he could to enhance this belief. He had a barometer, and he read the winds and weather better than the islanders could; he had a burning lens with which he kindled fires to astonish them, and there was his far-seeing eye, the telescope, and the twin eyes of his field glasses, which, it was reported, could make things large and small, near or far, according to which way you looked through them. The reports came from Filipino, who, alone on the island, dared to touch them, but even Filipino did not know how so much power came to be shut in such small space. Filipino looked things up in Mr. van Loomis's dictionary or encyclopædia, but he had not yet turned up the chapter on lenses.

Mario's mother had had no rights or titles in the island, but, after her death, Mr. van Loomis remembered that her unprepossessing son was half-European and had taken him into his home and tried to bring him up and teach him. Mario was not teachable; he was sullen and

25

stupid and simple. Mr. van Loomis took him fishing, tried to teach him good manners, a little English, to read and write, and some astronomy, which he believed all people should study to give them a sense of proportion. Mario caught new fish, he remained as uncouth as he had been before, his English was nearly incomprehensible, he hardly knew the first letters of the alphabet, and beyond knowing the moon from the sun he learned nothing about astronomy.

From the beginning Charis had disliked him; she said that he was hideous and thick. Charis was not tolerant, but Mario was thick-bodied, thick-necked, thick-jowled, thick-fingered; even his tumbling black hair was too thick; he looked like a young bull animal. He knew that Charis did not like him, and that made him follow her and tease her.

"This-a island belong-a me," said Mario in his peculiar jargon.

"It belongs to my father," said Charis proudly.

"No-a, mine. Mine. Mine but you-a not-a care," said Mario, teasing. "When you-a get big, I-a marry you."

"No!" cried Charis in horror.

"No else for you-a marry," said Mario, and that was true.

Whether those conversations shadowed anything in his mind she did not know, but, one evening a few weeks ago, she had met Mario in the corridor outside her room as she was going to bed. It was late. Mr. van Loomis was walking in the garden; Pheasant and the servants were gone to their huts; no one was near. Mario stood against the wall to watch her pass, and Charis stopped. She had sniffed a new smell on Mario. She knew the smell: it was the islander's drink, arrack. She was quite used to the islanders' drinking; when they were drunk they became merry and, afterwards, sleepy. She had not been alarmed or disgusted when she had smelled that smell on her pony groom or on the boatman, but she did not like it on Mario. Mario was not an islander. She stiffened and waited to let him pass her, but Mario did not move.

"You don't like me do you, Princess Charis," he said in Spanish. "Ya sé que no te gusto, Princesa Charis!" When he was tired or cross or distressed or drunk he lapsed fluently into his mother tongue. "Ya sé que no te gusto! You don't like me," he said.

"No," said Charis.

"Come here. Ven aquí."

Charis did not come. Her back against the wall, she looked at him with scornful eyes, but she felt her hands suddenly cold.

"Shall I come and get you, Santa Charis?"

Charis's usually good sense left her. She knew it was foolish to move from the wall, but, when Mario came at her, she screamed and ran down the corridor. Mario was slow on his great feet, but at her door he caught her and dragged her into her room. Charis could still see the shadowed quiet look of the airy white cave that was her bedroom, and she had still the horrible sense that Mario had defiled it. She could still feel his hands on her as he dragged her, undignified, to the bed, her feet slipping and sliding on the matting. At that moment Mr. van Loomis stepped out of his dressing-room next door.

She had not seen Mario again, but Pheasant had told her that he had been sent to the lighthouse on the rocks.

"Mario wanted to co. . . . cohabitate with me, didn't he?" she asked now, wrinkling her forehead. Mr. van Loomis winced; he had taught her to say what she meant in plain words, but these were too plain. "But 'co' means 'with,' from the Latin 'cum,' " said Charis thoughtfully, "and I wasn't with Mario, was I? I was against him. What is the word Blake uses?" asked the literary Charis. "You know, in the 'Daughters of Albion?'—'catch for thee girls of mild silver and furious gold.' " I wonder if I am mild silver or furious gold? she thought. She was afraid she was mild silver. "Yes, copulation is a better word, though it begins with 'co' as well." She leaned her chin on her hands as she sat with her elbows on the table (no one had ever taught her to keep them off); then she said to her father, "If we had copulated, would I have been his wife?"

"Good God! No!" said Mr. van Loomis, and his nerve broke. "You are not to talk like that."

"What would I have been then?" asked Charis, and this little question entered into Mr. van Loomis and rankled. He knew, now, what he had really known before and known for weeks, that the time had come when he must think seriously of the future of his daughter. He had brought her to the island quite forgetting that she would grow up, and here she was, grown. She was a young woman now, and he remembered with sinking spirits that young women were utterly puzzling; that, full of heart, they were curiously heartless; that, when there was no reason why they should not be plain as pie, they were deep as wells; that they were absurdly vulnerable and absurdly foolhardy. "Damnation!" said Mr. van Loomis.

Out on the sea, in the dinghy, Valentine and McGinty saw a canoe detach itself from the fishing boats and come paddling up to the dinghy. It came at flying speed, a long light canoe with a net shining and quivering from the pronged framework at its side. As it came level, four tall brown-skinned naked fishermen stood up, balancing on their feet, shading their eyes from the sun with one hand as they looked at Valentine and McGinty. They called to one another with excited cries.

What does one say to them? thought Valentine. One can hardly say "good-morning," but McGinty had already called out "Hullo." The men did not answer but stared naïvely and thoroughly.

"White man? Sahib?" called McGinty, tapping his chest and pointing at the house. The men shook their heads. Valentine and McGinty could not know that to shake the head in island custom meant "yes." One man also said what sounded to Valentine like "Ohé ." They stared again and then turned their boat and paddled away towards the island.

"Buggers!" said McGinty savagely.

"No. They have gone to tell," said Valentine.

"I have taught you as no other girl was ever taught," said Mr. van Loomis to Charis. "I have never let you waste an hour. No governess or school could have been as careful."

28

"No," agreed Charis listlessly.

"I should have let her be an islander, thought Mr. van Loomis despondently. Why did I teach and train her? Why didn't I leave her to grow as she could? As she would? He knew that it had not altogether been consideration for Charis. It was his need for someone to talk to, to talk with; a peer, thought Mr. van Loomis. Now that he had her, now that she approached to what he would have her be, this other unforeseen thing had come on their horizon. I should have foreseen it, said Mr. van Loomis in silent annoyance. Young things will grow. Will I have to take her away? Damnation! said Mr. van Loomis. Don't rush, said Mr. van Loomis to himself. Wait and see. Something may happen. He had a feeling that something would happen. He felt as if he had waved a little stick.

Charis knew she had changed. Pheasant told her she was always bad-tempered these days; her father said she was selfish and self-absorbed. If it were true, she could not help it; for her everything had changed. Nothing was itself any more; everything and everyone was tied to herself, and each had something as repellent as Mario, as attractively yearning as Filipino. Beautiful and hideous: those were her two epithets. Mario had touched her, and now his touch was the more powerful. Hideous! Hideous! thought poor Charis, and, suddenly, she wanted her mother. Mr. van Loomis and Pheasant were not enough.

"Was . . . Mother . . . like me?" asked Charis. It was the first time she had said that ordinary name. She said it as if it were stiff and strange. Then she said it again more naturally, "Am I like Mother?" she asked.

Mr. van Loomis was jerked back to the veranda and Charis. He stared. "Your *mother!*"

"Yes. Mother."

He drummed his fingers on the table as he always did when he was disturbed. "Your mother was a very beautiful woman," he said.

Then . . . not like me, thought Charis, and tears ran down her cheeks.

"Why are you crying?" asked Mr. van Loomis irritably. "She has been dead more than twenty years. You needn't cry for her now."

"I have never cried for her before," said Charis defiantly. "I want to know about her. I want to know who she was. I want to know who we are. I know nothing at all. It's time I was told. Who are we? Why did we come here? Who am I?"

Mr. van Loomis stared at her and then he stared far over the sea. It was so long since he had thought of his wife and the outer world that his mind had to grope after them, and they roused a strong emotion, stronger than he would have believed possible. I had forgotten, thought Mr. van Loomis. The squirrels ran up and down, the wind sent a windfall of acacia flowers onto the grass, the boys swept. Webster, seeing that neither of them appeared to wish for more toast, had silently gone away to the convivial courtyard; the bignonia creeper swayed and stirred, the fishermen's songs came faintly across the sea, and a school of porpoises passed, diving in and under and out of the water. Charis prompted him. "Father."

He was still silent, drumming his fingers, then he said abruptly, "Your mother was a Miss Burns."

That sounded so unlike the names of people as Charis knew them that her interest dried her tears. People on the island had one name, such as Serendipity, Niu, Hutchinson; a few had a double name, like Orange Flower, but the only people who had two distinct names were herself, her father, and Mario Fernandes. She had never thought of herself as Miss van Loomis, and she wondered if anyone would ever call her that. "Miss van Loomis," she murmured dizzily.

"No, Burns. Miss Burns," corrected Mr. van Loomis. "Yes, in a way you are like her. She came of a wealthy Edinburgh family. Yes, she was wealthy as well as beautiful." A smile touched his lips. "She married the Earl of Spey."

"Then . . ." Charis opened her lips, puzzled. "But . . . you are my father?"

"I am the Earl of Spey." Mr. van Loomis seemed curiously oppressed and troubled by it. "It brings it all back," he said. "Yes, child, I am the Earl of Spey. Our family name is Fyffe." And he said wearily, "The Earl of Spey, K.T.—that is a Knight of the Thistle in case you don't know—K.T., G.C.V.O., Viscount Ardlamont, Baron Stapleford in the county of Shropshire."

"All that?" asked Charis, marvelling, and then she asked, "And who am I?"

"Your real name is Grace Elizabeth Constance Fyffe. Lady Grace Fyffe," and he said pleadingly, "Charis is a prettier name."

Charis did not hear that. "Then . . . if I went to England now—"

"Scotland," said Mr. van Loomis.

"If I went to Scotland now, I should be Lady Grace Fyffe?"

"If you went to Scotland now you would probably have to work in a factory."

"Would I *really?*" asked Charis ecstatically. Her father did not ask her how she had this rosy vision of factories; he was busy with his own thoughts.

Charis felt uplifted and widened to a new horizon. She wanted to say to her father, "That is enough. Enough for today. Don't tell me any more today," but her thoughts came back to her mother. Her mother seemed real now, wealthy, beautiful Miss Burns, and dreamily she asked her father, "Was she mild silver or was she furious gold?"

The question took Mr. van Loomis off guard. "Mild silver," he said gruffly. Then he stopped, smiled, as if he had a remembrance. "No, furious gold. She . . ." There was a silence. Charis looked up and saw with surprise that her father was unable to speak. He stood up and pushed his chair away and went to the steps, standing with his back towards her, and Charis, at the table, had a glimpse of a difference that accounted for the difference in her, her difference from the islanders. On the island if you were sad, you wept; angry, you shouted and stormed; upset, you gave way. Now Charis saw grief, pent up and restrained, and this was something stronger than behaviour, it was deep. She saw that the feeling between her father and her mother had been more than the words that began with "co" from the Latin "cum"; it was concerned with faith and honour, and respect and love, but a love that she had not met, except that its reflection was between her father and herself. She saw this only dimly and felt more than she saw. This was what books are about,

31

thought Charis. This is what poems mean. This lies behind it all. I didn't understand before. Is that what I am waiting for? asked Charis, and she knew that, if she could not have that, she would take nothing less.

She sat looking at her father with a new kinship until he came back and put his hand on her shoulder. "Charis," he said, "she was silver *and* gold."

The answer pleased Charis. He had said she was like her mother; she did not mind being mild silver, but she wanted to be furious gold.

"It's a long story," said Mr. van Loomis, and he seemed to go back a long way from Charis in his mind. "I didn't take much interest in life after she died."

"No?" said Charis gently.

"No, that is not quite true. I had removed myself from life, perhaps, before. While I was up at Oxford," said Mr. van Loomis, his voice changing from nostalgia and alive with interest, "I became interested in conjuring."

The new romantic Charis stared at her father disapprovingly. Then her inherent coolness balanced this; after all, a propensity for conjuring may, quite easily, be as important as one's life as a wife.

"I found I had a gift for it," said Mr. van Loomis. "I became more and more interested. Conjuring to you means Maskelyne's and children's parties." (It did not. Charis knew the word only though the dictionary, as she knew most words, but Mr. van Loomis had forgotten where he was.) "It is an incredible art!" said Mr. van Loomis. "I use both words in their highest form; incredible and an art! No other art touches it. It is the power to transform; the power of the miracle, absolute." A look came into Mr. van Loomis's eye, a look that she had seen before but had not understood; it was visionary, determined and fixed. Then he pulled himself back to the breakfast table. "When you come to think of it," he said apologetically, "the whole world conjures, every man-jack of us." He paused, and an older look of sadness came into his face. "Then you learn," he said, "to go without it. That it is better to go without it. I have tried to learn that, Charis. I try to have nothing to do with it, but sometimes . . ." He paused, and that look came back
32

into his eyes, but Charis prompted him. "Father, you were telling me . . ."

Mr. van Loomis sighed and began again. "You must know," he said, "that we are shipping earls. Our family fortune was originally made in shipping and in whisky. Your mother's father was whisky. The earldom, of course, was given to my grandfather for his services in the Sudan. He was a great soldier, Charis. You should be proud of him. He was, of course, already a baronet. His father, your great-great-grandfather, started as a carpenter in the yard of Munro Macdonalds of Clydeside. That is now one of our concerns. He rose by his own efforts entirely. We are a wonderful family," said Mr. van Loomis. "We can do anything."

Could I, if I were given the chance? thought Charis. It was the first time she had thought of doing anything, but how would she get a chance? There were no chances on the island, shut in by rings of sea.

"We were often very foolish," said Mr. van Loomis. "In each generation, it seems, one of us had to have a folly. It was my grandfather who built a Greek temple at Spey, a Greek temple in Scotland. He put it on the top of a steep hill where no one could get at it; it must have been devilish to build. They use it for picnics now; they call it Spey's Folly. My father bought orchards in Tasmania; he bought them without advice or seeing them; they proved barren."

"And you?" said Charis.

Mr. van Loomis paused. He was not sure which was his wisdom and which his folly; if, for his father and grandfather, it had not been a groping after wisdom that ended in a folly. "I don't know," said Mr. van Loomis and sighed. "It was a complicated world, complications and chicanery. You don't know." He sighed. "There were the firms, and we had large estates. Your mother brought us more land and distilleries in Tobermory. It was all very cumbersome," said Mr. van Loomis, and he sighed as if he felt the immense weight of it still. "The Scottish are not like our islanders, Charis. One can't be despotic there. The simplest agricultural labourer is not simple at all. There everything is complicated. They have forgotten how to live. I didn't have time for it all. I didn't make

33

time. I didn't do my duty by the estates or by the firms. I didn't take my place in politics or the affairs of the country. Then there were strikes—"

"Strikes? Against *you?*" This was quite a new idea to Charis. She did not like some of the things he did on the island, but this was the first time she had seen him as a tyrant and she stared. "Did they starve?" she asked dramatically.

"People don't starve if they strike," said Mr. van Loomis. "They get strike pay." That was too intricate for Charis to follow and she let him go on. "There was trouble after trouble. I admit I didn't give my mind to it. I found it very tiresome and uninteresting and I shut myself away more and more." His eyes gleamed. "I was gaining a secret knowledge that would have astounded . . . Scientific: social: philosophical," said Mr. van Loomis longingly. "You may ask me how the practice of magic can be philosophical . . ." He saw Charis looking at him but he could not quite relinquish it. "They would have astonished, old Gilbray, Fitzadams, Hoestler—" He broke off. "I forgot," said Mr. van Loomis, "that to live your life successfully you must have life, and to have life you must live." That was so exactly Charis's own thought that she looked at her father with surprise. "You can't live by shutting yourself away," said Mr. van Loomis. But isn't that what you have done again? thought Charis. We are shut away on the island. He sat down at the table and ran his fingers over his beard, smoothing it down. "I am afraid I was a very selfish man." But for Charis sitting opposite him he might have asked, "Am I selfish still?" He did not believe that a parent should belittle himself in front of his child and he went on with his story. "I had a brother Archibald; he was clever, energetic, charming, and astute; he was plausible too. I was fond of him. Too fond." He sighed. Even now it hurt to think how a brother could hurt. "After the last war came the slump of the twenties—you wouldn't remember that. You weren't even born. It was acute economic depression."

Charis nodded. "There is always a period of depression after each war," she said. Having read much and been concerned little, Charis took an historical view of such things as ruin, war and famine, earthquakes and troubles,

34

that was afterwards to earn her the reputation of being unsympathetic; history is unsympathetic.

"We had troubles among the men," said Mr. van Loomis. "In the yards, at the works, everywhere. Archie managed them. He was very helpful. Soon he had everything controlled. As I told you, he was astute and energetic. Little by little, bit by bit—" said Mr. van Loomis and broke off. "He used to bring me things to sign, you wouldn't understand, but documents, contracts, agreements, deeds. I was very busy and I often signed them without looking. When you sign your name over and over again, and all the letters as well, it is hard to find time to look. Your mother warned me but I wouldn't listen. I didn't want to listen. He was too convenient and I didn't greatly care. I was immersed in my own work and didn't want to be disturbed. Then she died and I woke up. It was too late," said Mr. van Loomis, taking out his handkerchief and wiping his forehead, where, Charis was surprised to see, drops glistened though the morning was still cool. "It was too late. In the end, after the affairs had been settled, I was left with nothing but Spey. They couldn't take that from me."

"Spey?"

"Yes, Spey." Mr. van Loomis sat still at the breakfast table, but he seemed, in thought, to be again a long way away. "Spey. You have never known a grey country," he said.

"No," said Charis gently.

"Spey was the village our forefathers came from; it went with the castle. Our forefathers did not come from that, but my great-grandfather bought it when he bought —was given," Mr. van Loomis corrected himself and corrected himself again, "no, bought, his peerage. Never forget," said Mr. van Loomis, "it's no shame to have bought what you have. You buy it with your heart and mind if you earn it. He made himself a peer, and my grandfather, his son, was the first Earl." There was silence for a moment and then he went on, "Spey was a grey place, in the mountains with the glen below; the castle was grey; the battlements were still there and the keep and the four towers. You can have no idea, Charis, how tall those towers were; you had the same feeling there as you have here

35

on the mountain, but, remember, those were built by men." Mr. van Loomis paused. "The only things here that remind me are the rainbows in the waves. You should have seen a rainbow over the castle above the mist when the sun was shining even though the air was wet with rain." He looked at Charis, who was sitting with head up, looking past him at the sea with shining eyes. "You are not listening," said Mr. van Loomis.

"I am. I am," said Charis, and now she looked at him. "Why did you leave it if you loved it?" she asked.

"Your mother died and it felt empty," said Mr. van Loomis. "Besides I wanted . . ." He did not say what it was he had wanted. Was it the same thing that built the Greek temple? He said instead, "How could I stay? It needed a fortune to keep up a place like that, and I had given my fortune away. I was a ruined man; so I made it complete. I renounced my title in Archie's favour."

"In *his* favour! After he had treated you like that?"

"There was no one to blame," said Mr. van Loomis. "No word was ever said against Archie; only, mysteriously, after those years, I was ruined and he was rich, blamelessly rich. All the same, there were one or two people who didn't like the smell of him." He paused and then went on, "He was my heir; you were a girl. I knew I should never marry again, and I thought it would rankle." He smiled. "Archie was never robust enough to be wholly bad. He was sneaking. He used to steal jam and then be sick. If I stole jam," said Mr. van Loomis, "I kept it down. So he became the fourth Earl, and, yes, it rankled. Poor Archie has never been easy. He writes to me still." He did not say it was more than a year since he had picked up his mail. "Phaugh!" said Mr. van Loomis. Then he remembered what lay behind this conversation and said, "I should have left you with him."

"Not if he was sneaking," said Charis decidedly, and Mr. van Loomis felt cheered.

"I determined to get away from them all," he said. "Not to bring a soul with me, except you. You were a pledge from your mother. I had heard of this island. We had dealings with the Puerto company and I bought it and we came. I brought books and household goods and

36

trees and seeds and stock and tools, left the rest and came. I have not regretted it," said Mr. van Loomis.

"Wasn't I a great nuisance to you when you brought me here so young?"

"You were my greatest interest," said Mr. van Loomis. Tears started in Charis's eyes again, and he found them not far from his own. "I didn't bring a nurse for you. I thought it would be simple to look after you myself." The remembrance of the voyage came back to him. "Well, on the ship, yes, you were a nuisance," said Mr. van Loomis. "You used to eat oranges and put out the pips and pulp into my hand. Yes, I was glad when we found Pheasant at Puerto. Still . . . Here we have made a simple good life, Charis. It is fundamental. There is no conjuring here."

"Conjuring?" That word seemed to Charis to haunt her father. She asked, "What is the difference between conjuring and magic?"

"All the difference," said Mr. van Loomis shortly. "Conjuring is clever tricks. That is why the world is sick."

"*Is* the world sick?" asked Charis, interested.

"Yes. Sick with its own cleverness," said Mr. van Loomis. "I tell you, Charis, cleverness is a disease."

It was the first time Charis had heard that. "But . . . if people *are* clever?"

"Clever tricks are all the same," said Mr. van Loomis. "An atom bomb or a coffee machine. We crush our berries with stones and make coffee in a pan. Invent a coffee machine and you are on the way to the bomb. There is none of that here on our island."

Charis opened her lips to speak and shut them. Filipino had invented a coffee machine. Seeing how often the coffee boiled and was spoilt, he had thought out a different way: he had made a pan of the island clay fired hard, over which fitted another with holes in its base; the coffee was put in this, and the water from below bubbled up, and the coffee was made without the grounds being boiled.

"You invented the coffee," said Charis to Mr. van Loomis.

"I didn't. The coffee was here. I only used what was here."

So did Filipino; he used clay and fire and his wits. Everything was here, in the world, or it could not be . . . reached, thought Charis. She felt dizzy, overwrought and overtired; she had travelled a long way since the night and yet, for all this, she was still the same, still lonely Charis on the island.

Mr. van Loomis stood up. "I am going out to the lighthouse to see Mario. Would you like to come?"

"To see *Mario!*" After such a conversation as this! Charis was astounded at her father's insensitivity. Then she remembered that he did not know how she must feel. How could he? He was not a girl, young, bewildered, and alone. Charis began to cry.

Mr. van Loomis saw he had made a mistake, and he saw dimly, what was the matter. He remembered the collision with Flora Annie, and he looked at Charis sharply; there was nothing he could say. When he was uncomfortable or his own words failed him he often took refuge in proverbs. "There is an old Hindu proverb," he began.

Charis's shoulder twitched impatiently, but Mr. van Loomis went on. "When the pupil is ready," quoted Mr. van Loomis, "the teacher will come."

It was at that moment that the dinghy came slowly round the headland.

CHAPTER IV

AFTER he had taken Charis to her room and persuaded her to lie down in the quiet, Mr. van Loomis came and stood thoughtfully on the veranda.

It was a long while since he had helped a woman to bed after an emotional scene. The women on the island did not need beds except for sleep or love, and not always then—a mat, the sand, or the grass did as well. Their nerves were not torn by scenes: they had no nerves. Mr. van Loomis drummed his fingers on the veranda rail and ruffled his beard. "Phaugh!" said Mr. van Loomis crossly. "Damn!"

It began to dawn on him that there were unusual sounds and movement all round him. Shouts and calls were coming from the beach; a small cook boy, a slice of melon still in his hand, darted through the garden to the beach; three garden boys ran after him, and then the groom. No one was allowed to come that way, and Mr. van Loomis stepped indignantly down onto the terrace. Niu appeared at his elbow. "Look, Tsula! Look!"

Mr. van Loomis looked down on the beaches where a crowd was gathering. He looked along the jetty clustered with people and at the sea where fishing boats had gathered. The far fringes of the beaches were alive with people, and more boats were coming in, paddled so fast that white spray rose round them. Then, following the line of Niu's finger, he saw a small yellow boat out to sea. He supposed it was a boat; it might have been a raft but it was not a native one. His heart began a peculiar pounding in his chest. He sent Niu for his field glasses. When he had looked through them he stood very still on the terrace.

Along the terrace there were plumbago bushes, small and feathery, with milk-blue flowers, that grew with white oleanders in tubs. The air was balmy with the smell of grass and flowers warming in the sun; the wind blew in the acacia trees. But Mr. van Loomis noticed none of these things; he stood so still that a swallowtail butterfly, tempted out by the sun, hovered past his stomach and a lizard scuttled across the sun cracks by his toe. Mr. van Loomis brought the glasses down, startling the butterfly and the lizard away. He said, "Send Filipino to me."

His first impulse had been to order out his great canoe and go after the two men he had identified through the glasses as white men, but on second thought he decided to send Filipino. Why should I go after anyone? thought Mr. van Loomis grandly. This is my island. Let them come to me.

39

〜〜〜〜〜〜Filipino was probably the last person on
the island to see the dinghy. He had been down in his
hut, lying on his bed, reading, while the other servants
smoked and chattered. Filipino had learned that familiari-
ty and chatter take away its strength from the mind. That
was odd in such a talkative boy as Filipino, but that was
the strange thing about Filipino: he was everything; he
was talkative and not talkative: quick and slow; cruel and
gentle; bad tempered and sweet; while, for instance, Flora
Annie was simply a chatterbox and Resurrection was a silent boy.

Filipino had discovered a book he had not read, a
small brown book tucked away on Mr. van Loomis's
shelves. It was called *The Rights of Man*. He had bor-
rowed it and read it the night before, lying on his bed and
making a shield with his hand round his saucer light; the
little wick floating in oil gave only a feeble light, and Filipino's eyes ached, but he read the book through, and in it
he had found so many of his own thoughts that he was
exhilarated. He felt confirmed in all his beliefs; they were
true; they were there in print, and print was gospel to Filipino. When he had finally blown out his lamp and lain
down to sleep, the thoughts wove themselves with his
sleep in his brain and he woke giddy with overtiredness
but so exhilarated still that he had kissed Flora Annie for
sheer joy. Now, to make sure he had not been mistaken,
he was reading the book again. "Oh, but I should like to
meet someone, now, who knows the world, the whole
wide world!" said Filipino. Niu hailed him, and he had
looked up and seen the dinghy.

"Take these and look," said Mr. van Loomis when Filipino arrived out of breath, and he handed the glasses to
Filipino. The way Filipino took them and adjusted them
struck Mr. van Loomis; could Filipino have used those
glasses before? The boy would not dare! thought Mr. van
Loomis, but he did not feel quite sure. He looked sharply
at Filipino. He was strangely unsure of what Filipino
would not dare. "What do you see?" he asked.

"Two Tsulas, Tsula," said Filipino. They all knew

there were two white men without the glasses. At least a dozen people had told Filipino that between the beach and the terrace. "Two white men in a fat boat the colour of the sun." One or two ingenuous ones had suggested that it might even be the sun. "Two gods come down on the sea in the sun," they said reverently. Filipino pointed out that the sun was in the sky and came on up to the house.

"You can speak some English?" said Mr. van Loomis now to Filipino.

"Ohé," said Filipino politely, his eyes cast modestly down. He had the little book tucked into his waist knot; he wondered what Mr. van Loomis would have said if he had seen the English in that.

"You are quick and you can use your head," said Mr. van Loomis. "Take a boat and go after the Tsulas and find out who they are and what they want and bring them back. Don't bring them to the house beach; I may not want them here. Bring them to the second bay below and keep them there till I come."

Filipino was silent. He was filled with solemnity and a great purpose. Soon he was to meet other white men, men of the world, it might be young white men. He felt he must assert himself now or never; the little book pressed his waist. *The Rights of Man!* Filipino breathed quickly through his nose, his cheeks flushed hot. He pressed his lips together and said nothing.

"When I give you an order you will say, 'Yes, Tsula,'" said Mr. van Loomis.

Niu murmured concurrence and gave Filipino a small kick on the calf with his slipper. He too was very strict about island manners. "Tsula" was the island name for "white man." Mr. van Loomis was pleased to know that it had also come to mean "honourable." "Tsuli," the feminine, was Charis's title on the island.

"When I give you an order you will say, 'Yes, Tsula,'" said Mr. van Loomis.

"I will say 'No,'" said Filipino.

It seemed to him that the silence stretched away from the terrace, over the lawns and under the trees, past flowers and bushes and Charis's bamboo swing, past the summerhouse and the clump of morning glory, down the steps to the sea; it ringed out past the paddock and the flowering hedges, the servants' quarters and the kitchen, the stable and the lodge hut by the gate; and, as if the silence had spoken, it seemed to Filipino that everyone lifted his head to listen: the crowds on the beach, the villages, the people on the mountain; even the squirrels seemed to wait, bright-eyed; for a moment, no bird flew. The palms of Filipino's hands broke out into sweat, but to make sure he had said it, he did it again. "I shall say 'No,'" said Filipino.

"Did you say 'No?'"

The four small words started a tumult of fear in Filipino. "No," he said. "I mean 'Yes.' Yes, I said 'No.' Mister," began Filipino pleadingly in English. He had meant to conciliate and say "Master," but in his agitation he used the objectionable "Mister," and he saw Mr. van Loomis's look darken still more. He shook back his hair and touched the book with his hand and tried to take fresh courage. Suddenly he was glad that he had said "Mister." "I joined as houseboy," said Filipino loudly. "I am not your messenger. It is not my work to go."

Mr. van Loomis seemed to tower over Filipino, and his breadth was immense. Filipino had not known that his face was such a network of purple lines or that his eyes could stab . . . like a swordfish, thought Filipino, with blue strength and power. One man, alone, could fight a swordfish, but it was unlikely that he could bring a large one to land. Mr. van Loomis looked very large to Filipino, and he quailed and his bare toes moved uneasily on the terrace earth. "Very well. I go," said Filipino hastily. "I go." Then he remembered and wavered and retrieved himself. "If you ask me nicely," quavered Filipino, and words from newspapers seemed to come to him though he did not realize what they meat. "If you pay me overtime."

"Slap him," said Mr. van Loomis.

Niu, his dark face darker with emotion, stepped forward and slapped his grandson on both cheeks. What kind of emotion Niu felt Mr. van Loomis did not divine; he never knew with Niu, but the slaps were hard. Filipino did not resist; the slaps stung, tears smarted in his eyes, but they made him angry and that was easier.

"I don't care," said Filipino proudly, his voice brimming with tears. "I, sir, am not your slave."

Mr. van Loomis was outwardly unmoved; his feet were set wide and firmly on the terrace, his bulk was large and calm, but inwardly he was in turmoil. The yellow boat was passing steadily down the bay. He wished to send this tiresome boy after it. What is in them all this morning? thought Mr. van Loomis. It's a ferment. Aloud he said, "What did I take you from? What were you, knuckling under to Mario's mother, a woman? Were you free? In that witchcraft and degradation and abuse? You were slaves! Slaves!"

"No," said Filipino. He could not explain, but the submission to Mario's mother, the submitting to her abuse, still left them, in a way, free. Mr. van Loomis's demand for co-operation for their own good took far more from them and was far more forceful.

"Everything I have done here has been for your own good," said Mr. van Loomis.

"No," said Filipino. He still could not explain. It was too subtle for him, he could only feel it.

"You say 'No,' " said Mr. van Loomis. "I can only say 'No' too. Is there a man or woman now under the evil eye? No. Is there misery and poverty and disease? No. Is there any tribute to pay? No. No tribute. No taxes."

"There should be taxes," said Filipino. He struggled to explain. "We should do our own good." He knew what he meant. "Our own good or bad. Our good should *belong* to us," said Filipino.

"Is there anyone hungry or whipped?" Mr. van Loomis continued as if Filipino had not spoken.

"No, but—"

"Is there leprosy or beriberi or plague?"

"No, but—"

"Well then?" asked Mr. van Loomis.

Filipino began to feel desperate. He felt as if he were speaking with a loud voice and nobody heard. "But to be whipped or hungry *isn't*. I—"

"You have never been whipped or hungry," said Mr. van Loomis. "Try it and see."

"I should *willingly,*" cried Filipino.

Mr. van Loomis's temper broke. He felt he had had

43

enough to try him that morning. "If I have any more of this you *shall* be whipped," he said. "But I shan't whip you. I shall send you to Zambun."

Niu gave a little cry. Zambun was the penal settlement on the nearest island to Terraqueous, a hundred and forty miles away.

"When I bought the island," Mr. van Loomis told Valentine later, "I took the precaution of becoming its magistrate. It gives me great power." It gave him such power he sometimes forgot that, when he bought the island, he had not bought the people as well. But something was in the air today, and now he suddenly knew that, magistrate or no magistrate, he did not send people to Zambun, they sent themselves, and he had an equally sudden sense of the limitation of his own power. He was nonplussed and he found himself turning to Niu. Niu was standing and looking at Mr. van Loomis with his eyes set and with such hardness on his face that Mr. van Loomis felt cold. There was a pause; then, "I shall not send you to Zambun," said Mr. van Loomis. "I shall turn you over to your grandfather."

Niu gave a sigh of satisfaction and lowered his eyes and looked at Mr. van Loomis's feet. Mr. van Loomis still had that sensation of coldness. Good God! thought Mr. van Loomis. Surely I'm not afraid of Niu?

Filipino was not satisfied. He had now wound himself to such a pitch that he could not accept this tame ending. "Send me to Zambun," he cried. "I like to go! Starve me! Beat me! I am not afraid!"

They turned to look at him. "But I have never beaten anyone," said Mr. van Loomis, bewildered. "I have had them slapped but nothing else."

"I shall hunger-strike you," shouted Filipino. "I shall call the young men out. There will be a riot, I warn you, sir. You are a tyrant," shouted Filipino. "You must come down. We want government. Not your government. We want that it should be of the people, by the people, for the people," gabbled Filipino. He had to stop for want of breath.

Mr. van Loomis looked at him with eyes that seemed to drill their blue sight into Filipino. "You have been reading," said Mr. van Loomis. He took thought. Someone else had spoken to him of strikes that morning. Char-is! "Tsuli Charis has been teaching you to read. What have you been reading?" said Mr. van Loomis.

Mr. van Loomis had guessed right. In thoroughly educating his daughter he had educated Filipino as well.

One afternoon long ago Charis, coming out to play, had found a small boy sitting among her toys where she had left them on the grass (no one had ever taught Charis to tidy her things away). The boy was holding his big toe and scratching it in the island way with one hand, but with the other he was turning over the pages of one of her books page by page. When he looked up he was too enthralled to drop the book and leap to his feet as he should have done; he continued to scratch his big toe and said, "Tsuli, what does this mean?" Charis, looking over his shoulder, saw a picture of King Arthur pulling the sword out of the stone. Sitting down by Filipino, she told him the story of King Arthur. Presently Filipino noticed that the text went with the pictures, and presently Charis began to point out to him the A's and B's and C's. They were sitting beside a hibiscus bush, its root spread in a circle of sun-baked earth, and, breaking a twig, Charis had scratched an A and a B and a C in the earth. Soon he was scratching them for himself. The next afternoon he was there again, waiting for her with glowing eyes, and they had progressed from scratching on the earth to writing on Charis's slate and then to Mr. van Loomis's precious paper and pencil and ink. The ink was made from an indelible island stain. "Ink is better," said Filipino. "I want that what I write shall never die. You have the pencil," said Filipino.

Charis thought he was a very conceited boy, but she was amazed at how quickly he learned. At first she had taught him as one teaches a pet, for amusement, then less and less amusingly, until it was deep, hard work. They became like a proud sister and young brother, but as Filipino grew up he began to show his range and he grew to be separated, even from Charis. It was not that he knew more than she—a good deal of what he knew was glib and parrot-like—it was his imagination and invention. The coffee pot was the least of the things he had imagined; at a spark he took flame. Charis had sometimes

45

thought that he was so fierce he must burn himself out, but there was something inexhaustible in Filipino.

Now, "What have you been reading?" asked Mr. van Loomis.

Niu gave Filipino a push to make him answer. It put him off his balance; he staggered and *The Rights of Man* was jerked from his waist knot and fell, with a thud, face downwards on the terrace path at Mr. van Loomis's feet.

Mr. Van Loomis looked down at it. "Pick it up."

Filipino picked it up, a cold sensation in his ears. A plumbago petal had stuck to the page, which was brown and wet from earth and dew. Humbly Filipino brushed the petal off, but the wet brown patch remained.

"Give it to me."

Filipino gave it and shrank back. He was afraid Mr. van Loomis would lose his temper again at the dirty marks on his property. Filipino was afraid he would be slapped again, and he was a coward over being hurt, but Mr. van Loomis only said with irritation, "Why don't you read what you can understand?" He had not for one moment guessed that the boy could read books such as this. "When I learned to read, we read 'The cat sat on the mat,' which at least was fact and sense. This is half-baked, indigestible, theoretical jargon. Phaugh!" said Mr. van Loomis.

"I like it," said Filipino.

"No one could like it," said Mr. van Loomis. He was forgetting that, for the book to be on the island at all, he must once have liked it himself. He often told Charis how carefully he had chosen each book he had brought. "You don't understand it," he said.

"Tsula, I *do* understand it," said Filipino earnestly, his face aglow. "I understand, sir, every word. I . . . I drink it. I *believe* it! Every word!"

"Phaugh!" said Mr. van Loomis. "You are trying to fly before you can walk."

"Then I can fly," said Filipino.

Indeed Filipino made strange flights for an island boy. If he had actually gone up in Valentine's Water Star and flown over the islands and seen them scattered wide in the sea, they would have given him no surprise. To the islanders, their island was the whole world, except for

Zambun, from which none of them ever returned and which corresponded to hell; the Hat might have been the moon, attendant on the earth; the earth was the island and the sun; the real moon and stars were, the islanders knew, attached to the island to shine on it and give it warmth. Filipino alone had a sense of other islands, of the world, even of a magnitude of worlds. It was through books, but it was not only through books that he had it; he seemed to drink the air and know. At night, lying on his bed, in his open-sided hut, he would look up at the stars, and his significance would dwindle, and the island dwindled too and seemed to dissolve in the sound of its own surf into the air. This did not frighten him but gave him a strange melting joy as if he too had become the air, and then often he sang or wrote his songs. His ideas were not phenomenal to Filipino; he was a phenomenon himself, one of those who went from idea to idea as if they walked on the tips of mountains, if they walked at all. They did not have to learn to fly: they had to learn to walk.

"You don't want to go into that world," said Mr. van Loomis as if he were arguing about a possibility. "Into all that trickery and mess."

"I do! I do!" said Filipino.

"You don't know what you are talking of."

"I do."

"How do you?"

Filipino took a deep breath. "I read your newspapers." And he said humbly. "Please to excuse me for it."

Four years ago Charis had discovered a drawer full of newspapers in her father's study. Mr. van Loomis had meant to lock the drawer; he had meant to burn the papers as he read them; he had always done this before, but had grown careless. It was two years since he had been out to the barrel to pick up the mail, and he had forgotten about the newspapers in the drawer. They were old, but that made no difference to Charis and Filipino. They read them avidly; unconsciously they learned a new idiom. If Mr. van Loomis had not been so busy he would have noticed that Charis's words and thoughts had changed. Though they did not understand more than a quarter of what they read, a shutter opened in the minds of Charis and Filipino, and they looked on a new world. "And it *is* the world," said Charis. "It isn't made up, like a book. All that it says happened has happened."

"Oh, you children!" said Mr. van Loomis now, and he asked Filipino, "What do you *want?*"

"I want to meet with a man," said Filipino slowly and shyly.

"What man?"

"A real young man."

"What do you think you are yourself?" asked Mr. van Loomis, but that had not dawned on Filipino; he did not feel at all like a real young man.

"I want to go among other young men and rub their shoulders," said Filipino. He thought there was something not quite right in the way he had said that but he swept on. "I want to meet men from all over the world. From everywhere." A thought came to him that made him breathless, and, for a moment, he stopped. A dazzling thought had come to him; suddenly he saw the way clear before him. It was something he had not thought of before. "Colleges are where you learn. Send me to a college," said Filipino.

Mr. van Loomis looked at the house behind him where he had led Charis to her bed in tears; he looked at the distant lighthouse rocks where Mario was interned and at the sea where the dinghy was still gaining slowly on the town; perhaps there in the dinghy, was Filipino's real young man. He sighed. In making himself responsible for this island he had made himself responsible for something unfathomable. Or should I have fathomed it? asked Mr. van Loomis. Should I have known about all this if I had been more aware? Whether he should or should not, he felt helpless. He was held in something he did not understand. What, for instance, had brought those two strangers as if from a spell? "I didn't make a spell, did I?" asked Mr. van Loomis.

"Tsula?" Filipino did not understand.

"I abjured . . . yes, that is the right word. I abjured magic," said Mr. van Loomis. "But . . ." He looked at the house, the garden, the rock, the sea. "But did it abjure me?"

No one, nothing, answered him.

48

WHEN Mr. van Loomis had dispatched the now glowingly obedient Filipino after the dinghy, though he was burning with curiosity and impatience himself, he went slowly across the lawn, past the morning glory and down the steps, along the jetty, and stepped into the canoe that waited for him at the jetty head. He felt it was only dignified to go on with his morning's programme rather than wait at home for the strangers. Why should they upset my plans? asked Mr. van Loomis.

The boatmen greeted him with respect. He looked big and imposing, shining with whiteness, the whiteness of his beard enhanced by his tanned face and his blue eyes and matched by his white eyebrows and thick hair. He wore white trousers and a singlet with a wide cummerbund round his waist that was growing portly.

His boat was imposing too. It was like a great war canoe with outrigging to steady it over the surf. Mr. van Loomis had bought it from the chief of another island on his way to Terraqueous; he paid for it in kind with one of his imported boars, the smaller of two photographs he had brought out, and a Victorian necklace of silver mesh that had belonged to one of his wife's aunts, the old Miss Burns of Edinburgh. It was a heavy price but the boat was worth it. It was native-built of wood inlaid with mother-of-pearl, and its eyes, in the prow, were ornamented with silver and coral. It was rowed by a crew of eight picked men, who sat two by two in the stern; they wore loin cloths of island-dyed crimson and a long rag of the same colour wound round their heads to catch their sweat. It was Mr. van Loomis's first island attempt at uniform; he liked to see them smart and all the same, but the islanders did not take easily to smartness or to uniform;

49

the boatmen often came in other colours or with flowers in their hair. They rowed fast, their paddles flashed exactly together in the sun, and, on a little platform on the prow, the head boatman, Luck, kept the rhythm, standing, balanced on his feet, as the boat flashed through the waves, chanting rhythmically, "Hé, hé, hé, hé." Charis always knew when her father was coming and going by the approaching and receding "hé's."

At first the men had thought they were going after the dinghy, and when Filipino went racing out alone there were disappointed murmurs. "Our Tsula can't go after them," said Luck. "He is a great chief. They must come to him." And the men said, "Ohé," satisfied.

The canoe turned out to sea and met the glassy green swell, deeper since the storm. From the sea, the island and its mountain made one shape to the skyline with colours of white and green and brown and lavender streaked with pumice and white, rising from the white beaches to the white cloud. The colours were pellucid in the sun; it was too early still for the heat haze which would presently rise from the pockets of inland valleys that were stiller and warmer, more lush, than the rest of the island. Mr. van Loomis could identify every colour and shape, predict each change.

Sounds came to them clearly as they ran along parallel with the shore. Mr. van Loomis knew every sound: the sound of the waves breaking, of parakeets, of the island women threshing out their corn in hollow wooden blocks with a corn pole. He could put a name to the sound of the husking of the maize in wicker trays, to the creak of the small handmills grinding the grain into flour. He heard the scream of a well rope and the slapping of wet cloths in the wash places in the river; the sound of oxcart wheels and the crack of whips; of children splashing one another in the sea; of the drums of a funeral.

He could identify all the smells, from the exact brand of the stinking fish to the peculiar sweetness that was to puzzle Valentine and came from the flowers on the chema tree, a tree that was peculiar to the island and had white chiselled flowers and long sharp thorns.

Fishermen stood up in their boats for him as he passed, though the wash of the heavy canoe was dangerous to their light craft. Mr. van Loomis lifted his hand in acknowledgment, and his signet ring caught the sun and sent a shaft of light into their eyes; such shafts can be seen from the aureoles of saints or supreme beings in holy pictures, a shaft like the eye of God. On land, if the islanders met Mr. van Loomis, they stepped off the road; a few ignorant ones lay down in the dust, but they came from the back of the hill, the island's hinterland, and had been tormented by Mario's mother. After reading the newspapers and talking with Filipino, Charis had grown to be hotly ashamed of this, but Mr. van Loomis thought it not unfitting.

On the island Mr. van Loomis still ordered the world, and he felt he would continue to order it. "At least a place can't be treacherous," said Mr. van Loomis now. "Places have no secret springs. They don't grow." As he said that he had a strong feeling that he had waved the little stick, a magician's wand, and that the opposite would happen as it did in the magician's trick, the unexpected, the rabbit that could not have been in the conjuror's hat, and that the island, by some unexpected twist, would, in the end, order him. "Nonsense! Phaugh!" said Mr. van Loomis. "I know the island, every inch of it. It can't play tricks on me." Still the island seemed to shimmer into changes. In all his acquaintance with it he had not learned that the island was always inexorably itself.

Mr. van Loomis had no doubt but that he had benefited the island. He had given it back its tranquillity; he had made the islanders prosperous and kept the beauty of their island for them; he had kept it outside the world, away from trade, so that it was not spoilt: there was no corrugated iron, no cement, no asphalt, none of the things that the near-savage dearly loves. "They don't know what I have saved them from," Mr. van Loomis often said. There was no cinema, no radio, no electricity. There was no money: the islanders traded in kind with one another and Mr. van Loomis. He had guarded their indigenous industries, ideas, and customs; he had added only a few of his own. The island houses were built of woven bamboo like wickerwork or else of beaten earth, leeped with lime wash in white or native colours, and thatched; Mr.

van Loomis had built his house of the same earth, the same thatch, only he had made it larger and embellished it with wooden floors and windowboxes, bathrooms, verandas, kitchens, and gates. The island roads had been simply paths where jungle or grass or earth or sand had been trodden down with usage; Mr. van Loomis's roads were the same, only widened by the same simple process of treading; he had gangs of men and women stamping the earth in, and he had taught the people how to make and use oxcarts; they had not seen a wheel till then. He had planted trees along the roads so that the people walked in ordered shade. He had brought seed and fruit trees with him from Scotland and Puerto and taught them to irrigate and augment their crops; he had introduced all kinds of startling crops, some of which, though the islanders did not say this to him, made heavy work. He had weeded out the sick and poor stock from the cattle and sheep and pigs and improved the breeds with a prize bull, two rams, and a boar (the one left from the buying of the canoe), which the islanders felt they should worship for their size. Even the cocks and hens had grown bigger since Mr. van Loomis came; the very gourds on the gourd vines had swelled.

Stocks of cotton and copra and wool and timber and gold had accumulated on the island for Mr. van Loomis; he had no means of sending them away, and he did not intend to destroy his peace by getting a means, and he kept his stocks in bamboo warehouses behind the little town. It gave the islanders, he thought, a healthful business to collect these stocks, and they were impressed by the visible signs of increasing wealth. Only Filipino wondered what was the reason for this pile and, seeing no reason, felt its uselessness. He often thought of those sheds of Mr. van Loomis's. They should be divided among the people, thought Filipino; but what would the people do with them if they had them? He felt sure that something ought to be done.

Among other industries on the island, Mr. van Loomis had revived the pearl fishing that had thrived long ago. In the creeks and bays of the island and its satellite rocks, and in two banks out to sea, in certain places were oyster beds.

The native divers went down for the pearls, naked and unprotected except for a sharpened dagger of ironwood that they wore round their necks and used against the attack of a shark. Long accustomed, they could walk and swim under the sea for minutes together without anything to help them but their muscles. Now, as the canoe drew near, Mr. van Loomis could see the little fleet of boats and, in the middle, the large barge to which the divers clung when they came up.

Prem, the head man, came paddling up to them in his boat. As he neared them he sent it shooting forward with a strong stroke of his paddle and stood up in one graceful movement from heel to head, balancing, holding with his toes on the narrow fast-moving little boat. "Tsula!" he said in greeting.

"Prem!" returned Mr. van Loomis, and Prem smiled broadly. Mr. van Loomis liked his broad, smiling face. Prem had been down with his divers; his black hair was wet; the water streamed down his back and thighs and dried on his brown skin in lines of salt; he wore nothing but an old thin cloth tied between his legs and knotted round his waist with plaited grass. Now he undid a knot in the corner of his cloth and held out, on the cloth, five or six small pearls and one larger for Mr. van Loomis to see. Mr. van Loomis thoughtfully took the large one and weighed it between his finger and thumb while Prem watched his face.

"It *is* the one, Tsula?"

"I believe it is," said Mr. van Loomis.

"It is like the Tsula's other ones," said Prem. "Only larger, Tsula! It is one of the largest I have seen."

Mr. van Loomis had been collecting pearls for a string for Charis. One day he would sell all his pearls, but certain fine evenly matched ones he was keeping for her. Charis's twenty-first birthday was near, and the string was almost ready; it wanted only the centre pearl, and this, by its size and weight (as far as he could estimate it), its shape and lustre, seemed to be the pearl for which he had waited. Prem was right: it was one of the largest he had seen. "Who found it?"

"Tinpal."

"He shall have a goat," said Mr. van Loomis, and he

took the pearls from Prem, gave him one or two orders, and called to Luck to go on.

Mr. van Loomis had his completed string of pearls, but, after the morning's scene with Charis, he was not as elated as he might have been. He now thought of something he had not thought of before: he remembered how, once, he had shown Charis some pearls as a child, and she had run and brought him some little egg-shaped seeds, half red, half black, and brilliant, that fell from a bush near the stables after it had flowered; the islanders used to pierce them and string them. Charis plainly thought they were prettier than his pearls. The older Charis would probably see the beauty of the pearls and like them for their own sake . . . but that would still not be quite as pearls, thought Mr. van Loomis. Would they be of any use to her? Do pearls need people, other women, to give them value? he asked. He could not decide. A savage might treasure an emerald for its water, but he might equally well keep a pebble. "I don't know," said Mr. van Loomis aloud and unhappily.

In the sun-filled morning he felt wrapped in gloom. He was seriously perturbed. It was a strange feeling. For twenty years Mr. van Loomis, until that night with Mario, had had nothing to perturb him, and Mario was easily brushed aside like a troublesome fly, or so he had thought. Even the war had passed him by. "It's nothing to do with me and my island," he had said. "If it comes here, it comes; then I shall consider it." It had not come. He had sat on his island away from the tides that had washed the world; now he was caught up in a larger tide that was even more ruthless: the tide of time. 'Something is beginning," it said. "Time goes by. You must, inexorably, be swept away." He looked through his glasses to where the small speck that was Filipino was gaining on the larger yellow mark of the dinghy.

They themselves were getting near the lighthouse that, as they drew near, separated itself into a small pillbox standing on rocks that lay by themselves, out to sea. The sun caught the lens of the lamp and flashed on them. Mr. van Loomis could see Jéo, the young keeper, a dot on the rocks, watching them. There was no sign of Mario. "Mario!" said Mr. van Loomis.

54

It was only now, after the scene with Charis, that Mr. van Loomis could trust himself to speak to Mario. Mr. van Loomis had been judging the islanders for twenty years, trying to show them how to control themselves and not lose their tempers and let off blowpipes or open veins when they were angry; he had even tried putting down cockfights and stopping the kid and calf sacrifices, but there he had been defeated; the island gods were stronger than Mr. van Loomis, and he wisely paid tribute to them, but he had tried to show the islanders, by example, what they should and should not do to keep themselves energetic and temperate. Now he found himself intemperate; he wanted to do what he would have had to send anyone of them to Zambun for doing; he could have strangled Mario with his bare hands; he would have liked to cut Mario's throat. "Mario!" he said and gritted his teeth.

He felt, also, that Mario had started this unrest. It was Mario who had upset Charis, and, though he had nothing to do with Filipino, Mr. van Loomis was now linking together several little things that he had seen and not really taken notice of before. Perhaps Mario had upset Charis and Charis had set off Filipino. Mario had made Charis, who up to then had been a little girl, suddenly desirable . . . and desirous, thought Mr. van Loomis. At the thought of Charis being desirable, or desirous, Mr. van Loomis trembled with strange feelings of rage and fear. He thought of Flora Annie, running full tilt into him; of her giggling laughter, giggling even at him; of the way her cloth was drawn tightly over her small hams; of her dimpled shoulders and full little bare breasts; of the red flower flaunting in her hair and her inviting smiling eyes. He had boxed Flora Annie's ears but he had smiled. Flora Annie was easily settled; soon, perhaps this very moon, the sooner the better, a husband would be found for Flora Annie. But a husband for Charis? How to find him? I should have brought her up as an islander, but I couldn't have married her to an islander, thought Mr. van Loomis; the thought made his blood run cold. I should have left her behind, but it was too late to say that. He sighed. If Mario had left her alone there might have been another two or three years of peace, and Mr. van Loomis cast round in his mind for an epithet for Mario but it was so long since he had had need really to swear that he could not find one; he thought of Mario's mother, and her son seemed to him as coarse and potent. "The—the hagseed!" said Mr. van Loomis aloud and saw Luck look at him. He was cold with anger and cold with nausea to think how nearly Mario . . . How can I protect and keep her? thought Mr. van Loomis, and a sickening thought came to him: what would happen to her were he to die and leave her alone? He made a wish, the wish and prayer of every good mother: I wish that she could marry well and happily. I wish that, in that boat, one of those two strangers could be a good and personable unattached young man. I wish that he and Charis could fall in love and marry and live happily, not ever after of course, no one does that, but for most of their lives. That is what I wish, so help me God! said Mr. van Loomis.

He had wished so intensely that he had shut his eyes. Luck, facing him, wondered if he were cross or unwell; then Mr. van Loomis sighed and opened his eyes. "The young are very upsetting," he said.

"Tsula?" said Luck politely.

They had come to the lighthouse. It was not really a lighthouse but a lamp of the kind that are usually on buoys; here, on this rocky point, the surf was too full for a buoy, and the lamp had been built into a pillbox on the rocks and was lighted at dusk every evening and shone with a steady beam out to sea. It was more friendly, less lonely, than most lighthouses; the keepers were allowed to come ashore in the daytime to eat in their houses and sleep with their wives, but, to Mr. van Loomis, it was a thorn prick: it was the only part of the island that was not his. Here the Inspector's ketch had to call, and Jéo, the young keeper, and his father were responsible not to Mr. van Loomis but to the Inspector. Jéo had not dared to use his advantage, but Mr. van Loomis was careful not to provoke him by inquiring too closely into his doings and he resented having to be careful. This made the business of Mario doubly difficult; without the extreme of Zambun, there was nowhere else to banish him and . . . I don't send people to Zambun, said Mr. van Loomis to himself again. They send themselves. Mario had done nothing that sent him to Zambun. He was safe enough on the lighthouse; he was not a skilful boatman, as the island young men were, and he would not have dared to try the passage between the rocks and the mainland alone; but Mr. van Loomis felt he had put himself into Jéo's hand, and that made him uneasy and irritable.

Jéo came now, down to the landing rock, and stood ready to catch the rope that Luck had in his hand to throw. Jéo was smiling. Then he is still glad to have Mario, thought Mr. van Loomis, relieved.

The current raced round the rocks, but Luck brought the big canoe round to run with it, and, back-paddling, the men brought her in without a graze to lie beside the large flat rock used for landing. Jéo caught the rope and fastened it to a ring riven into the rock. He saluted Mr. van Loomis. "Tsula!"

"Jéo!"

Stores, maize and vegetables and bananas and rice, were put ashore, and Mr. van Loomis stood up and came out from under the awning, which was stretched where he sat, and passed Luck, who stood steadying the prow of the canoe against the racing water with a long pole. One of the boatmen had sprung out and was now in the sea between the canoe and the rock, with the water washing round his waist; he put his hands on his knees to steady himself and bowed his back so that Mr. van Loomis could use him as a rail. Helping himself with one hand on the boatman's back, Mr. van Loomis stepped ashore.

He had seen Jéo two days ago on the mainland. This spring month, while the moon was rising, was the courtship month. Jéo, young and stalwart and well-to-do, was seeking a second concubine. Mr. van Loomis knew that, and knew that Jéo wanted to be much ashore this month, and he knew that was why Jéo was glad to have Mario on the lighthouse. Mario, for all his stupidity, could be left to watch the light. Jéo's father, the old keeper, was ill on the mainland, and Jéo was very glad of Mario. He had told Mr. van Loomis that the Inspector was coming, and the day before they had seen the ketch come in. Mr. van Loomis had forbidden the Inspector a landing on the island itself, and there was no love between them. Now Jéo reported that the Inspector had said that Mario Fernandes was not to stay on the lighthouse, that he was not a fit person to be near the light.

"Mario Fernandes will stay on the lighthouse," said Mr. van Loomis.

"Ohé," said Jéo in perfect agreement.

"Send Mario Fernandes to me," Mr. van Loomis was about to say when he remembered that Mario would probably not come. He said instead, "Where is he?"

Mario was fishing at the back of the lighthouse, hunched on a rock, his big dark head turned towards the sea. He only hunched himself more closely as he heard Jéo's call. "Stay here," said Mr. van Loomis to Jéo and picked his way over the rocks to Mario. "Good morning," he said, and as Mario did not answer he said it again in Spanish, "Buenos días."

Mario looked round and scowled.

"Fishing?" asked Mr. van Loomis for something to say.

"Sea not belong-a you," said Mario rudely in his thick blurred voice.

"You have baited your line too high," said Mr. van Loomis. "That makes it too heavy, and your hooks are too big. You will lose it."

Mario scowled again. He was not a good fisherman and he knew it.

He is like a great bullock, the way he moves his head from side to side when he is worried, thought Mr. van Loomis. Mario was worried now. He wished that Mr. van Loomis and the boatmen would not come and look on his shame. The heavy mat of curls on his forehead made him look more like a bullock than ever, but it did not hide the dumb unhappiness of his eyes. "I am unhappy, unhappy," Mario would have said, but he could not say it; he did not know how to, he could only feel it. He was sent away from the island where he had grown up, where people were tolerant of him; away from the drink that lifted him up into another Mario who was braver and more articulate, even if he were sick next day. Now he was penned here with himself, usually only with himself, for Jéo went ashore; at times he was frantic and beat his head against the pillbox wall to make something else, if only a hurt, to

58

help Mario to get away from Mario. This Adam loneliness was worst for Mario, as it was best for Filipino who needed to be solitary. Mario needed people; he was gross and lustful; grossness and lust thrive on people. Now he was cut off and he felt as if he were dying. "What did I do?" asked Mario, and his eyes filled with tears so that the sea and the line, with its dancing pieces of white shark flesh on the big hooks, blurred in front of his eyes. He could not remember what it was he had done except that it was something to do with Charis. "I didn't want your nasty daughter," he flung in Spanish at Mr. van Loomis.

The sea roaring in the caves below the rocks sounded loudly in Mr. van Loomis's ears and he had to drive his nails into his palms. He remembered how Charis had thought sea lions were actual lions, wet and sleek, with waves for manes. Lions were roaring in him now; he shut his eyes so that he would not see Mario. "Why did you touch her then?" he asked, controlling himself.

Mario did not know why, as he did not know what else he could have done. He had been drunk and she was near and a girl. Mario had always wanted a girl; the island girls threw water in his face and laughed at him. He had a fleeting remembrance of Charis that night; her skin was white and soft, he remembered that clearly, and from that white skin something dim came into his brain, something like a reason, and all at once he knew he had a reason. He said, "I-a thought you-a meant her for me."

"For you?" Mr. van Loomis shouted, and he shuddered.

Mario saw the shudder and his hurt eyes glowered. "I-a man!" he said with dignity, then he lapsed into Spanish. "You can't be a favourite and then not a favourite," he said.

"You never were a favourite," said Mr. van Loomis curtly in Spanish too. He opened his eyes and looked at Mario with loathing. "I never could bear the sight of you."

There was silence while the line shook and quivered with the pounding of the waves and slid a little farther off the rock into the sea.

"I thought you were kind," said Mario. "I thought you

were wonderful. Yo creía que usted era un bueno hombre! Que idiota! You took the island from me—"

"It wasn't yours."

"It was my mother's. You took it. You didn't ask her to give it to you. No! No! Jesús! Usted era demasiado listo! You were too clever!"

"I bought it from the Puerto company who owned it and never fished it," said Mr. van Loomis. "Nobody wanted it. It was too far away."

"I wanted it," said Mario, and his big lips trembled.

"You and your mother were allowed to live here, that was all. I was a fool to let you stay."

"Now you won't let me," said Mario. "You won't let me live. Pheasant taught me about Our Lady. Our Lady will punish you. You wait and see. Dios lo castigará! Ya verás. . . ! Ya lo verás. . . ! I thought you were wonderful. I tried to learn . . ." He could not think now what it was that Mr. van Loomis had tried to make him learn.

"Everyone has more than I have," he said in a torrent of Spanish. "Every little garden boy. They all laugh at me. Why? Why? I always obeyed you. You didn't tell me not to touch Charis. I thought you meant her for me. One minute you tell me I am different, like you, next minute you say I am not. How am I to know? I shall do something to you," shouted Mario. "I shall do bad. If ever I can do anything to you, I shall. To her and to you. I hate you. You wait and see what I shall do. You wait. Espera! Espera . . . mal hombre!"

Mr. van Loomis turned to go, and Mario scrambled to his feet. He had not realized that Mr. van Loomis was only paying a visit. "You-a take Mario?"

"Certainly not," said Mr. van Loomis.

"Not?" Mario shook his head as if he had not quite heard, and his hair fell into his eyes. "Not?" bellowed Mario.

"I told you, not."

"Please-a. Please. Por amor de Dios! Please-a van Loomis. Please! Please!"

Mr. van Loomis walked away.

Mario stood a moment, doubling and undoubling his great fists, then he bent and picked up a stone, a small rock, and hurled it straight at Mr. van Loomis, at least Mario thought it was straight, but it fell harmlessly on one side. Mr. van Loomis did not even turn his head. In a few moments Mario heard the sound of the canoe going away.

He sank down on his rock, sniffing and rubbing his hands into his eyes. In the sunlight he saw them going away towards the mainland, the paddles flashing together, Luck's "hé's" coming across the waves, Mr. van Loomis sitting under his awning on the red cushions, going towards his island that was Mario's island.

Mario shook his head from side to side and then gave up; sobbing a little, he bent down to pick up his clumsy fishing line, but it was not there. Mr. van Loomis had been right; baited too heavily, it had slid down into the sea.

Then Mario really burst into tears.

CHAPTER VI

When Filipino, followed by all the island eyes, went speeding after the dinghy, he was not thinking only of the two strangers; with the wonder of them was a new wonder at himself, Filipino.

He felt he was a new Filipino. He thought even the strangers must recognize him as different. Before they would have treated me as an island boy, thought Filipino, as a servant; now they will see I am a young man. Mr. van Loomis had said he was a real young man, and he had argued with Mr. van Loomis and, what was more wonderful, Mr. van Loomis had argued with him. "Yes, we had an argument, we *argued together!*" said Filipino aloud and dizzily. He felt he was now capable of arguing with the two strangers, no matter who they might turn out to be. Before he would have been simply at their beck and call, as he had been at Mr. van Loomis's. "Do this.

Do that. Fetch this. Take that. Go there. Come here," murmured Filipino. Those days, of course, were not yet over, but release had begun; the promise of release. "He will send me to college," said Filipino.

Colleges were in America or Europe. Oxford was a college. Mr. van Loomis had been at Oxford. He had etchings of Oxford in his room, and Filipino had stood in front of them often, gazing into them as if his soul would rake out their meaning; he had tried to puzzle out their buildings, spires and towers and quadrangles. In England even the villages had spires. They must have done a very lot of building, thought Filipino.

Now as he went after the dinghy he studied the empty sea air, trying to imagine it pierced with spires, but he could not. He looked down into the glassy depths of the sea where he could see fish swimming, pale and coloured and rainbow-striped with a sudden shot of silver as one darted behind the clear fronds of weeds; far down below were anemone beds, but no towers such as had been in King Arthur's sunken country underneath the sea, the same Arthur who had pulled the sword from the stone in the picture in Charis's book that first day. King Arthur's country had passed away; it was lost under the sea, but from it you could hear bells ringing. Filipino had never heard a bell as he had never seen a spire. "But I shall," said Filipino. First he would go to London, London lying upon its river: *"Sweet Thames, run softly till I end my song."* Filipino imagined the Thames, and he did not imagine far wrong: on the island river a haze hung in a mist in the early morning: Filipino imagined the Thames like that but wider and, of course, built over. *"Ships, towers, domes, theatres and temples lie":* Wordsworth is a very good name for a poet, thought Filipino. He had once said that to Charis and added that, if he ever came to be a poet himself, he should like to take as his name Wordsworth the Second. "You can't do that, it's too well known," said Charis. "But I should be well known and I should *honour* it," said Filipino in rebuke.

Who was Filipino? He often wondered that himself; meanwhile he was a fine young male, beautiful and tall, slim hipped, loose haired, with an extraordinary virility and brilliance and simplicity (the only person who had

62

not seen him yet was Mr. van Loomis, and even Mr. van Loomis had begun to have inklings). But Filipino was uncertain; anything distracted him, and he varied from day to day. He was already the island songmaker and sang the old folk songs to the long-necked sitar that was not unlike a guitar and that he played better than anyone else on the island; but he was not content with songs. "I shall be an explorer," Filipino had often said, but he was exploring all the time. Now he looked across the sea to the dinghy he was rapidly overtaking; in it were two real unknown men; they would open new worlds to him, worlds of which he and Charis had dreamed and thought and read. Suddenly he was a little frightened. Not very nice things happen, thought Filipino, and his eyes looked scared. Suppose they are not nice men? he thought. Suppose they are bad? There are many bad people, thought Filipino.

Mr. van Loomis had ordered the *Times,* the *Spectator, Punch,* the *Illustrated London News,* and the *Magician's Monthly* to be sent with the island mail; none of them was a sensational paper, but in each of them, plain enough, were tales of pain and hate, fighting and killing, hanging and shooting, poverty and disease. Sometimes they had frightened Charis and Filipino so that they felt they would rather not read; Filipino had sometimes felt he must shut his eyes and stop his ears and go back to his peaceful little hut and his songs, but "I want to be serious," he told Charis. "We must be con . . . con . . ." "Contemporary," said Charis, and they read on without flinching.

"Then . . . are people not good?" he had asked Charis.

"No," said Charis. After a moment she said, "Yes. Yes and no. Good and bad." Charis was both more mature and less enthusiastic than Filipino; she did not catch fire but, as she read the papers, she saw something he did not. She saw a weight of judgment and taste and a steady sanity that helped to balance the horrors. Filipino saw only one thing at a time, Charis looked more widely, if not widely enough. She had pronounced primly, "Good and bad, like you and me."

"But we are good," said Filipino in surprise.

Charis shook her head. "No one is good," she said. "My father says man has tamed everything but himself."

"What has he tamed?" Filipino asked immediately, but he did not listen for an answer; taming, to him, had brought a picture of the little monkey Resurrection had tamed; it was wild, but Resurrection had made friends with it, and it came when he called it and sat on his shoulder and ate nuts from his hand. There was, Filipino had read, a belief that man was descended from a monkey, and now he had a sudden thought that every man had a monkey in him still; now Filipino saw Mr. van Loomis as a great white ape; Charis was a rare white she-monkey; a dark spider monkey was Niu, and a plump pollen-yellow female was Flora Annie; and I have a monkey, thought Filipino. That was not a funny thought, it was uncomfortable; I stole those cigarettes, thought Filipino now; I didn't want to steal them, but I stole. I go from one thing to another, he thought hopelessly, just like a monkey seizing and throwing away. He saw the monkey looking at him with its shallow eyes, and the eyes reminded him of a look he had seen in a real person; with a shock he realized that the person was Mario Fernandes. "But there is nothing in me that is like Mario *Fernandes!*" cried Filipino, shocked, but still the monkey's eyes persisted in looking like Mario's. "Then is Mario Fernandes sad?" asked Filipino. That was a new thought; he had always treated Mario as a clumsy joke. I don't understand what I am thinking, thought Filipino.

Still paddling, he began to think again about his twin brother. He had always despised Resurrection a little for being content to remain a gardener; now he began to wonder about his strength and gentleness; Resurrection was stronger than Filipino, but he was always gentle; that was why the monkey came to him and not to Filipino; but there was no trace of any monkey in Resurrection; no trace of Mario. Filipino could not imagine Resurrection stealing cigarettes. An uneasy thought came to Filipino: had the quiet young brother tamed himself better than he, the brilliant, boastful Filipino? But Resurrection had nothing to tame, said Filipino in contempt. I am wild. Again he had a quick thought of that monkey, but he turned his mind hastily away from it and began to chant,

"O wild West Wind, thou breath . . ." I am informed with poetry, said Filipino proudly.

He meant that he had learned it, but there was more poetry in Filipino than that; there was poetry in his songs, in his music, in his bones, in his feeling for the island, in his feeling for himself and his twin brother, in his visions of places far beyond the sea, in his dreamings and torments and passionate longing. He need not have worried as to what he meant to be. Filipino, that uneasy burning being, was born a poet; everything he saw or felt was spun into that; it was that that gave him at once naïveté and wisdom, that made him catch fire and burned him out, so that he needed his long spells of quiescent dreaming. "Where do you fly?" they asked him, teasing, but, without teasing, he knew that he flew. He was also a very robust and greedy young man, easily side-tracked, interested in too many things. "You will get into trouble," said Niu. "You make much trouble," said Niu.

Now, as he sent his boat flying over the water to catch the strangers, splashing his back with drops, he pretended he was in England. England was set in a silver sea; the sea round the island was a deep dark blue, green in the swell, but Filipino knew the colour of silver, he cleaned it every day, and he saw the English sea as immeasurably shining. England itself was green, he knew that too, and it had primroses, but he did not know what they were. London was the chief town, and England was very cold. Filipino tried to imagine what it was like to be cold; sometimes, bathing in the river before the sun was up, he had been chilled, but in England you woke and the world was frozen and all the green was white. *"When men were asleep, the snow came flying . . ."* He had not, of course, seen snow. Charis said snow was like manna, but they had not seen manna either. "It is very snow," said Filipino aloud, trying to imagine what it was like. He tried to think of the island covered in snow; the people would think the gods were furiously angry, and they would tremble and beat drums and make a sacrifice, one of the sacrifices that Mr. van Loomis had forbidden but that went steadily on. "A cock," said Filipino lingeringly, "or a white kid." Blood on a white skin was very decorative. The English took snow in their stride, thought Filipino

65

and sighed; he was not aware that he took many things in his stride that would considerably have upset the English.

He paddled on more slowly, and now he was thinking that snow, white and pure and cold, must be akin to the cloud on the mountain; the cloud made him think of Charis, and he began, in his head, to make a song about snow; he heard its music, the words came to him. He knew now that he should not have said "it is very snow." That was incorrect; it came from thinking in the island language, Terraquenese into English; how often had Charis told him he must think directly in English; but "very snow" seemed to suit what he would say.

The snow is very snow of very snow this morning . . .

and Filipino paddled on in the hot sunshine, which, unshaded as he was, was sending sweat pouring down his back.

Snow is absent and pure and cold . . .

If the snow were absent it would not be there, thought Filipino. That was a nuisance because it sounded well; he meant absent as Charis was often absent, absent-minded, but you could not say snow was absent-minded; snow did not have a mind. How difficult it was to write a song! thought Filipino. He knew he was not going as fast as Mr. van Loomis had intended him to go but he still dallied;

*The snow is snow of very snow this morning,
  absent and pure and cold . . .*

He decided to sing it aloud, and he was still singing as he caught up with the dinghy and circled round it to show off a little, travelling fast now, and then back-paddled suddenly and stood up, carried past it by the impetus of his boat. "Good morning," he said politely.

"What were you singing?" asked Valentine, and McGinty stared with his mouth half open.

Filipino did not answer. He had forgotten his song: it was suddenly brought home to him that he was here, in the presence of two wonderful strangers, and that they were really two real young men. A thudding came up into his ears, and, while he had not felt the rocking sea or the buoyant jumping of his boat, this made him dizzy. He dropped down on his knees in the boat. "Please," said Filipino dizzily and shut his eyes.

"Please what?" said Valentine. This almost naked boy, with his black hair flying and the drops gleaming on his brown skin, with his well-turned English, was like an apparition.

"A moment," murmured Filipino. Then he opened his eyes and stared long at Valentine and McGinty, looking into their faces with shining eyes, caressing every feature of them until McGinty blushed.

"Can't you ask him what he wants?" growled McGinty to Valentine. "Go on! Speak to him."

But Filipino had begun first. "What is your name? How old are you? Where do you live?" he was asking Valentine. They were the questions that children ask one another, but Filipino did not know that; he wanted to hear the answers. He fixed his eyes on Valentine and asked again, "Where do you live?"

"London," said Valentine briefly. "Now—"

But Filipino interrupted him. "London!" Filipino cried. "Not *London!* Excuse me," he said. He felt dizzy again, and once again he had to kneel down in his boat and keep his eyes closed. Then he opened his eyes. He felt elated and full of joyful omens; this was a joyful omen, and he could not contain himself. "That was one of my own songs I was singing to you," he boasted to Valentine in joy. "Could you write a song in our language?" He surveyed them both with amused eyes and said, "No, I bet you you could not, but I can nearly write a song in English. I shall be able to write one quite when I have been to college."

"Are you going to *college?*"

"To Oxford," said Filipino happily.

Valentine looked at Filipino's bare wet torso, at his knotted-up blue and white cloth and his bare brown legs and feet and the chema flower behind his ear.

"Do you know what I shall do when I have my degree?" asked Filipino, quite unaware of Valentine's look.

"Or is it more than one degree?" asked Filipino. "If so I shall get them all. I intend to do everything. And I shall be a musician and poet as well."

"Being a musician and poet is a whole-time business," said Valentine sourly.

"I shall be both," said Filipino. "But first—"

"You will have no time for first," said Valentine; he did not know why he went on arguing but he did. "No time for anything," he said severely.

"For Christ's sake!" interrupted McGinty. "What *is* all this about? Are you going to talk to him all day?"

"I shall come back here and be indigenous," said Filipino to Valentine, taking no notice of McGinty. "I shall collect the relics of my people and all of them will be printed. We shall see them in *print!*" said Filipino reverently. "No one has ever written them down. Some of our island songs are very beautiful. Listen." And, standing up in his canoe, he began to sing again, looking over Valentine's shoulder at the cloud on the mountain while the dinghy floated buoyantly on the waves.

The song was a light nasal chant that changed to a minor key and held an underlying sadness. It seemed, to Valentine, to gather up all that the fringes of the island had held for him that morning; he sat, rocked by the floating dinghy, and listened entranced while McGinty fidgeted and groaned impatiently until it ended.

"That is our rainbow song," said Filipino. "You will hear it all over the island, everywhere. All the people sing it, but we have songs more beautiful than that. We have blood songs, very old. This island, they say, every year gives fruit and corn and salt and gold and blood of its own earth. All these are in its earth."

"Surely not blood," objected Valentine.

"No. Blood is shed," agreed Filipino.

"Is blood shed here?"

Filipino dropped his eyelids. "Now we are not allow," he said primly, and as if that made him remember he said, "I have come to take you to Mr. van Loomis." He saw the mail bags and his eyes widened. "We not allow to touch those," he said.

"We found them broken loose and brought them in," said Valentine.

"We not allow to touch," repeated Filipino.

"Listen," broke in McGinty. He could wait no more. At least this talk of songs and salt and blood proved one thing, that English was spoken on the island, and that promised civilization. "Listen," said McGinty. "We're in trouble. We had to come down behind that island there; had no fuel, no juice." Filipino did not look as if he understood. "No petrol," said McGinty.

"Petrol?" repeated Filipino politely. "Oh! *Petroleum!*" said Filipino. "That is used for motors?"

"Ours is a plane," said McGinty.

"An aeroplane?" Filipino's eyes were bright with interest. "A wind-machine!"

"Wind-machine!" said McGinty.

"It is partly a wind-machine," Valentine pointed out.

"Is it down? On the sea? Can we see it? Is it here?" asked Filipino, dazzled.

"No, or we shouldn't be sticking to these bloody paddles," said McGinty tersely.

Filipino looked with pity, but the paddles were not bloody. He found McGinty hard to understand.

"Listen," said Valentine in his turn. "We want to get away from here, urgently."

"But you haven't been here yet," said Filipino, disappointed.

"I have urgent business. We have to get away quickly." Valentine's voice was authoritative, and Filipino instinctively became obedient. "What island is this?" asked Valentine.

"Mr. van Loomis call it Terraqueous," said Filipino noncommittally.

"Earth and Water," murmured Valentine, and he asked Filipino, "What is its island name?"

"Island name Mānoa," said Filipino with pride.

"Mānoa." Valentine tried the sound and liked it. "What does it mean?"

"Earth and Water," said Filipino.

"Terraqueous, Mānoa," said Valentine, looking at the island.

"Never heard of it," said McGinty as if that were a reason why it should not exist.

"Is there any petrol here?" asked Valentine.

"For what?" asked Filipino, amazed, and then he saw by Valentine's face that he was getting cross. "Is no petrol," said Filipino hastily.

"Not even a garage?"

"Is no garage." "Garage. Petrol." Filipino tried these entrancing new words over on his tongue. "Petrol. Garage. Garage. Petrol."

But Valentine was speaking. "Does a plane ever come?"

Filipino shook his head.

"Then when does the steamer call?"

"Is no steamer."

"There must be *some* means of communication," said Valentine crossly. "How do you get to the other islands?"

"Don't get," said Filipino. "Unless you want to go to Zambun. Ha! Ha!" They did not laugh, and Filipino had his first lesson in the provincialism of jokes.

"Listen,' said Valentine, and he spoke in a slightly hectoring way to show he was determined. "Your Mr. van Loomis isn't an islander. He didn't grow on the island. How did he come? Something must have brought him here." Filipino nodded. "Very well then," said Valentine. "When was the last time a steamer called?"

"Twenty years ago," said Filipino. "Before that I was born."

There was silence from the two in the dinghy. They were leaning on their paddles. Neither spoke. They looked tired out, bewildered, draggled.

"Come," said Filipino gently. "Come. I will take you to Mr. van Loomis."

After a moment, still in that silence, they turned the clumsy dinghy round. Filipino fastened his boat to theirs and helped to steady them against the current, and they began to paddle back the long way they had come up the bay.

CHAPTER VII

CHARIS had come down to walk on the beach. She had
ceased to cry; she had changed her cloth and sash and
blouse, combed her hair, washed her face, and calmed
her mind. She had also thought a great deal about her
mother, and about herself, and accepted her lot.

Charis had pondered and thought, in a way that Filipino had not, over the books and newspapers they had
read. Filipino was concerned with himself. Charis was
concerned, in a way that was almost painful, with other
people, other girls, people and girls she had never met but
read about; she thought about them and compared them
with herself. For instance, she had tried earnestly, from
illustrations and photographs, to make out their dresses
and coats and shoes and hats; then, "What should I look
like in a hat?" she said to Pheasant.

"Yo' has a hat," said Pheasant. The island hats were
large, of plaited straw, but, like Filipino and the real
young man, Charis did not count hers as a hat.

"I mean a real hat," she said. Now she despaired of
ever wearing one.

She was hopelessly alone. Most disheartening of anything she had read, to Charis, because they made her feel
most separated, were the commercial advertisements.
*"Study at home for a degree, now more than ever neces-
sary for you in your career. Take the Home Economics
Course and become important to your work.
Accountancy: Advertising: Bookkeeping: Business
Management: Commercial Art. Send stamp for free book-
let."* On her father's desk lay her thesis on "The Origin of
Art in Primitive Man" with which he would presently be
well pleased; Charis could speak Spanish, French, and
German besides the island dialect and her own well-in-

flected English; she was thoroughly grounded in mathematics, history, literature, geography, biology, botany, astronomy, and any of her father's subjects, but she had no knowledge of these things that the advertisements said were necessary; she did not even know what they were; she could not take a course, she had no money; she could not send a stamp for a free booklet; there were no stamps on the island, the only mail was her father's and that went by bag. Now she had learned who she was, she had, in a way, met her mother, but that did not make her any more like any other girl, any more like Anya, Rosalind, or Emma: though they probably knew nothing of commercial art or business management, they at least had stamps and letters. Charis had never had a letter. One day she had written a letter, to try it. She began it: *Dear* —Dear who? In the end she had had to write it to herself: *Dear Charis*. At least it had given her a forlorn identity, but it was forlorn. "Father said the teacher would come," said Charis. "What teacher?" There were no teachers on the island, and she knew now that the island was to ring her round for ever. "For ever and ever and ever," said Charis aloud.

In a way she was right. The sediment of the island was in her bones, in her no less than the islanders, and they, if they were sent to Zambun, died of homesickness. Filipino had been right; it was a sediment of coral and salt and soil, a vein of gold, a core of fire, and a cool surface of dew. The strata of the island held all these things from fire to dew and had an interesting interwoven covering of growing and living things that shimmered into a whole as exquisitely as the weaver birds' nests that hung on the palms. The wind blew through the island in an arcade of sound in which all its storms and winds, songs and voices, living and elemental, were blended in a cool perpetual echo of the fringe of all these sounds.

In the first morning light the fishermen sang as their boats drifted down with the nets, down past the house to the bay; that lazy, gentle singing had woken Charis ever since she could remember. Then came the higher, shriller singing of the herd children driving the goats and cows up the valleys with songs and whistles from boy to boy and the little pipe of a bamboo flute. Charis had early learned to play on those flutes herself; the flutes were sad, all the island songs had cadences of sadness, as Valentine had heard in Filipino's song; this happy easy life was tinged with sadness and, as in all life, sorrow was never far away. The island was old, how old could be seen in the temple on the mountain where the old vestments and shields and masks were kept for the ritual dances. On festival days there were drums sounding from the sea and land, in the villages and courtyards, in the small streets of the town, in the fields and down from the temple. Charis had often met the drummers, naked, with their faces whitened and a red noose on their hair and vermilion paint between their eyes; they had frightened her as a child, and a drum was always to mean fright and excitement to her. Every year new eyes were painted on the boats, new patterns on the house walls and the wheels of the carts, and the whips were tufted with new bright cotton. The dyes for the whip tufts were gaudy, but the dyes for the cloths were the old, trusted vegetable dyes, and the only colours were dark, though rich and lasting. Cloths were printed with hand patterns of red and deep blue, blankets were dyed red and dark saffron, and the pottery was brown and grey, deep blue or its natural brown-red.

The people worshipped the elements and the sun, the moon, earth, and the rain; the rainbow, they believed, interceded for them. They believed that they themselves were spirits and that the spirits of the dead were more powerful than they.

Charis was tinged with this worship but she could not see the need for complication. If one worshipped the sun, what did one need but the sun? Why the temple, these symbols, these drums? Charis had not yet learned the significance of the fact that nothing can go near the sun and not be scorched, that man cannot even look at it with his naked eye. Charis was young and very convinced.

"What religion is Charis?" Valentine was to ask later.

"Charis has studied comparative religion with me since she was ten years old," said Mr. van Loomis.

"Yes, but what religion is she?" asked Valentine, and Mr. van Loomis realized that, for all he had carefully taught her, he had omitted to give her a religion of her own.

"All she needs is an open mind," said Mr. van Loomis, but Valentine still seemed to think she needed a religion.

It had not occurred to Charis that any of the comparative religions were to do with her. Impersonally she had learned of the teachings of Christ, Buddha, Mahomet, Confucious, and the Greek and Hindu philosophers; none of them had seemed personally for her. Neither was she touched by the magic that interested her father—or was she? Or was it a different magic? She thought how the spark came out of the tinder on the dry wood and made a fire . . . and no one knows what will be wood to what tinder, or what fire they light, she said to herself. There is magic in that; but I shan't light any fire, said Charis. She was too cool, and she thought of Filipino, how if he walked on the shore he would kick the stones, pick up shells and throw them away, with a perpetual inner restlessness, sit down on a rock, dreaming, gazing, with his thought flowing in and out like the waves, like the tide. Filipino, sitting on the rock, had fire in him; he smouldered. She was cool, but it seemed to Charis that there was this to be said for her: she saw magic where nobody else did. "Isn't it magic, this that is in people, that deep fire?" asked Charis. "The rest is conjuring," she might have said. Her father had told her he had given up conjuring, but he had said that we all conjure a little. Because we must, said Charis, her eyes on the sea, unless we have enough magic. She saw this clearly in Filipino: that he would have to choose between conjuring and his own original magic.

Her attention was caught by Resurrection, who was walking along the shore towards the garden bay. He had come down on the shore to collect the smooth white pebbles with which Niu liked to edge the flower beds in the kitchen courtyard. Mr. van Loomis had forbidden them in the garden, and everyone thought that a very singular taste. Charis watched the tall boy walk along. She had not particularly noticed him before; now she saw that he was very like Filipino, but taller, more strong. Resurrection walked along, choosing a pebble here and there and sometimes stopping to wash one in a pool and then put-

74

ting it in the basket he carried on one hip. As he walked he looked so quiet that Charis thought he seemed to have the power to melt into the air, the clouds, the flying birds, the palm leaves in the breeze, and the tumbling sea, and yet still be Resurrection walking calmly along. The sun shone through his thin white cloth as he walked, lighting its edges, and Charis had the curious thought that what was fire in Filipino had turned to light in Resurrection.

She looked away from Resurrection and saw Valentine.

It was as if the sea had drawn back for a moment, a long moment, leaving the shore bare. The moment was held in time: the sun shone, the white sands stretched, the wave held back like glass: nothing moved. There was no sound but the sound of a sigh from the wave; then Charis knew it was her own sigh, and the wave ebbed back and another came up, washing nearly to her feet as she watched Valentine walk towards her on the beach.

There were some little monkeys chattering in a cotton tree that stood behind the palms; the wind blew in the palms, making whispers that mingled with the monkey chatter as if it were an urgent voice trying to tell something through all the little broken monkey words; the voice seemed to be in Charis as she watched Valentine draw near. Charis had an inner ear, and she had proved, honestly and beyond a doubt, that if she listened to it she did not go wrong. She might not do right, but she would not go wrong. When she listened she was aware of something in herself larger than she, a feeling of being allied. It had not struck her that this had anything to do with the comparative religions. Now she felt it say, "Look well, look deeply at this young man." "But . . . it's impossible," said Charis. "A moment ago he was not here." And it answered calmly, "He is here now."

Charis was often grave, but as Valentine came nearer she watched him with a peculiar gravity and a mounting happiness. The wind blew the folds of her cloth against her legs; she was glad that she had changed and put on a cloth of soft raw white silk and not the usual cotton; it blew against her, softly and reassuringly, and she knew how gracefully it wrapped her thighs and hips and caught her at the waist where the matching white silk sash was wound over her loose blouse. She hoped there were no tear stains now on her face, and she was glad that her hair was drawn back smoothly and caught behind her ears with two beaten silver pins; Charis's hair was not long enough to twist into the usual island knot, and she wore it loose and straight to her shoulders. She had taken off her great straw hat, there was shade here from the palms, and she held it against her and smelled the scent of the chema flower she had pinned in her blouse as Valentine came up to her.

Charis looked well and deeply at Valentine and decided he was beautiful. He was taller than anyone she had ever seen except her father, but where Mr. van Loomis was broad and heavy Valentine was slim, and the effect, to Charis, was of a wand, or a tree walking. He was tired, rumpled, and unshaven, but Charis did not see that; his clothes fitted, which Mr. van Loomis's and the islanders' did not; Valentine looked, to Charis, as if he were poured into his clothes. His paleness seemed wonderful to her after the deep island skins; she had seen that paleness before only in her own mirror; Valentine's hand, when he put it out, was almost as white as hers; he had a gold half-hunter watch on his wrist; the only other watch Charis had ever seen was her father's large fob watch; but, with all the revelation that Valentine was to Charis, she immediately saw something his mother and his sister and his friends had not seen, the honesty and trouble in his eyes. There is something the matter, thought Charis; his eyes looked as if he were hurt and puzzled, a strange thing in a polished, successful person like Valentine.

As for Valentine, then and ever afterwards, he saw Charis as gentle and strong; even when he learned that she was also a little shrew it made no difference; and, from the beginning, there was something else that tied him: Charis at once reminded him of his grandmother, and, to Valentine, his grandmother had been, as well as the sternest, the most interesting, the most romantic person he had known. Those qualities soothed him because they fulfilled all his needs; even as a little boy he had been the same.

"You are ruining that boy," his grandmother had told his mother.

76

"Why? He is an unstable, nervous, highly strung child I know, but I do everything I can to encourage him."

"He shouldn't be encouraged," said Valentine's grandmother. "And I don't agree; he isn't unstable, he is amazingly constant; he is a nervous, highly strung child and, I repeat, he shouldn't be encouraged; he is like a violin bow, and you tighten him up and up; what he needs at home is a letting-go, a loosening; he needs to loosen."

As Filipino had guided the dinghy to the shore, for Valentine the island had grown more and more like all coral and treasure islands. Flocks of bright birds rose up out of the woods and flew inland, like arrows, with staccato cries; they were green parakeets, and after them, silently, in a flash of scarlet and yellow, flew small and even brighter birds. He had caught a glimpse of the monkeys, brown and lithe when they were swinging, looking like large brown burrs with long tails when they sat still in the branches. There were flowers growing round the houses, hibiscus and marigolds and rioting gourd flowers that were canary yellow; there were creepers too, of a white flower that hung between the trees. Valentine had found he was thinking they were white passion flowers. Why? He did not know if passion flowers could be white; he imagined they were purple, but now he saw what he thought were white passion flowers, clear among the vivid scarlet of poinsettias and cotton trees.

Fishing boats had put out to them, and Filipino proudly brought them in through a floating crowd of laughing, shouting, gesticulating men. There seemed to be a great deal of fishing; nets hung from the boats and nets hung in the villages too. Valentine saw fish scales glittering in a net hung from the branch of a cotton tree under the red flowers that were blossoming where presently the great burst cotton pods would be. Other trees were flowering in the woods, more cotton trees, cassias, mauve bauhenias. "It must be their spring," Valentine had said.

"Spring? Would they have a spring?" asked McGinty, surprised. The only spring he recognized had primroses and thrushes' eggs and cool sunshine tempered with rain. "I don't call this a spring," said McGinty, but Valentine was right. A smell of honey and scent had come lightly over the sea from the trees and seemed to him to give a premonition of new life and happiness; with it came a smell of earth that was mingled with dew drying in the sun and fish drying on the shore, of burning grass and wood and dung; and as he landed he had smelled a whiff of peculiar sweetness that he could not identify; could any flower smell as strong and as sweet as that? Now, standing by Charis, that scent came to him again, and he saw it came from a small white wax-petalled flower she wore pinned to her blouse.

Charis held out her hand and said, "How do you do?" as she had read they said in books, and Valentine did not guess till long afterwards, when he saw it must have been so, that it was the first time she had said it. Except for a faint pink flush on her cheeks the colour of the island oleander, there was no sign that this was new to her.

"How do you do?" said Valentine, shaking her hand gently. "My name is Valentine Doubleday. Are you Miss van Loomis?"

"I am Charis van Loomis." Charis was not sure if she should have said Miss van Loomis, but, as he had given his two names, she did that too. Valentine Doubleday? Lines from the papers came to Charis from that. She tried to remember, and all at once she knew. "Valentine Doubleday. The playwright?" she asked smoothly, and Valentine was tickled and a little pleased to find himself known even here, on this far island. "Welcome to Terraqueous," said Charis.

Though she could not have been more surprised to see him if the sky had opened and he had descended in front of her, she knew from the books and plays that she had read (she wished she had read one of his plays, but in the days when Mr. van Loomis had chosen his books Valentine was learning his first lines in *Pelican Pie*) that strangers, to begin with, talked of things that did not really matter and that were nothing to do with themselves or the moment in hand; it was called conversation, and now, though she was burning to ask Valentine why he was here, where he had come from, and how he had come, she said, turning back to walk along the beach, "I'm glad you were able to come now, in spring. This is the best time for our flowers."

More than ever Valentine was reminded of his grand-

78

mother. Just so, when he had come in avid with some desire or project of his own, his grandmother had made him wait and not fidget, while she talked lightly or austerely or charmingly of something else that did not matter at all. It was not till long afterwards that he had realized how valuable those moments of control had been or how they put the project in its right perspective; it was Valentine's capacity for waiting without fuss, his extraordinary patience, that had helped to bring him where he was; but he needed that reminding still.

Valentine missed his grandmother more than he knew. She had died when he was seventeen, and no one had taken her place. His mother was devoted: his grandmother had never been devoted; she kept herself outside Valentine and then she could see him clearly. She had soothed him; someone as brilliant and busy as Valentine needs to be soothed, and he can be soothed only by firmness and the truth. Of late years, though he was still young, he had filled the eye too much to be told truths (and there were no home truths because he had no home; instinctively he lived apart from his mother). That was the difference in Charis from the first; she held back from him and saw him clearly.

"Very soon," Charis was saying now in her clear soft voice, "our wild lilies will be out and the quisqualis. I hope you will be able to wait for those." So would his grandmother have talked, but with this difference. "Have you seen the larkspurs?" she would have said. "The sweet peas? The snowball tree?" The homely flowers, the faint pale hues of Valentine's childhood; this girl stranger, cool and clear as she was, was yet exotic. Once again Valentine smelled the sweetness of the chiselled flower she wore; he liked her clothes: in some ways she did not remind him of his grandmother. Valentine was surprised to find that his blood was beating a little more quickly. As he walked beside Charis the sound of the surf and the waves sounded in his ears with the chattering of the monkeys and the whispering of the palms. Valentine heard that whispering clearly too.

The waves, as they swept up and back, left patterns of themselves in the wet sand from which bubbles winked in the sun and burst into the sand with a little plop that no one heard. The bubbles and the wet sand showed, momentarily, all the colours of the rainbow. A soft wind blew from the sea, and a breath of air blew back, spiced, from the island to the sea, and the cotton tree, where the monkeys were, dropped its scarlet petals on the sand. Charis and Valentine walked at the waves' edge, talking of nothing at all until Charis stood still and said, "Here is my father."

They had been so absorbed that she had not heard the "he's" coming back across the sea and Mr. van Loomis had landed and had been watching them from the garden for some time. When he had first seen the shape of Valentine standing beside Charis, it had been so exactly the shape of the young man he had prayed for that he had been afraid. Now he stood, watching them walk along by the sea, their heads turned to each other, Valentine bending a little to Charis. "Even the right height for each other," said Mr. van Loomis with as great a conceit as if he had made them.

When Filipino had brought the dinghy ashore and saw Charis some instinct had made him indicate her to Valentine and keep McGinty with him. "That is a rare good boy," said Mr. van Loomis, forgetting how troublesome Filipino had been, but when Mr. van Loomis looked at McGinty he immediately felt out of temper. McGinty affronted him; he did not like the way McGinty stood, leaning against a palm, and smoking; it looked laconic, and then he saw another thing that did not please him: Filipino was carrying something up the beach from the sea. The shapes were familiar to Mr. van Loomis: they were mail bags. Mr. van Loomis swelled with anger. "Who has touched those?" he said to Luck. "Who has dared to touch them?"

"The Tsulas, Tsula," suggested Luck.

A strange perturbation rose up in Mr. van Loomis. Now I shall have to read the mail; it will upset me. He was sure it would upset him. The outer world of intricacies and intrigues, of wars and finance, kings and duties, repelled him more and more. "Phaugh!" said Mr. van Loomis aloud. He was very angry. He tried to calm himself. "I have read dozens of mails. There is nothing in

80

them," he said. The thought still persisted that this time there might be.

Near Mr. van Loomis someone else was watching the strangers. It was Niu, come out from the kitchen where he had stirred up Serendipity and the house servants to proper hospitality. Niu looked down at Valentine and McGinty and his face was hard. Mr. van Loomis, looking at him, thought for a moment that Niu looked resentful, but as Niu turned to him his face was smooth and polite. "Tsulas are hot from the sun, Tsula," said Niu. "Better not open wine. I serve fruit drinks and coffee?"

"Ohé," said Mr. van Loomis, but his eyes followed Niu as he went back to the kitchen, his slippers flapping on the path.

Valentine and Charis walked towards Mr. van Loomis as he came down the steps onto the beach. As they drew near he forgot Niu. He saw that Valentine was indeed a personable young man, but, as he looked at the set of Valentine's head, it seemed arrogant to him. That is a very conceited young man, thought Mr. van Loomis. I shan't know what he is like until I test him. I mustn't let it be too easy, thought Mr. van Loomis, not for him and not for her. He believed Charis to be fastidious as well as romantic, and that would make her more difficult to please. I must give it an interest, thought Mr. van Loomis, something for them to cut their teeth on, a little opposition, and, as he went forward to meet them, he frowned and made his face set and grave.

"Good morning, sir," said Valentine.

Mr. van Loomis did not say "Good morning." He frowned again and said, "This is private property. May I ask what you are doing here?"

"Your boy brought us ashore," said Valentine, surprised.

"I sent him to bring you. I wanted to know what you are doing in these waters."

"Father!" said Charis. "Father!"

"Hush, Charis. I'm afraid we don't welcome strangers," said Mr. van Loomis.

"So I find," said Valentine with an edge to his voice that cut Charis sharply.

"Since the war we have had to be careful," said Mr.

van Loomis, inventing sentences that sounded well to him. "I shall have to ask to see your papers."

"Father!"

"Hush, Charis."

Charis looked at him in bewildered anguish.

"I am quite in order," said Mr. van Loomis. "I am magistrate here. I must ask to see your papers and those of your man—I am told you have a man—before I allow you to land here on Terraqueous."

"We have landed," said Valentine. He could not believe that this pomposity was serious, but Charis was aghast.

She left Mr. van Loomis and turned to Valentine. "I have never known my father to talk like this," she said in distress. "He *isn't* like this."

Valentine took his wallet out of his breast pocket and said stiffly, "I will get McGinty," and walked away down the beach.

"Father," said Charis urgently and softly, "why are you behaving to him like this? Father, isn't he our guest?" They had never had a guest before.

"Don't be foolish, child," said Mr. Van Loomis. "We have valuable fisheries on this island. I can't have every Tom, Dick, and Harry landing here."

"He isn't Tom, Dick, and Harry," said Charis nearly in tears. "He is Valentine Doubleday, the famous playwright, Father."

"I suppose he told you that."

"He didn't. He told me his name and I recognized him," said Charis with pride.

"Then you have been reading the newspapers too?"

"Yes," said Charis as if that were nothing, and she said, "Or I shouldn't have known who he was. He is a marvellous young man."

"What do you know about men?" said Mr. Van Loomis. "Don't be a fool, child. You haven't met any man except Mario and the islanders; you think he is marvellous because you only know Mario. You should have seen some of the young men I knew in my day—the McDugdale of McDugdale or Dundas's boy in the Argylls.

82

That was a young man if you like! Why, this is a Mario compared to them!"

"I don't believe you," said Charis. "I don't want to see any more men."

"How do you know?"

"I know," said Charis, and she might have said, "I seem to know him with my whole heart," but she could not say that, not yet. "I . . . I like him," said Charis.

"Phaugh!" said Mr. van Loomis, enormously pleased.

Perhaps it was the mention of the McDugdale of Mc-Dugdale, or the thought of the pearls for Charis's twenty-first birthday, but Mr. van Loomis seemed to see a shining floor, the lights shining down from chandeliers and the lines of lustres on the walls, shining on well-brushed heads, broad shoulders in velvet coats and the colours of the heavy, swinging plaids; they shone above bare shoulders, gleaming pearly-white ones, white against the tartans, and he had a sudden feeling that Charis ought to be there. He could feel the pearl that Prem had given him, it was in his pocket, between his fingers; it was his gift to Charis and now he thought with infinite regret that it was not enough. If she could have had her twenty-first birthday at Spey, a ball for her coming of age. She ought to have had it, thought Mr. van Loomis in dismay, and then Valentine came back along the beach, and Mr. van Loomis's spirits lifted. But there was one question to be settled, and he felt he could not wait to settle it. "Are you married or single?" asked Mr. van Loomis as he took the papers that Valentine gave to him. The answer was so important to him that his hand trembled.

"Single," said Valentine briefly. He had brought Mc-Ginty with him and introduced him now. " 'Lo," said McGinty pleasantly.

"Good morning," said Mr. van Loomis distantly.

"Good morning," said Charis gently. Though she was gentle, she could not help comparing McGinty unfavourably with Valentine. Poor McGinty had not a chance; no more than an islander, could he look happy when he was not happy; his beard was not fair like Valentine's but ginger, and his hair did not lie down but rose up from his haircut that had already given him a quiff; his skin too did not tan in the sun but turned pink; now he looked as if he had been boiled all over. Not as good looking, said Charis to herself. Not good looking at all.

Mr. van Loomis, having looked through their papers, was firing a hail of questions at Valentine to cover up his question as to Valentine's married state. "Your name is Doubleday? You are English? Where do you come from? How did you come? What happened?"

This was a little hard on Valentine. As he had been a king's son, he was used to being more than recognized, hailed and courted and flattered. He did not exactly want this, but he was used to it; people tumbled over themselves to meet his smallest wish; he had not know till now how spoiled he was. "You see our papers," he said stiffly. "We were flying from Sydney. I had flown out from London for my sister's wedding. Last night, making for Surabaya, we had come down at Atemboea and, just after taking off, we ran into a storm and were blown off our course. The radio failed, and we don't know where we are, and I'm afraid the name of your island doesn't tell us. We ran out of petrol and came down in the bay of that rock island and paddled ourselves across. I'm a playwright and I have a play just going into production; we open at Birmingham on the twenty-third, so that you see I must get back."

"You . . . you act in your plays as well as write and produce them, don't you?" asked Charis.

"Yes," said Valentine.

"You see, Father," said Charis, her eyes bright with interest. And she asked Valentine, "Are you in this one?"

"Yes."

"In the . . . chief part?" asked Charis with a sidelong look at Mr. van Loomis.

"I take the lead, of course."

"You *see*, Father."

Mr. van Loomis snorted.

"It's urgent I get back," said Valentine again. "Your boy says there is no petrol here."

"No," said Mr. van Loomis.

"I suppose that we can cable?"

"We have no cable station."

"Then wireless a signal?"

"There is no wireless."

"Then—"

"We are dependent," said Mr. van Loomis, "I should say, rather, that we *should* be dependent—did we need anything, which we don't, we are quite independent—on a chance yacht or fishing boat passing. We take our letters, if we have any, out to a buoy, and any ship that comes along takes them to the nearest office, probably Puerto, but that is four days' sail from here. She may have a bag for us, in that case she leaves it at the buoy. It is seldom or never that a ship puts in here. Our only regular caller is the lighthouse ketch, but, since we feed the crew from the island and they are islanders, she only calls four times a year. She came in yesterday. What a pity!" said Mr. van Loomis blandly.

McGinty gave a long rude whistle. Valentine looked at Mr. van Loomis, but Mr. van Loomis met his hard gaze kindly. "And if there is anything urgent?" asked Valentine.

"When you have lived as long as I have," said Mr. van Loomis, "you will know that nothing is urgent."

"Oh, don't be ridiculous!" said Valentine, his patience breaking. He turned his back on Mr. van Loomis, kicking up the sand with his foot. He felt like an ineffectual small boy. Charis looked at him with hurt and pitying eyes. Mr. van Loomis waited blandly.

McGinty went to Valentine and said urgently under his breath, "It doesn't matter what the old bastard says. We'll find a way to get out of here. They'll be looking for you, don't forget. Soon as it gets round, they'll be out after us. Don't let's argue. Let him talk all the cock he wants."

"I repeat, nothing is urgent," said Mr. van Loomis. "What you do in your world is your affair. This happens to be mine, and I refuse to have my peace disturbed. You will have to wait and see what comes. You have told me your story. Very well. Now you have landed, you may stay on the island, provided you do as I say."

"Thanks for nothing," murmured McGinty.

"This is my island," said Mr. van Loomis, "and you will do as I say. You will both of you go to my house, and you must give me your word," he said to Valentine, "that you will not try to leave the island, either of you, without my permission, or try by any means to reach the outside world. No rigging up of transmitters," he said severely to McGinty.

"What does he think I am?" McGinty murmured to Valentine, "a bloody W.E.M.?"

"Meanwhile I shall go out and find your flying boat," said Mr. van Loomis, "and verify your story."

"It happens to be true," said Valentine coldly.

"In that case I shall be able to verify it," said Mr. van Loomis. "Then I shall arrange to put out a signal, but first you must give me your word."

Valentine was looking at Charis.

All this time she had kept quiet, not interrupting her father though she was distressed. Valentine appreciated that quietness; presently, he guessed, when they were alone, she would deal with her father, but she kept his face for him in public. Valentine liked that too. He felt too weary to compete with Mr. van Loomis; suddenly it appeared that Mr. van Loomis was right and that nothing was urgent; London, Birmingham, the play, the whole business, seemed far away and more improbable than this improbable landing. He capitulated. "Very well," he said, "I give you my word. What else is there to do?"

"Nothing else," said Mr. van Loomis cheerfully. He turned and looked down the beach, beckoning Filipino. "And you should tell your man that he should wear a hat. A red head is a dangerous colour for the tropics."

McGinty scowled. "Why can't he speak to *me?*" murmured McGinty to Valentine. "I'm here, as good as him!"

"And now," said Mr. van Loomis, "my daughter will take you up to the house."

When they had gone Filipino emerged from behind a palm tree. "Did I do what you told me, Tsula?" asked Filipino. "Tsula, will you send me to college?"

"Very well. Very well," said Mr. van Loomis, answering the first part of the question. He was turning to follow the others when Filipino stopped him.

"Tsula, what is this?" and Filipino held out something on the palm of his hand. It shone small and round and white in the sun, and Mr. van Loomis took it and looked at it; it was an Australian sixpence. Filipino watched it, anguished while it was in Mr. van Loomis's hand.

"Where did you get this?"

"The red Tsula gave it, Tsula. Please to give it back!"

Mr. van Loomis was angry. Till that moment no islander on the island had touched a piece of money; even Mario's mother had had the sense to keep that from them. The island currency was barter and work. It seemed to Mr. van Loomis to fit McGinty that he should have come strolling in amongst them and at once tipped Filipino. Yes, given him a vulgar tip, thought Mr. van Loomis in fury.

"Tsula, give it back."

"You don't want it," said Mr. van Loomis.

"Tsula . . . please!"

Mr. van Loomis would have sent the sixpence spinning into the sea, but he remembered how tiresome Filipino had been about nothing that morning. I mustn't give the boy a grievance, thought Mr. van Loomis, and reluctantly he gave the sixpence back to Filipino.

"Tsula, is it money?" Filipino's tongue came out and wet his lips.

"Yes. Curse it and him and you!" said Mr. van Loomis, thoroughly out of temper, and walked away up the beach, but Filipino had not heard him.

He had never seen any money, but it was in every book and newspaper that he and Charis had read, and he knew it was important in the outside world. There came to Filipino, from the sixpence, a sense of freedom and power; also a great sense of responsibility; it was not for nothing that he had heard Pheasant tell the story of the Prodigal Son. Filipino tied the sixpence carefully in the corner of his cloth and tucked it deep down in his waist knot against his skin. "Money! I have money," said Filipino.

CHAPTER VIII

VALENTINE felt as if he were charmed. All through luncheon he listened to Mr. van Loomis's urbane conversation, watched the clear-cut shape of Charis's small head in the dining-room's shaded light, where Niu and the boy Filipino came and went behind them. McGinty did not speak; he looked pink and sulky in spite of Charis's efforts to talk. Mr. van Loomis did not notice McGinty at all; McGinty appeared to have offended him, but none of them knew how. Mr. van Loomis talked to Valentine, whose head was beginning to swim. The dining-room was restful; the windows were shaded from the noonday light by slats of wickerwork held away from the sills with sharpened bamboos; on each sill was a cascade of white orchids, their roots bound on the wood; the flowers hung down over the sills inside the room; their scent was heavy. There was grass matting on the floors, and against the walls were wooden chests. The table was carved, Mr. van Loomis told them, in a single piece from the roots of a tree; they sat on stools of the same shape; the wood was reddish brown and hand polished. The table mats were grass, woven like the floor mats but fine and of the same green-white colour. The soup was served in wooden bowls of the hard red wood, but there was French flowered china and the silver was old-fashioned, heavy and crested. Valentine looked at the crest, a stag's head in a coronet, and looked thoughtfully at Mr. van Loomis.

There was a smell in the room that was homely in its strangeness, the smell of fresh brewing coffee. Then he must get stores, thought Valentine.

Niu and Filipino went backwards and forwards. They wore clean cotton cloths, their hair was immaculately oiled and brushed back with a flower behind the ear.

As soon as Niu had set eyes on Valentine and McGinty he had hurried to the kitchen and stirred up Serendipity. One boy had gone scuttling down to the beach for live crabs, another up the hill to the vineyards for grapes; to Niu, the only way they should be eaten was when they were still warm from the sun. One boy was sent to fetch cream and a fresh pumpkin for Serendipity to make a dish of pumpkin in curd; Niu himself had made a sauce for the chicken. "First time Tsula have his own guests," said Niu with his inscrutable face. "It must be all good. Nothing must be wrong."

Now they ate a clear strong soup, crab scallops in their shells, chicken with rice and fried vegetables, the rice brought in first in wooden bowls with the hot sauce over it, then fruit and young bamboo shoots crystallized in sugar. On the fruit plates fresh leaves were laid and Niu brought bowls of water and fringed napkins for their fingers after it.

In a corner Webster, the cook's son, stood holding a huge palm-leaf fan with its stick resting on the ground between his legs. He swished it rhythmically, stirring the air. Webster, named for Webster's English Dictionary, wore a clean cloth too, and a garland round his neck. The swish of the fan and the soft padding of the two men's feet made Valentine feel more than ever in a sleepy dream.

They came out on the veranda for coffee. "How do I get coffee?" asked Mr. van Loomis. "I have a plantation. I found coffee wild here and cultivated it. We roast our own berries." He stopped and frowned. Walking unexpectedly round the back of the house before luncheon, he had come full upon the coffee machine bubbling over a brazier with Filipino squatting beside it. Mr. van Loomis was angry, but for twenty years he had not been host to anyone and he was enjoying it too much to be put out for long. "This evening you shall taste our wine," he said. "The islanders make an arrack which is very raw. We have a rice wine not unlike the Japanese, but I planted vines. Twenty years ago I brought them from Touraine, and the climate on our mountain seems to suit them. We make a white wine, medium dry; it has a reasonable bouquet."

"You seem to have everything here on this little is-

89

land," said Valentine, batting to keep his eyes open. He sat facing the light, and the chinks that showed between the blinds struck spears of light into his eyes and worried him. Charis quietly stood up and drew them closer. Valentine looked at her gratefully. Now he sat in shade and his lids grew heavy. It seemed a long while since the morning, since the moment when this surprising morning had broken into light and he and McGinty had begun to paddle themselves in the dinghy with their new unused paddles away from the Water Star. He saw McGinty give a large yawn and had to stiffen the corners of his mouth not to follow him.

Mr. van Loomis was still talking. "For all its smallness our island is big," said Mr. van Loomis. "I wanted it to be vast, and, as you see, it is. You may smile"—Valentine had not smiled—"but it has vast resources. You see the surf on our beaches; the thunder comes from caves far down under it where the water surges up. There are deep growths of coral and holes reaching fathoms down into the sea; the mother rock is ingeous, but it is a mass of hidden caves and water. The sea stretches to the horizon all round us," said Mr. van Loomis. "And you will scarcely see smoke or a sail. We don't need them," said Mr. van Loomis; "we have all we need. Our mountain head is lost in cloud so that its height gives us a proper perspective a feeling of infinity. It gives us our variation in climate too; down here it is balmy, tropical; up there it is temperate." Mr. van Loomis stood up and put his coffee cup down on the tray, stood upright again and stretched his arms. They have the span of an old prize buffalo's horns, thought Valentine.

"I wanted my island to be vast," said Mr. van Loomis again, "and I made it vast. Think of our crops; we have the crops of a whole continent: we have palms and rice fields and jute and groundnut, bananas and copra on the plain. We grow our own tobacco, coffee, Indian corn; on the lower slopes we have tea terraces and orange groves; lemons and vines and olives farther up, and, towards the summit, the fruit trees I brought, almonds and apricots and peach and apples; there I have pruned and cultivated a species of wild raspberry; if you came to tea with us in summer you would think you were having tea in

90

England, raspberries and cream. I planted trees," said Mr. van Loomis, "along the roads and in the forest as I felled; they are saplings still, but one day they will be . . . mighty," said Mr. van Loomis, stretching again. "For building we have bamboo and palm leaves and our own wood. We have little metal on the island; the smith works his smithy only when he is not farming; we work with wood, and wood is a peaceful thing; it's not destructive, it's not too hard, it's strangely human; it has life, it will die; metal doesn't die, it rusts and tarnishes. Beware of anything that cannot die," said Mr. van Loomis. "It has no chance of greater life."

"Pity you haven't any petrol," said McGinty.

"Petrol, refineries, all the rest of it—conjuring, sheer conjuring!" said Mr. van Loomis shortly. "We want no conjuring here."

To McGinty that seemed almost like blasphemy. "They are inventions," he argued.

"That is what I said," said Mr. van Loomis, and Valentine laughed.

McGinty did not know what they meant. He understood less and less of the conversation and cared less and less to understand; besides being sleepy he was bored, and he showed his boredom. He fidgeted and yawned until Charis, coming to the decision that there are some guests who have to be dismissed, said, "Wouldn't you like to go and lie down? We all have a siesta here in the afternoon."

"Don't mind if I do," said McGinty. With a commiserating look at Valentine he went in.

In spite of his sleepiness Valentine was beginning to be fascinated. As Mr. van Loomis described it, the island seemed to rise for him again, as it had risen to meet him from the sea. Filipino came in to take the coffee tray. Valentine wondered how the laughing, boastful, flying boy with the boat on the sea had transformed himself into this skilful mute; he thought it would be interesting to hear about the island from Filipino too. "You have your islanders very well trained," he said as Filipino disappeared through the door. "Are they happy?"

"*Happy?*" Mr. van Loomis almost snapped. The sight of Filipino had pricked him sharply. He saw that coffee

91

machine again, bubbling on the fire; he remembered *The Rights of Man*. Damn the boy! He is becoming a menace, thought Mr. van Loomis, but it was too soon after luncheon to be disturbed. He frowned and said shortly, "They are contented," and put Filipino out of his mind. "Their life is the shape of a round," said Mr. van Loomis. He was beginning to be sleepy too. "That, my dear Doubleday, is the true shape for everything. Everything is a round; the universe—"

"We don't know the shape of the universe," said Valentine.

"The world is round," went on Mr. van Loomis, ignoring him. "The world's path round the sun, the year that comes round again to the same day, the day and the night that grow through the hours and come back to the beginning of the day—it is all a round. That is the pattern we are meant to follow. The cycle is the shape of wisdom."

Charis gave a little yawn.

"Then you don't think we should choose a line and stick to it?" said Valentine.

"Mr. van Loomis shrugged. "If you like," he said. "But it is very fraying for the nerves."

"It is," said Valentine, and Charis noticed the edge in his voice.

"A line has no beauty and no end," said Mr. van Loomis. "When it's gone, it's gone; you will never see it again. A circle is bounded, it has discipline. The great things of the world are always disciplined. Look at a sonnet—"

"A sonnet?" asked Valentine, trying to fight the drowsiness in his voice and eyes.

"Yes, a sonnet. The greatest poetry in the world has been written in a sonnet," said Mr. van Loomis and walked away to the other end of the veranda.

"Doesn't your father ever qualify what he says?" Valentine asked Charis.

"I can*not* tell you how much I believe in discipline," said Mr. van Loomis, coming back. "Man must accept a limit, recognize a law, to work and live in peace. We are human, not to be endowed with freedom. That is why I chose a little island that I could control. You will find discipline all through it, in it, itself, in its daily life. Here

92

you will find limitation and you will find beauty and simplicity. Men have forgotten how to be simple. Take sewing," said Mr. van Loomis. "What need is there to sew? Here there is no need. There is nothing that needs sewing on the island. For instance, excepting mine," said Mr. van Loomis, "there isn't a single pair of trousers on the island."

"Filipino has a pair of trousers," said Charis.

CHAPTER IX

WHEN Mr. van Loomis went in, the veranda was very quiet. The yellow tropical mid-day light hung over the garden and the sea; the beaches shimmered in a haze of heat, and the sound of the breakers made a low booming sound that seemed to Valentine to go far away and come near again and go far away. With the sun beating on them from outside, the grass-blind mats gave off a soporific hot grass smell; his eyes were lidded with sleep, his legs felt drugged with it.

"What do we do now?" asked Valentine.

"Sleep," said Charis.

That seemed to him the most beautiful thing he had ever heard. He stood up and went to her and took her hand; it felt cool and light, in the universal heaviness. "You are an angel," said Valentine and kissed her hand and went away to his room.

Charis caught her breath sharply and stood up; she lifted her hand and held the back of it, where Valentine had kissed it, against her cheek. "Don't be a fool," said Charis to Charis, but already she knew she was a fool. She was tingling from head to foot. "Don't feel like that," said Charis sharply to herself. She tingled still. Then as another thought came to her, though she was standing on the veranda, the warm air, spiced and balmy with sun, blown to her on every breeze, fanning against her skin, Charis was cold with misery. She was thinking of all the other women and girls whose hands Valentine had kissed. He did it so lightly and easily that she was sure he had kissed hundreds; someone as famous as he would have kissed all kinds of hands—duchesses', princesses', beauties', thought Charis miserably; hands of dozens of other girls, competent, worldly-wise girls; real girls, not Anyas or Emmas. She began to have a terror of them.

"Mis' Charis, ain' you goin' foah to lay down?" It was Pheasant come to look for her. Charis did not notice that it was strange for Pheasant to be awake and dressed at this time of day.

"Pheasant, when you saw girls, young ladies, before you came here, did they seem . . . very . . . clever and pretty?"

"None purty an' clever as you," said Pheasant.

But she only *says* that, thought Charis bitterly. She says what she thinks I want to hear.

Impatiently she told Pheasant to go in. "I shall come in a little while," she said, but she did not go.

"It's interesting for you to have met him, that is all," said Charis to Charis severely when Pheasant had gone. "Tomorrow, soon, he will go away again. He must go away." Her lips trembled. "What do you *expect?*" Charis asked herself fiercely, but her eyes filled with tears and the bars of sunlight on the shaded floor from the blind cracks slid together in a blur. Poor Charis! It is no use telling yourself to arm, if you have no armour.

She stood there on the warm veranda, so still that a lizard came out and moved vertically down the wall behind her, then rested on its pads and flicked with its tongue at a fly.

Each moment of the days and the nights on the island, except in the chill of the early morning, was interwoven with a mesh of insects and lesser reptiles, like life itself proceeding, busy and unnoticed. There was always the tck tck of lizards and the whirring of a cicada in a tree. The maids swept down countless cobwebs from the corners, and other cobwebs gleamed across the lawn and on the bushes in the morning dew. There were the great winged evening beetles, and every evening too, at dusk,

Niu went from room to room in the house waving a bowl of lit malodorous incense against the mosquitoes, while Filipino and Webster ran ahead to close the slats on the windows. In the drinking trough by the back door, or in the garden coiled under a bush, there was sure to be a little brilliant grass snake; there were beetles with polished green and peacock backs like scarabs from Egypt, and there were swallowtail butterflies and the wild island bees. At night, in every creek and over the marshes and along the paths that led through forests up the hill, there were fireflies. Now Charis stood so still, her hand against her cheek, her eyes filled with tears, that the lizard tcked fearlessly and caught his fly. Suddenly he flicked back into the corner: Charis had raised her head. Then she walked quickly to the steps and lifted a crack of the blind.

In the heat of the day, when normally he would have been stretched out on his bed, sleeping heavily, Charis saw her father stepping off the jetty into the canoe; she saw him step down and bend under the awning to reach his seat; she saw Luck push off from the jetty poles; the paddles were held waiting for his cry, and then they all dipped and flashed together, dipped and flashed, turning the canoe away from the shore. Luck's "hé's" rang out, and the canoe headed quickly towards the open sea. Then, from the corner of her eye, she saw Pheasant and Niu walking away from the steps deep in talk. They should have been sleeping too.

"Hé, hé, hé," came Luck's cry across the sea.

I wonder what they are up to, thought Charis.

CHAPTER X

"You understand," Mr. van Loomis had said to Niu, Pheasant, and Luck in his study. "Understand, Tsuli Charis must not know."

"Yes, *sah!*" said Pheasant jovially, rolling her eyes. Pheasant insisted on being jovial. Mr. van Loomis gave her a displeased look. The time had not yet come to be jovial. "Yes, *sah!*" said Pheasant and smacked her lips.

"Yes, Tsula," said Niu.

"Yes, Tsula," said Luck, but less certainly.

"And the two young Tsulas must not know."

"No, sah!" Pheasant's chuckle filled the room, and Mr. van Loomis frowned and held up his hand.

"They are asleep," said Niu.

Valentine was asleep in a room that sounded to him in his sleep like a cave, one of those underground caves that Mr. van Loomis had spoken of. He tossed restlessly, too tired and stiff to rest; he had pushed open the window slats before he lay down, and there was too much light in the room and the heat came in. McGinty slept dreamlessly, tired out. Filipino too lay asleep on his bed on the shore; above him the palm leaves moved, endlessly whispering. Filipino smiled in his sleep; he was dreaming of Oxford.

Charis was on the veranda, but Niu, Luck, and Pheasant faced Mr. van Loomis across his desk in the study. They all looked unwilling and, except Pheasant, a little sullen. This was the time for sleeping, and they felt they should have been asleep; instead they had been roused up when they had hardly eaten their mid-day meal; they had had to re-dress themselves, a light task with Luck and Niu, but for Pheasant it meant getting into her top petticoat and dress and retying her head-handkerchief and putting on a clean apron, but Pheasant still looked jovial. They had all understood perfectly and at once what was in Mr. van Loomis's mind for Charis, but it was only to Pheasant that it seemed a cause for rollicking excitement. Luck and Niu had had occasion to marry their daughters in due season, there was nothing uncommon in that, but to Pheasant it was life made suddenly vivid. She thought Valentine pale and uninteresting; for her, any male should be full-blooded, noisy, and rumbustious, especially any male who was to marry Charis whom she loved. "But we doan' ketch no husbands hyah," said Pheasant philosophically. Valentine was a good deal better than no one.

"You understand, Pheasant. It's more important for you than anyone; you talk to Missy most."

"Yes, sah."

"And don't you go talking to her now."

"Lawd-a-mighty! Sah! Jest as if Ah'd think—"

"That will do, Pheasant." Mr. van Loomis hoped that it would do. Pheasant was bridling her neck with indignation.

"Now, listen to me," said Mr. van Loomis.

"Is it the wind-machine?" asked Niu.

Mr. van Loomis nodded. "The machine won't go by itself on the wind," he said. "It won't go without the oil that it eats."

"We have plenty of good nut oil," said Niu.

"Not that oil," said Mr. van Loomis and explained the needs of aeroplanes. "I want to put it in a safe place until a ship comes," he said.

"Why should a ship come?" asked Luck, but Niu looked at Mr. van Loomis and understood him perfectly. "No ship will come," said Niu.

"Ohé," said Luck, understanding.

"Now, listen," said Mr. van Loomis again, and he outlined his scheme to them.

"Can't do," said Luck promptly.

"Must do," said Mr. van Loomis.

Niu was silent, looking at his slippers.

"When the lighthouse ketch comes," said Mr. van Loomis, "we can tell the young Tsulas it is the day for a bow-and-arrow contest at the back of the hill. We can say there is a wild-cat hunt, or let them wash gold in the streams. One year, two years, might pass."

"But first we must hide the wind-machine," said Niu.

"To keep it safe," said Mr. van Loomis.

"To keep it safe," said Niu without expression. Niu had always been compliant. Now, suddenly, Mr. van Loomis wondered what would happen if he were not. For a moment the question seemed to hang in the balance, then Niu began, in a soft undertone, to argue with Luck. Mr. van Loomis waited. Luck began reluctantly to be convinced. "Might do," said Luck. "But first we must get Prem." Prem was the strongest swimmer on the island. "With Prem we might do."

"We shall get Prem and all the divers," said Mr. van Loomis.

"Might do," said Luck.

Mr. van Loomis stood up. "Come then."

"Now? At *this* time?" asked Luck in dismay.

"Now," said Mr. van Loomis, and Niu added, "While the young Tsulas are sleeping."

In the doorway Mr. van Loomis stopped. "Niu," he said, "tell Filipino he is not to talk." Both Niu and Mr. van Loomis knew that Filipino was inflamed with the idea of the Water Star and the talk of Valentine and McGinty. Mr. van Loomis had seen him, at luncheon, stand transfixed with a bowl of soup in his hand, almost letting it run over on the floor. Twice, absent-mindedly, he had taken away Mr. van Loomis's plate before he had finished. Niu looked at Mr. van Loomis and nodded. They both knew that Mr. van Loomis would have to keep a tight hand on Filipino.

Mr. van Loomis wondered whether Niu thought this new plan a rightful part of Mr. van Loomis's power or if he were shocked at a breach of island hospitality and manners. Mr. van Loomis knew the island courtesy: the fattest lamb, the best chicken, the largest bowl of rice, must always be given to the guest; but he remembered Niu's face that morning. He looked at him again and, as always, he did not know what Niu was thinking. He had never known what Niu thought; in all these years he had had at his elbow someone gently acquiescent but inscrutable. He looked at the old man, standing politely before him, his cloth looped and pleated round him, his hands folded, waiting. Mr. van Loomis thought that for twenty years Niu had been waiting. Waiting for what? Niu's eyes were indecipherable under their wrinkled lids. He looked immeasurably dignified and patient; and I have been giving him orders for twenty years, thought Mr. van Loomis. I have made this old chieftain my servant, and I have been in the hollow of his hand. Niu had given him nothing but courtesy and care, but Mr. van Loomis suddenly felt cold. The thought had come to him again of what would have happened to Charis if he had died here. He had not the least idea; she might have been well cared for, honoured, thought Mr. van Loomis, but on the island a woman was owned by her man, she was a bearer of children, a mender of nets, a cook, a worker, and a plaything. Mr. van Loomis felt weak and giddy. He thought now that Niu would be ruthless in getting his own way. What was that way? Mr. van Loomis did not know, and he thought that Niu embodied the island itself, with its balmy surface and unsounded depths, its balms and breezes, its gentle conprehensible customs and its hidden thoughts and rites.

There were dark things on the island. Every now and again someone died mysteriously and quickly, and a little dart, fine as a needle, was found in his neck or arm or back; sometimes found, more often not. Once Mr. van Loomis had come across a scene he was not meant to see; in the stream, far up the mountain, above the temple, where he seldom went, he had found a blood-stained stone; this was where the sacrifices he had been unable to stop were made. That morning there had been a cock there, struggling with its wings, its breast slit open and its heart still beating; and there had been something else than the cock: as the blood ran down into the water two streams of blood had mingled; what Mr. van Loomis had picked up beside the cock had been a baby's hand. That was a time when he had not used his powers as a magistrate. He came down from the mountain and pretended he had seen nothing, but that night, and for many nights, he had not slept. He had remembered what he had once read of savages: *"charming and innocent and murderously cruel."* Charis had been six years old then, and he had vowed by her bed, in those nights, that he would take her away, but days passed, slipping away into other days, and all had been ease and content and he had not taken her away. Now the back of his neck was wet and he had to use his handkerchief. He was thinking how sure, how exact, Niu's hands were; they could do the most delicate things. Mr. van Loomis had seen them rig a walnut-shell boat with a cobweb-fine spun-silk rigging for Charis; he had seen them peel an apple and leave the peel as fine as silk; he had seen Niu win from all the young men at the archery feasts with his great bow and arrow. Mr. van Loomis had always thought of them as kindly, clever hands; now he shuddered. He had held those death darts

99

himself and wondered at their delicacy and lightness; a light blow, one little prick, at any time of day or night, and it was done; and I am one white man, alone among them all. Why did they suffer me so long? asked Mr. van Loomis. He did not think now it was because he was a magician; he thought perhaps it was because he had served the island, taken it from Mario's mother and worked for its good; I have . . . chiefly . . . served the island, thought Mr. van Loomis.

He went to the window and touched one of the white orchids that cascaded there; his finger looked red and coarse and gnarled against its purity. In that moment Mr. van Loomis was nearer humility than he had ever been in his life.

He felt tired and melancholy. What is the use? thought Mr. van Loomis. I am still an alien. He felt, all the same, that if they did not love him it was ungrateful of the islanders; he had done much for them, but . . . It's not what we do but what we are that makes us loved . . . or not loved, thought Mr. van Loomis. He thought he was not loved. He looked at his fingers against the orchid; his finger did not look fit to touch it.

He stood very still. He had remembered, in that moment, a turret room high up in the south tower at Spey. It was a small room, so small that, with its whitewashed walls, it was almost a cell. It had a narrow slitted window that looked down on the battlements and elms and countryside; the room held only a table and chair and books, and, for pacing, there was the small walk on the battlements that led to the other turret of the tower. It seemed to Mr. van Loomis a haven, quiet and withdrawn. If I could go there and leave everything, he thought, and he remembered suddenly that it was the room he had begged as a workshop when he was a boy and where, in secret, he had begun to practise his first conjuring as a young man. Now, with a feeling of sickness, he felt he had turned away from all conjuring. If I had that room now I should use it for different work, for quiet thinking, for reading, for study and meditation and quiet; but, as he said it, the old fascination seemed to rise up in him and he remembered a trick he had found out in secret there.

100

"This eternal *lust!*" said Mr. van Loomis angrily and put on his hat and went out to play his trick on Valentine.

The canoe headed first for the pearl fishery where it had gone that morning. Like Luck and Niu, the crew were sulky and indignant at being taken out in the hot sun; they paddled slowly: it was too hot with the sun overhead to paddle fast. Mr. van Loomis, under the shade of his awning, kept taking off his hat to wipe his face. The men had no hats; their flat wickerwork hats would have blown off in the stiff sea breeze. Their faces and backs and chests were soon wet and their palms blistered with their own slipperiness on the paddles. Mr. van Loomis felt them flagging. "Tell them," he said to Luck, "that we shall have a picnic day for the whole island tomorrow!"

"Not if we die today," called a young wit, and they all laughed. The boat moved faster, and Mr. van Loomis smiled.

When they reached the pearl fleet everyone was asleep. The whole fleet had drifted slowly with the sea, as it did every afternoon; a sixth sense told them when it was too far out. The light boats rocked on the swell without a sign of life; in the prow of each lay a heap of dark shells, and in the stern was a large wicker shield, and under each, curled on the boards, naked and cool, a diver slept.

Mr. van Loomis woke them ruthlessly. He was in a hurry, and, dazed and sullen, they followed the canoe. It was hard, sleepy as they were, to keep up with it. Prem had put them three to a boat, leaving the other boats drifting and unguarded. Mr. van Loomis told them curtly that they could pick them up on their return. Across the sea they raced after the canoe, farther than they cared to go, a storm might always sweep up and catch them here away from the main island. They looked back uneasily at the boats they had left as the island grew small behind them and the bare rocks of the Hat grew near, rising up from the sea as they swept round it. They came round the point where the current raced out and left the bay almost as smooth as a lagoon, and then they stared, their crossness and their sleepiness forgotten, their paddles held with the drops flashing off them until the boats were

101

drawn back into the current again and Prem and Luck shouted.

On the calm water, where Valentine and McGinty had left her anchored, large and white and strange, lay the Water Star.

They were half afraid. When Mr. van Loomis ordered them nearer they paddled gingerly, one eye on him, one on the plane. They trusted him to deal with anything strange and bad that might be lurking there, but they kept their eyes anxiously on the Water Star as well. When he ordered the big canoe to come alongside the Water Star and stepped from it onto a float and then up on the wing, a low murmur went round. Mr. van Loomis could not, at first, find out how the cockpit opened, and as his hands went over it and he slipped and swore, it looked to them as if he were saying incantations; then he found it, and they watched breathlessly as the door swung open and he pressed his large bulk into the cockpit. He spent a little time there. Valentine had left the key in the locker, and, looking in, Mr. van Loomis found papers, books, maps, a little silver wedding horseshoe with a sprig of white heather, a tin of cigarettes, a torch, and the sextant; the luggage locker was open, and two pairs of flying boots were lying on the floor. Mr. van Loomis gathered up anything that could be moved and pushed it into the locker on top of the suitcases; he did not want anything from the Water Star to find its way onto the island, and he locked both lockers and put the keys in his pocket. Then he called to Luck and Prem to come up.

They came up beside him, their eyes sliding in their heads, their hands feeling and running over the white paint and woodwork and steel and glass and chromium, the shining array of switches on the instrument board and the velvet cord of the upholstery. Mr. van Loomis had difficulty in making them listen to what he said. He looked up at the sky; the sun was moving towards the west behind the Hat; already it was full afternoon. He turned and spoke sternly to Luck and Prem. After a few moments' colloquy, ropes were brought from the canoe.

Mr. van Loomis stood out on the wing, steadying himself with one hand on the fuselage; all the faces in the canoes were turned up to him as he explained what it was he wanted. "It is my idea," said Mr. van Loomis, "that we shall take this wind-machine from the sea and put her safely in the big cave. The cave now, at this tide, is full of water. We can float her in."

"Ohé," came assenting murmurs, and they eyed the Water Star, thinking of handling her. It did not seem strange to them that Mr. van Loomis should speak of her as female; she had, for them, the attributes of a goddess; they sensed power in her. "Ohé," they said.

"But we shall not leave her in the cave," said Mr. van Loomis. "The tide might float her out. No. We must put her somewhere safer than that. We shall not tell the young Tsulas where we have put her," said Mr. van Loomis, looking at the sky. "They don't understand our tides here, or our ways. They might wish to get her out. I want to put her," said Mr. van Loomis, "where no one will find her." They looked at him blankly. "You know, or some of you may know," said Mr. van Loomis, "that the earthquake river, the fall, comes down inside the cave, and it flows out to meet the tide, and together they make a big wave—"

"Very big wave," said one of the men.

"Very big wave," said Mr. van Loomis, "but not too big for us. We can go through that wave. We can go through that wave and we can go through that fall," said Mr. van Loomis. "We can go on the wave *through* the fall," said Mr. van Loomis.

"That isn't possible," said one of the younger men. "It isn't possible to go through the fall. At the back of the fall is rock."

"At the back of the fall is not rock," said Mr. van Loomis. "At the back of the fall is another cave."

Murmurs went from boat to boat. Not many of them had known that he knew that; some of the young men themselves did not know it. They looked at him with added respect. They began to understand.

One of the men stood up. "Tsula, the wind-machine will not go through the wave and the fall."

"She will if we take her," said Mr. van Loomis.

"She is too big."

"Too big for twenty men?" said Mr. van Loomis.

"What little men they must be!" There were fresh murmurs.

Here, in the bay of the little island, if they were still, they could hear very faintly the thundering of the fall in the cave; it came down from the inner crater and broke through the roof at the back of the cave with a wall of green water that churned the cave pool to white. When the tide was down it ran out in a river that had made a channel for itself through the rocks. It was strong, but not so strong, thought Mr. van Loomis, that it could not be met with enough men, men who could dive and swim like his crew and the divers. "Of course," said Mr. van Loomis aloud to the sky and the sea, "it isn't work for boys—or for girls," he added. A murmur went round. "Men could do it," said Mr. van Loomis thoughtfully to the sky, "but only those who are strong swimmers," he added, more thoughtfully still.

There was silence. The boats rode with the plane on the calm water.

"If the wind-machine were safely inside the cave," said Mr. van Loomis, "I should give two bullocks for the picnic day tomorrow and some sheep. We could have a feast."

"We have never been in the inner cave," said one of the men.

"My father went," said another, a large young man, indicating his father beside him. "He says the bats are as big as eagles."

"Boys are afraid of bats of course," said Mr. van Loomis.

The young man scowled, but the others laughed.

Then one of the boatmen stood up and, with a shout, dived over the side of the canoe and swam round the Water Star. Luck began to fasten the ropes, and Prem threw them down to the divers, who caught them one by one, treading water, swarming round the Water Star. When the ropes were ready Mr. van Loomis came down into the canoe, where he stood on the prow and held up his hand to Luck and Prem. Prem dived into the sea and swam round the men, exhorting them, while Luck stood up on the Water Star, keeping a watch on her direction and to see the wings and tail were clear. She swung

104

slowly round on the water, the men easing her gently as Prem led them towards the entrance to the cave.

The ropes swept down into the sea like water snakes, the weeds bent and waved and rose again round the swimmers' legs, and when one of them went down and touched bottom, a funnel of gold sand spread upwards in a cloud and shoals of small bright fish fled in front of him. When the men dived and swam below, their black heads seemed fixed into their bodies as if they had no necks, their shoulders widened and glimmered as if the water had taken off their edges, they were widened and then elongated and their legs showed, wavering, flattened, and foreshortened. They came up to breathe, shaking drops from their heads and flat brown faces, spitting water through their lips and squeezing out their noses between their gers and thumbs and dived again. Slowly the Water Star moved across the sea until she came opposite the entrance to the cave, and here the men rested, steadying the plane, while Luck and Prem talked together, measuring the distance and the race of the tide with their eyes. Mr. van Loomis watched them gesticulating and arguing, but he did not interfere; if anyone could, these two would get the plane into the cave.

He could see the difficulty; each wave, with its surf, rushed with its force into the cave, met the force of the fall and ebbed back; could the men be quick enough to ride in with the plane on the wave and hold her against the stronger rush back? That was what Prem and Luck were arguing. Then he saw them divide, and Prem, with half the men, left the Water Star and swam into the cave. "You will need all your men," Mr. van Loomis wanted to call, but he held back the words. Instead he beckoned the young boatman who was left with him and, stepping into one of the small boats, told him to follow Prem. "Tsula, be careful," shouted Luck. "Take care we don't sweep you down."

Mr. van Loomis raised his hand; he meant to land on the rock ridges at the side of the cave. His man sent the boat forward with a strong sweep, raised his paddle, steadying it, and he and Mr. van Loomis rode in the cave on a flying wave crest and were hurled into the cave, washed round so that the boat was almost on its side, and were brought up with a strong steadying force, held by Prem and two boatmen.

Here was an abrupt change of light; the cave was shadowed; the light from outside came in through the arch at its mouth and struck upwards again from the water on its floor, so that its ceiling was an arched reflection of wave light, shadowed by deep rock crevices. The air was filled with spray and the thundering noise of the fall. Mr. van Loomis saw with relief that the fall was not as heavy as he had feared; it was the enclosed space in which it fell that gave it its enormous roar; the echoes of the cave came back to reinforce it and made it seem more powerful still. It was, all the same, a heavy fall of water, wide enough for a river, falling in sheer green-white streams into the pool. Mr. van Loomis measured its width with his eye to see if he had been right and the Water Star would go through it. "Will she go through?" he shouted in Prem's ear, pointing to it, and Prem nodded. Prem dived off the ledge where he had stood and swam to the fall, struggled in the water, dived again and came up behind it. Mr. van Loomis could see the dark shape of his figure veiled and sometimes blotted out behind the water; then Prem dived again and came back gasping. "She will go, if we can get her through," he said. "But it comes down like a boulder on your head."

Now Mr. van Loomis saw the plan that Prem had made with Luck. He saw why they had divided the men. Those in the cave were standing along the narrow rock ledges at the sides; as the others rode in with the Water Star on the rush of the wave, these would leap to meet her and hold her. Long ropes were passed in from the plane outside, and men stood, their feet braced ready to hold firm. Others would dive in and help the men who came in with her. Some stood on the wing tips to fend her off; some steadied the tail. Mr. van Loomis stepped up on a ledge; his small boat was lifted and put up on a ridge. They waited. From far, almost too small to hear in the boiling noise of the fall and the upflung spray, came Luck's shout, echoed by a man at the entrance of the cave, and, before the sound of it had died, with cries and fierce shouting, the Water Star was swept in, immeasura-

106

bly huge and unwieldly and white, the men swarming round her.

"She will be smashed!" cried Mr. van Loomis. It seemed impossible that she should not be as she came down on top of them, enormous above the small, struggling brown bodies with their shouts and cries. They had first to steady her rush inwards; the impetus flung the water high up to the cave roof, deluging and blinding them; and then, stronger still, came the rush back, dragging the men from the ledges like flies, but here Luck had foreseen, and some of the men had dropped off at the entrance as she came riding in and braced themselves against the rock walls and passed ropes behind her to make a barrier which four of them held. The rush came back, and with it the Water Star. They were borne nearly to the roof, but the ropes held, the ropes at the back, the ropes from the cave walls. Though some men were dragged, others took their place, and, as the wave ebbed, the Water Star was left on the cave pool, safe, a little battered but safe. But the next wave was to come; gasping, dripping, bleeding, they had only a few moments to prepare for it while they steadied her to take her through the fall.

The ropes were still held at the mouth of the cave, others from the side; men swam round her, holding her, to act as buffers, and now two, holding the first long ropes, prepared to dive under the fall and come up on the other side, while Prem, with a shout to show them, went through it. He came back under it, shaking his head, half stunned for the moment. There were shouts of dissent from the men, a warning shout from Luck, and the next wave came in. It was a huge wave and carried the Water Star forward so that her nose hit the fall; she recoiled against the wave and the surf boiled up. Prem shouted and Luck shouted, there was another surge forward, and almost before they knew what had happened, men and plane were tumbled through the fall. Mr. van Loomis saw one wing tilt up and then right itself; he saw the water hit the plane, and saw a turmoil of arms and legs and heads; he saw Luck clinging to the tail, and then they were swept, whole, from his sight.

He waited for Luck to come and tell him a man was

107

drowned, the propellers smashed, a wing torn off. "You have done it now," said Mr. van Loomis to Mr. van Loomis. "It was too much of a trick. You traded on the men's docility; you made them ashamed of not doing it; you egged them on, like boys. Now, if anything has happened to them, you are responsible. This is what comes of your tricks!" He shut his eyes, giddy and sick with shame, and the thundering noise seemed beating into his head.

"Tsula." It was Luck shouting into his ear. Mr. van Loomis opened his eyes. Luck was standing, dripping and gasping, as Prem had, in front of him; he had a large bleeding graze on his left cheek and the blood ran down his neck to his chest. Mr. van Loomis instinctively put out a finger and touched the blood, but Luck only shook his hair back and smiled. "Well?" said Mr. van Loomis, seeing only the blood.

"Tsula, come, see. Tsula can go through the fall." Then Mr. van Loomis saw that Luck's eyes were merry and that he seemed elated in spite of the hurt. "Come, Tsula. All done," said Luck. Mr. van Loomis dropped off his hat and cummerbund and shoes.

When Mr. van Loomis, beaten and giddy from his dive under the fall, came up in the inner cave and saw the dim form of the Water Star floating in the murk, he could not help it, he had a feeling of enormous triumph and enjoyment. The men were fastening her, weighting the ropes with rocks and dropping them, but, shut away by the falling water, there was little drag here at the end of the pool. The pool was long, shallow, black; there was only a murky filtered light, and Mr. van Loomis swam a few strokes, touched bottom, stood up and slowly walked the length of it. The men had dragged the Water Star as high as they could; he could make out her shape, hardly floating, but resting on the sand. She was beyond the reach of the spray, and here she could remain, thought Mr. van Loomis, safe and dry, with one chance in a thousand of anyone finding her. He did not think that either Valentine or McGinty would dream of penetrating the fall; they would see it sweeping down at the end of the cave; had not some of the islanders themselves thought it was the

108

back wall? "Are all the men safe?" asked Mr. van Loomis.

"All safe, Tsula. Some a little hurt," said Luck, "but all safe."

"Two bullocks, five sheep, and twenty young cockerels," said Mr. van Loomis.

He reached the end of the cave, which narrowed and ran back into the rock in a knife cut. He could see a faint glimmer in the darkness, and, standing, balancing himself between two sheer rock walls that ran up like a funnel, he saw that he could look through a slit to the sky. Here they were far down below the top of the Hat, and, as from the bottom of a well, in the far tiny round of blue-black light where the sky seemed pressed down on the earth, he saw a few stars faintly shining. He looked and then he smiled and went back to Luck and Prem. "Come. I shall show you something wonderful." He took them and showed them. "Stars," he said.

"Stars!" breathed Prem and Luck. "Stars, but is it night?"

"No, it is afternoon," said Luck, and they made the deep island obeisance, their hands joined together before their faces.

"Tsula!" said Prem.

"The stars will know what we have done today," said Mr. van Loomis.

"Tsula!" said Luck and Prem.

He could see the whispers going round from lip to lip though he could not hear them. One by one the men tiptoed up the cut and stood and looked up at the stars. Mr. van Loomis watched them and saw the round black heads, so like children's heads, lift one after the other to look and heard the low exclamation of wonder, and he felt magnanimous and good. He had not, of course, actually said that he had put the stars there, turned daylight into stars to commemorate the day, but, "Tsula!" the men breathed in reverence. "Will we always see stars there now, Tsula?" they asked.

"Always," said Mr. van Loomis graciously.

They swam back, diving under the fall, letting themselves float out easily on the wave, tired but elated and filled with wonder, leaving the Water Star moored to her stones and resting in the water on the sand, hidden at the far end of the cave. Their heads were filled with the accomplishment of this great deed, the promise, earned, of two bullocks, five sheep, and twenty cockerels, and the wonderful appearance of the stars. Last of all, Mr. van Loomis looked round in the sounding murk-filled cave and, more than pleased with himself, dived and swam out to join them.

CHAPTER XI

VALENTINE was woken by something very fragrant under his nose. It was the flower in Filipino's hair as he bent down to arrange a pair of new grass sandals for Valentine on the floor by the bed. Through his half-shut eyes Valentine saw Filipino's distinguished head close beside his pillow; the flower was the same creamy-petalled flower that Charis had worn. He remembered how on the veranda, when the blind chinks struck into his eyes, she had quietly risen and pulled them together; now he saw that, as he slept, someone had come and closed these too, and covered him with a light cotton shawl. "Who did this?" he asked Filipino, and Filipino smiled and shrugged and said, "Niu?"

In the shaded room, lulled by the sea, Valentine had slept as he had not slept for months; he had woken to a deep sense of peace and, a word he had not thought of in connection with himself, of healing. "What is it, on this island?" he asked Filipino.

"Is what?" asked Filipino back.

"Is . . . the island?"

"Mānoa only a little ordinary place," said Filipino.

Valentine lay, with ease in his bones, not tired but blissfully lazy, lazy and comfortable. "Perhaps that's what I need," he said. One would think of this as an extraordi-
110

nary place, but the boy is right, it is ordinary like anywhere else. Perhaps I have been extraordinary too long, thought Valentine, yawning, and watching Filipino as he moved about the room and went to the window to open the slats. "I have forgotten . . ." He was interrupted by another yawn and he forgot what it was he had forgotten.

"Now bath," said Filipino, coming and standing by the bed. "Bath in bath or sea?"

The slats were open and Valentine saw that it was sunset in the garden. A richer light lay on the lawns, turning them deeply green; the tree trunks shone. He could see a clump of hibiscus flowers, and their trumpets glowed. He could see a strip of sky that was a soft refulgent blue; in it was an apricot cloud. There was a sound of splashing water and a gardener came into sight carrying a goatskin swollen with water on his shoulder; he was splashing the flowers. The small boy, Webster, whom Valentine recognized, was flying a kite; the island kites were made of paper, thin and gay to fly. The kite was out of sight but the bamboo roller danced and spun in his hands. Some fan-tail pigeons were strutting, stretching their necks and arching them, swelling their chests as they pecked insects on the grass; they were white as silk or seed-pearls in the light. Valentine could hear the sound of a lazy little flute and, behind the splashing water and the click of the bamboo roller and the pigeons' throaty murmurous croons, he heard the surf.

"Bath or sea?" asked Filipino.

"Sea," said Valentine. He was wide awake.

The half-hour in the surf with Filipino was such exhilaration as Valentine had not known. He had surfed in Australia and Vancouver, but this was more exhilarating still; the water was, not warm, but cool and clear, and the sand shone white in it. When Filipino saw how Valentine swam he took him out of the netted enclosure and showed him how to dodge and hit if he met a shark. Filipino himself swam like an otter, shaking back his hair, which clung wet and gleaming to his head. They were both naked, and Valentine saw how white and soft his body looked beside Filipino's; if he touched the boy he touched something firm and springing, warm under his wetness. Filipino fetched a surfboard and they rode in on

111

the big surf waves. They dived under the breakers whose
roots were green-glassed water, and the cool salt stung
their eyes. They swam out past the surf where the water
was a smooth swell and they could see clear depths where
shells glimmered; they dived to get the shells, and fish
swam past Valentine, flicking against his bare skin with a
cool water-fanned tickling. When they were tired they
swam in and lay on their faces on the sand; it was still
hot from the day in the sun.

As they lay, Filipino said shyly, "That one called
McGinty . . ."

"Yes," said Valentine idly.

"Mr. McGinty is not liking me," said Filipino. "He is
not liking it here."

McGinty's face, obstinate and sulky as he had last seen
it at lunch, came into Valentine's mind. "Probably not,"
he said. He was pleasantly tired; it was dusk now and, in
the island's tropical twilight, it would soon be night. Valentine was thinking that a cigarette and a drink would be
good; on islands they drink something called a stingo,
thought Valentine. He saw a stingo as a whisky in a long
glass with soda and cubes of ice and a round of lemon,
though that is probably quite erroneous, thought Valentine, and, anyhow, quite unobtainable here. Mr. van
Loomis had talked of home-grown wine and rice wines,
but I could do with something that has a kick in it,
thought Valentine.

Filipino was still talking about McGinty. "It's better to
like," said Filipino.

"Much better," said Valentine. "If you can." And he
said, "McGinty likes his own people, you know."

Filipino nodded. "Perhaps he like them so much that
he can't like any else, or perhaps he hasn't such . . . *big*
liking."

"He has a girl," said Valentine.

Filipino was gratified; he felt Valentine was talking to
him as man to man, but he was not placated. "A girl
ought not . . ." He found it difficult to express himself
about McGinty and he changed the conversation. "Have
you a Tsuli?" he asked.

"No," said Valentine. "And you, are you married?" He
had an idea that the islanders would marry early.

Filipino shook back his wet hair and laughed. "I never want get married," he said. "I don't want that I be tied. I love everyone. I don't want that I love anyone too much. Resurrection too. He doesn't want," said Filipino.

"Who is Resurrection?"

"My twin. My brother." Filipino let the sand run through his fingers.

"Does Resurrection love everyone?" asked Valentine idly, scooping a handful of warm sand and letting it run through his fingers.

"Oh, yes!" said Filipino. "And everyone love him. *Everybody*. But they say I am too much trouble," said Filipino, and he said, "Presently Resurrection will marry."

"Even if he doesn't want to?" asked Valentine.

Filipino shook his head, which meant "yes." "My grandfather will say and Resurrection will do," said Filipino. "My grandfather wants sons to come after us on the island. What he wants, Resurrection will do, even if he not want it himself."

"But not you," said Valentine.

"Ressurrection is a stupid boy," said Filipino and laughed. He laid a finger gently on Valentine's thigh and asked, "You like it here?"

"I like it very much," said Valentine. "I want to get away, but I'm not sorry we came."

"Mr. McGinty is sorry," said Filipino and bent his head, whittling a stick he had found with the sharp edge of a shell. He had discovered that it was one thing to belittle the island himself, another to bear it when it was done by anyone else. "I think Mr. McGinty will be sorry he doesn't like that he came," said Filipino. Again he felt that was not well expressed, but again he found himself tongue-tied when it came to talking of McGinty.

~~~~~~~~~~~Valentine walked up from the beach with Filipino, but when they drew near the house Filipino melted away. Valentine went into his room and found shaving things ready with hot water and his clothes laid out on his

113

bed, cleaned and pressed, his shirt freshly laundered and dry. His body was chilled, and the dry, warmed clothes were a luxury. In a few minutes Filipino appeared in a fresh cloth with a fresh flower and his hair oiled again.

"Everything seems to be done very quickly," said Valentine, showing his clothes.

"There are many wash girls," said Filipino carelessly.

"This island is well run," said Valentine.

"We are glad that you are pleased," said Filipino primly.

Again from the slim young man and tumbling sprite of the beach he had become the wraith of the young servant. The room was nearly dark; Valentine could dimly see the folds of the white cloth wrapping Filipino's thighs and legs and the fresh white flower picked in the garden as they had walked through it; white flowers had gleamed in the garden as this gleamed now behind Filipino's ear. The boy was silent, sensitive to Valentine's quiet mood. He will always be sensitive, quick to life, thought Valentine. How fresh he is! He felt a pang of envy. Filipino made him feel elderly and stale; Filipino was beginning; Valentine was an—"anachronism" was the word that came into his mind. For a moment he was angry; he was only thirty even if he felt like fifty; he, Valentine, the most up to date, the before date, the antennae, an anachronism? "Your antennae tell you, you are an anachronism," said Valentine to Valentine, "and you swear they are always right." An anachronism means out of keeping with time. "But how? How?" he demanded angrily. "How has it happened?" And as he asked it, he saw how it happened. He saw it in his relationship to Filipino. Filipino seemed to him an amusing, scintillating boy. That was how Valentine himself had once appeared. Now he was no longer a boy. "It's time you were your age," he said seriously to himself. "You are a man, full grown, mature and serious. It's time you started on another stage." As he said that, he remembered what he should have liked to forget, the night when he had had to come on the stage to speak to the company after the last night of his last play, *Tinker's Curse*. *Tinker's Curse* had run for only six weeks, a thing that had not happened to Valentine Doubleday before.

114

He remembered, sharply now, the anticipation giving way to doubt, doubt giving way to a horrible surmise and then to a horrible certainty. It was a failure.

"A dead flop!" said Tuggie. He remembered still the hurt surprise that had been in Tuggie's voice. Tuggie Marks, his manager, had a perpetually worried fat face, but Tuggie was more than worried then; he was cut sharply, he still could not believe that anything Valentine wrote could be a failure. Tuggie was loyal; they were all loyal, thought Valentine irritably, all his faithfuls: Jos, Carlotta, Ellen Wayne whom he had found and made; faithful and loyal, and Valentine thought that disloyalty was sometimes a virtue; not one of them had warned him or censured him over *Tinker's Curse;* of course, being farce, thought Valentine, Jos and Carlotta and Ellen were out of it, but still they *should* have seen; they should have had that much wit, thought Valentine.

Now he saw the stage as empty and bare; it was waiting. He knew, of course, that that was nonsense; there was no empty stage for him in London, or anywhere else. Nothing waited: if he were to come back he would have to roll up his sleeves and work; work damned hard, thought Valentine. He left the window and bent down, peering into Mr. van Loomis's shaving mirror; he had managed to shave himself with one of Mr. van Loomis's cut-throats and had only nicked his chin; he wondered how McGinty had got on. Now, as he brushed his hair, from outside, in the dark, came the sound of a deep-throated singing. "That's a Negro," said Valentine, surprised. "Have you Negroes here?"

"It's Pheasant. Pheasant always singing," said Filipino carelessly.

Pheasant had dressed Charis and now she sat singing and threading fresh garlands, as she did every evening, for Niu, Filipino, and Webster to wear at dinner; she threaded the jasmine flowers and ate hot roasted nuts that Serendipity roasted on a little brazier and put in hot shells on the dinner table. When Pheasant had her mouth full she hummed, and it made a thick fruity noise in her throat.

"Ah've a li'l wheel a-turnin' in mah haaht,"

sang Pheasant.

"Ah've a li'l mmmmmmmmmmmmmmmmmm mmmm in mah haaht."

When her mouth was clear she sang the words lightly as she worked:

> *"In mah haaht. In mah haaht.*
> *Ah've a li'l wheel a-turnin' in mah haaht."*

It felt to Valentine like the beating of a happy, unconscious pulse, which is really what it was: Pheasant was not thinking in the least of what she was singing. To its light accompaniment he left his room and walked along the garden to the veranda.

It was hard to tell which were lights or fireflies on the earth and where the lights ended and the sky and stars began. A pinpoint of lantern moved away on some distant path; a star shot down towards the sea; Valentine walked to the edge of the lawn and watched the waves tumbling on the beach below, lit with phosphorus. The lighthouse beam shone out to sea and the air was full of sound: the surf, the waves, the twanging and shrilling of insects, Pheasant's song, and, from far off, the sound of a drum, beaten and stopped, beaten and stopped, in rhythm; a wisp of breeze brought the sound of laughter and voices.

Valentine was still tired; he still had that feeling of light-headedness but he was strangely still and peaceful. He walked round the veranda where, behind the tubs of flowers, he found Charis waiting for him in candlelight that came from thick white wax candles in branched wooden candlesticks along the wall. The veranda glowed with their soft light. Valentine sat down, stretching his legs, pleasantly tired, and, from a small table, she brought him a tall glass.

"I don't know if you will like it," said Charis, "but my father has one after bathing and I thought you should have one too."

116

"What is it?" asked Valentine.

"We call it a stingo," said Charis. "We make rum here from our sugar. It's a rum stingo."

"Charis," said Valentine, "you are a very excellent child."

This depressed Charis; she had thought, among flowers and drinks and spread candlelight, that the veranda looked not unlike the parties she had read about and that she herself was the picture of sophistication. She had on her very best clothes. There had been, surprisingly, no opposition from Pheasant about that. "What you gwine wear?" asked Pheasant, and when Charis showed her she did not say, "No, you ain'. You had a silk out fer this mawnin'." She said with admiring eyes, "Mah lamb gwine look lak a real laidy." It was the first time Pheasant had ever called her a lady.

She had brushed her hair back as far as she could and she had thought she looked dignified and grown-up; now Valentine called her an excellent child. I suppose I am as unimportant as a child to him, thought Charis and sighed. I suppose that's why he called me Charis. Ought he to call me Charis as soon as this? Shouldn't I be Miss van Loomis? Oughtn't he to have asked my permission first? Of course not, thought Charis bitterly; they call children by their first names.

Valentine saw he had depressed her though he did not know why. How absurdly vulnerable they are, he thought, thinking of her and Filipino together; he did not say it in criticism but tenderly. He looked at Charis, standing with her back to him, by a tub of white tobacco flowers, and he liked the small shape of her hips under the swathings of soft silk. Charis thought her hips too small, as, by island standards, they were; the islanders liked hips like two ripe gourds, but they pleased Valentine. He liked the glimpse he could see of the nape of her small proud neck and what he could see of a white, well-shaped but determined small ear. He saw he had hurt her and he wanted very much to go across to her and put his arm around her in contrition; he knew exactly how she would stand, upright in his arm, offended, and he knew that if he kept his arm there, presently he would find her quivering with an inward storm of feeling of which she would say nothing at all. But Valentine knew he could not do that, that Charis must be touched seriously or not at all, and he knew that she would presently swallow the hurt and turn back to him again with some gently hospitable remark. When she is a little older, thought Valentine, it will be impossible to know if she is hurt or not . . . unless you know her very well . . . unless you are very close to her, and the words that were in Valentine's mind as he sipped his stingo were "near and dear."

He could not say anything comforting to Charis because McGinty appeared. He had been sitting in his room until Filipino came in and said, "Dinner. They are waiting for you on the veranda," and added, "Better hurry up."

McGinty felt that Filipino was impertinent though his voice was perfectly respectful. McGinty had woken from sleep more chagrined than ever. Niu had brought him hot water to shave in; McGinty had cut himself three times with the razor; "Bloody nearly cut my head off," said McGinty. He had chosen to bath, not bathe, and he had found his bath ready, a wooden bath like a tub, lined with glazed earthenware, and a clean cloth, to wrap round him when he came out, laid ready on a stool. He too had found his clothes cleaned and dried and new grass sandals for his feet, but he was not soothed; he ignored the sandals and put on his shoes. Now he refused the drink Charis offered him and sat on the edge of a chair, hanging his hands between his knees and looking more than ever unwilling and bored.

Then Mr. van Loomis arrived. He was freshly burned from the sun and looked extremely well and genial and at ease. He took a stingo from Charis and drank it standing, looking down at them benignly; Charis looked back at him with suspicion; she knew that gleam in his eyes and he had an air of being too well pleased.

"Where did you go so early this afternoon?" she asked, hoping to take him down a little, but Mr. van Loomis looked more pleased than before.

"Where did I go? I went out to the Hat," he said, swirling the last of his drink round and round in his glass, and he said to Valentine, "I thought I should check up on what you told me as soon as I could."

Valentine and McGinty leaned forward eagerly; this

was better than they had expected. Mr. van Loomis raised his glass and finished his stingo. He never told a lie. Now he made two statements that were both perfectly true. "I went out to the bay of the Hat to find your plane," he said, and "It isn't there," said Mr. van Loomis.

CHAPTER XII

WE SHOULD have seen if he had sunk her," said McGinty. "The water is clear. He couldn't have burned her; we should have seen the smoke and there would have been shit all over the water."

"There was some oil."

"No more than what she made when we came down," said McGinty gloomily. "Wonder if he rigged a sail on her and sent her out to sea."

"He isn't a magician," said Valentine.

"Wonder if he got these blacks of his to lift her for him and roll her up the hill and tip her into the crater and down the bloody volcano. It's *possible*," said McGinty savagely.

"Don't be fantastic," said Valentine.

"The whole blooming island's fantastic," said McGinty.

Two days had passed since Mr. van Loomis had taken them out in the canoe and allowed them to search for the Water Star.

"Where did he take you?" asked Charis suspiciously, but Valentine's answer gave her no clue.

"Oh, up and down and round and round," said Valentine. "I must say he was most patient. We went on looking long after it was obvious there was no use in looking."

"Did you land?" asked Charis.

"Yes," said Valentine, and he said with acerbity, "But the Water Star couldn't land. She hasn't legs!"

"Did Father show you the caves?"

119

"Yes," said Valentine wearily. "We played hunt the thimble, but an aeroplane isn't a thimble."

"It's very strange," said Charis.

"Very," said Valentine. He tried to speak lightly but he could not, and he walked away from her and went and stood by the veranda rails with his back to her.

Charis sat in her chair, softly rubbing her nails to make them glow and look pink; she rubbed them softly and thoughtfully. Her father often told her he had a reason for everything he did. When they went out to look for the Water Star he had not allowed her to come. She had felt hurt and left out, but now she was beginning to guess his reason and she was glad she had been left out. I wouldn't want to know anything about it if . . . thought Charis. She stopped short on that "if." Now it was not her nails that glowed pink, it was her face. She stood up and went in. At that moment she felt she could not be near Valentine. Presently Valentine drifted to his room.

"He doesn't mean us to get off," said McGinty.

"Nonsense," said Valentine. McGinty had come to his room and was sitting on the bed. "We're not children or boys, we can't be made to stay," said Valentine.

"You gave him your word."

"That was only for a limited period," said Valentine shortly.

"What period?"

Valentine did not answer. He said, "If we are patient, we shall get off."

"We can't without him. Don't forget. He's God on this island."

"Nobody's God," said Valentine irritably.

If Mr. van Loomis could have thought of a way in which he could have left McGinty out of his schemes he would have done it, thankfully, but he had no choice.

From the first time he saw him he had disliked this laconic and cocksure young man; he did not like McGinty's manners or his accent, or the way he cut his hair, or his opinions. "And they are not his opinions," said Mr. van Loomis. "They are what he has heard, not what he has thought." McGinty could not put up with Mr. van Loomis's despotism.

"The old bastard!" said McGinty after listening to Mr.

van Loomis giving his orders. "He might be Hitler! I told you, he thinks he's God." They were each unjust to the other. Mr. van Loomis's blood boiled at the sight of McGinty; if McGinty's blood had ever boiled, it would have boiled at the sight of Mr. van Loomis. "*And* he's a bloody great liar," said McGinty. "He's lying to us about the plane."

It was the feeling of being held in a network of lies that made McGinty most desperate of all; he had no philosophy with which to meet it. If he had been at once more simple and more humble, like the islanders, he could have shrugged his shoulders and asked, "What is truth?" If he had been more sophisticated and alloyed with worldly knowledge, like Valentine, he would have said, "Ah well! Most of us tell lies." He would have known that truth, except as revelation, is not for humans, but McGinty insisted on absolute truth. It was an angry insistence because, as naturally he did not get it, he was always balked by a sense of disappointment that he could not name and that made him feel aggrieved. McGinty was always slightly aggrieved; now the disappearance of the Water Star was a palpable untruth, and it justified him in feeling angry.

The islanders had nothing but good will for the two strange Tsulas but it amused them and pleased them to see them both successfully hoodwinked by Mr. van Loomis. It made them sure their white man was the greatest; now his latest magic with the stars had passed from mouth to mouth and confirmed them. To see him confound Valentine and McGinty was sport to them; it pleased some age-old snobbish instinct, especially in Niu. Niu was very courteous, very helpful to McGinty and Valentine, but there was something hidden in the air. Valentine too had a strong sense of trickery, and yet he could not see how they were tricked. "A calm sea, no ship for miles, no petrol, and no one who knew how to fly her. How? How?" asked Valentine.

He tried to cross-examine Filipino, but Filipino had retreated into evasiveness; Valentine thought he was afraid to talk; if they talked to him, he stood, ready to fly off at the first question, and it was only when he himself had some very urgent questions to ask that he would speak to them. Pheasant rolled her eyes meaningly at Valentine and

121

waddled away as if she could speak if she would. "What is it, Pheasant?"

"Ain' nuthin', Massa Valentine," and she added, "You jes' stay hyah and let tha' air and sun eat into yo' skin. You sho' look peaked, Massa Valentine. Don't you fret. You stay hyah. You kain' help it." Even little Webster would study him at meals, until he leaned harder and harder on his fan stick and stopped it. Valentine began to think he was bewitched.

To begin with he had chafed and worried as much and more exquisitely than McGinty. How could he help it? He was worried about his play. Quite apart from the island, he knew now that he was worried about his play.

It was his new musical play, his operetta, *Rosalind*. Suddenly it seemed to Valentine that it was not like him to have written anything called "Rosalind." Names are very important," he said often. "They are very indicative." "Rosalind." He tried it over on his tongue and he did not like it. "Rosalind": paper roses and balconies and Edwardian dresses. His *Rosalind* had all these things. Why did I call it that? thought Valentine, staring at the sea. He began to think through the first act, hearing the opening bars in his head, and "Rosalind" seemed to suit it so well that he did not think he could have called it anything else. Well then? thought Valentine. Well then?

He saw Tuggie's face with the glasses pushed up on his huge forehead. He saw Jos Mayer, cross and saturnine, arguing over the score and fighting Ellen over her songs; Jos was guaranteed to argue from beginning to end. He saw Tony Adams, his young discovery, who was understudying him, and Ellen herself, his Rosalind, with her famous apple-blow skin and wide-open eyes and red-gold hair and the enchanting mouth that let through such clear fluting notes and such inane remarks. Poor old Ellen, thought Valentine, she has always had me behind her, she won't have a chance with Jos. Would Tuggie be able to hold them together? thought Valentine. He did not think Tuggie would but perhaps Carlotta . . . He saw his dear Carlotta, tried and true; Valentine had first acted with Carlotta when he was twelve; she had been with him, in and out of shows, all the years since, Carlotta of the great voice and perfect temperament. But perhaps, thought Valentine now, Carlotta, like Tuggie, had been with him too long; Carlotta should have known, but perhaps she had not been able to bring herself to be quite honest with him. "Are you pleased with it, Val?" He had said, "I don't know. Should I be pleased?" And Carlotta had said emphatically, "It's quite delightful." Or had she been honest? Was it quite delightful? That was not what he had wanted it to be. Quite delightful, thought Valentine and gritted his teeth. In Australia he had thought out several changes; he had written in a new song for Ellen, new business for himself, but still he was not sure. What would Tuggie do now? Would he go on with Tony? He would go on till the last possible minute of course, but if Valentine did not come? Would he go on then? Did Valentine want him to go on? Would he rather cancel the whole thing? Cut the loss? Valentine fumed, not over the borders of good manners, but in a volcanic way that was uncomfortable for everyone.

"That is a very spoilt young man," said Mr. van Loomis to Charis. "Nothing has ever gone wrong with him."

"Should it have gone wrong with him?" asked Charis, puzzled. She could not see how that could be an advantage.

Mr. van Loomis was right. It was a long time since anything had gone directly wrong with Valentine, though perhaps, in himself, he had not been right; he had the wit to see that, in the last two years, his success had not really been success at all, that he had been carried along by the impact he had made before, and no one could do that for long. The failure of *Tinker's Curse* had been the first outward symptom. No one had told him or given him a warning; no one would tell him till the critics and the public made it plain, as had happened over *Tinker's Curse*. "Did I write that?" Valentine was to say of it afterwards. There seemed no one he could trust. "Oh, Val! It's going to be wonderful," they said. His antennae told him it was not wonderful. "We shall have to be damn careful," he had told Tuggie. "We can't afford another flop."

"*Tinker's Curse* was bad luck," said Tuggie.

"Bad writing," said Valentine.

With the disappearance of the Water Star a crack had come in Valentine's certainty. The Water Star had nothing

123

to do with *Rosalind* but the loss had come as a shock. The Water Star had disappeared when she could not disappear; she was gone, without a trace, and he had no remedy. He was helpless.

He saw that his fuming and fretting hurt Charis. The evening before he had put his hand on hers as they sat alone on the veranda before dinner and said, "I think this is an enchanting place, Charis. At any other time I should have loved to have had the chance of being here."

"You are here," said Charis slowly, and the words she would have liked to say rang in the air. Why not love it?

"You see," said Valentine, "I should be in London."

"But you are not in London."

"No, and what can I do?" He shrugged, and there was a silence. Valentine felt there was something Charis wanted to say. He put his hand on hers again. "What can I do, Charis?" She looked at his hand, her lids down. "Tell me," said Valentine. She raised her eyes and looked at him."

"You could . . . enjoy yourself," Charis suggested timidly. Valentine stared at her, and she blushed but she went on. "It seems to me . . ."

"Yes?" His voice sounded faintly amused and that made it hard for Charis to go on. She blushed more deeply as she said, "It seems to me that you have been too busy."

Valentine took his hand away and stood up. "Think, my dear," said Valentine reasonably. "I have had to be busy. I have done a great deal."

"Yes." Charis conceded that. "But if you, or anyone, get too busy you lose touch with life, and that is fatal."

"Why fatal?"

Charis opened her eyes. "Because without life you die of course," said Charis.

"Then am I dead?" said Valentine, teasing, but it was angry teasing. He was remembering something that a critic had written after the first night of *Tinker's Curse,* a critic for whom he had a great respect. "Mr. Doubleday does not hear, he is too busy knocking the nails into his own coffin." Valentine winced. "Say what you mean," he said roughly to Charis.

For a moment Charis was intimidated. "You are dead tired," she said, avoiding the issue, but she was too honest to pretend and she took a breath and returned to it. "All

124

these plays," she said hesitantly. "Plays and music and writing and paintings, all work, are made of life."

"Yes. Yes," said Valentine impatiently.

"But . . . to give life you must have life," said Charis, looking up at Valentine's angry face. "And you haven't. How could you have? You don't give yourself time to breathe."

"The eve of a new production is hardly the time to breathe," said Valentine.

Charis considered that. "If I were on the eve of a new production I should take deep breaths, slowly. I shouldn't *gasp.*"

"I don't gasp!" said Valentine and turned his back on her.

This was one thing, among others, that Charis was learning, that people, however exalted and wise and gifted, were the same, that even princes and saints could be wrong, and that if you subscribed to the wrong, even through pity, it did not help them; that you had to be brave with them; princes and saints could be unhappy, bewildered, and cross. Her eyes as she looked at Valentine were very tender.

Charis was a comfort to Valentine in spite of her pricks. The very fact of her ignorance about the Water Star made her an ally. He often caught her looking at her father with a cynical look in her narrow grey-green eyes; the servants said Charis had snake eyes, and there was something of the wise, small serpent in her.

"If they come looking for us now they will be looking for the Water Star," Valentine burst out, going back to the thought of his play. "That would be bad enough. A plane not much bigger than this room in the whole of the Pacific. They will never find us without her; this island is an island among thousands, like pebbles," said Valentine, and he asked Mr. van Loomis, who came through the veranda on his way to the beach, "You have put out a signal?"

"You have asked me that twenty times," said Mr. van Loomis. "But who will see it? Who is there? I don't know," said Mr. van Loomis and spread his hands.

"You don't know anything," said Valentine rudely, and Mr. van Loomis raised his eyebrows and went out to the beach. Valentine was white; he dug his nails into his

125

palms. "I'm sorry, Charis. I shouldn't have been rude to your father. I was thinking of my play."

Charis's eyes hardened as they looked at him and grew narrow in a way he was to learn to know and she asked him in a voice like a needle point, "Is it a good play, Valentine?"

"Do you think I should write a bad play?" asked Valentine. He tried to speak lightly.

"It needn't be bad," said Charis. "That doesn't make it good."

He was suddenly more angry with her than he had been with anyone in his life. "You are amazingly conceited," said Valentine and he almost hissed. "So conceited that you are ridiculous and laughable. Laughable, do you hear? You don't know it because there is no one here to laugh at you. You little queen bee! You are absolutely ignorant," said Valentine scathingly. "Ignorant and pompous, as pompous as your father. You know nothing, nothing at all; nothing of plays, nothing of writing, nothing of people. You have never even seen a play, and you sit here on your throne and give your cold conceited little opinions and expect me to listen. How dare you?" shouted Valentine. "How dare you talk to me like that? You know nothing about my plays, and nothing about my writing, and nothing about me. Then . . . shut up!" said Valentine violently. "Shut up!"

Valentine felt exactly as if he were a shellfish and his shell had been broken and Charis had lifted it and with a long thin wire probe was unerringly exploring the soft crevices inside him; and there was a place, deep down in Valentine's firm sophisticated self, that was not sure or firm, and there he knew he was not pleased with his play. He knew he had been afraid and that it was the failure of *Tinker's Curse* after the comparative failure of the play before, *Lords and Owners,* that had made him afraid. "That is ridiculous," said Valentine. "What do any of them know about it? *Lords and Owners* was a damn good play. It misfired, that was all. I knew that. I know it now. Then why lose my nerve?" He had not lost his nerve—he had done worse: he had played safe. "But if you tell them you are afraid they think it's the end of the world . . . instead of, perhaps, making you aware and beginning fresh
126

worlds," said Valentine. In *Rosalind* he had put all the Doubleday ingredients, he had gone back to *Midwinter Spring* seven years before. "And seven is my lucky number," said Valentine. It had the same flavour, the same pretty witty wit. "But it is a better play," said Valentine. "Better, but the same," came to him like an echo. "It can't miss," said Valentine, "except . . ." Except that seven years ago is seven years ago, too far, not far enough; or perhaps a thing once done is done, for, deep down in those crevices, Valentine had a suspicion that *Rosalind* was dull.

"Dull. Dull. Dull," breathed the sound of the surf and the wind, and Valentine was completely miserable.

Charis sat quite still in her chair; though her head was high Valentine saw that he had smitten her. She too, now, was white, and her eyes were brimming in tears. It was so quiet that the sea sounded as if it were beating on the veranda. "Dull. Dull. Dull," it beat. Valentine made one last effort. *"Now* will you be quiet," he said and shut his eyes.

When, after a little while, he opened them, Charis had not moved. The sea still beat but the wind had taken the sound farther off. Valentine saw how very white Charis had grown, how stiff the bones of her face. "I'm sorry," he said. "You are too young to be talked to like that."

"I am not," said Charis clearly but a tear rolled down her cheek. "I am quite old. I am nearly twenty-one." She was right. Twenty-one was old on the island.

Valentine was strangely moved. He went across to her and knelt down by her and kissed her.

Charis sat even more still than before, but, when his hand found hers in her lap, her fingers held his. With his other hand he took out his handkerchief and gently dried the tear.

"You are very fond of the theatre," said Charis.

This small understatement touched Valentine. It showed him that Charis, even in a moment that was sharp to her, could think steadily and selflessly in a way he would hardly have believed a young girl could. He kissed her again, gently on the brow, and said a thing he would not have said to anyone else, that he would have censured if anyone else had said it, yet it was completely right and true. "You see, it is my kingdom," said Valentine and, kneeling beside her, as she held his hand, he began to speak to her of it.

⁓⁓⁓⁓ "Everything compensates itself," Valentine was able to say to McGinty afterwards. McGinty did not see it. "As we are here and have to stay here," said Valentine, "Why not enjoy it?"

"*Enjoy* it?"

"Didn't you ever read or dream about an island when you were a boy?"

"May have done," said McGinty without enthusiasm.

When McGinty walked into the little house in Hounslow where his girl Eunice lived and took two lemons out of his pocket and gave them to her mother and said, "Here, Mum. I got these for you in Augusta, 's morning," he did not feel he was participating in anything wonderful; to McGinty to be in Sicily in the morning, Hounslow in the evening, was not second nature but first. Perhaps he had lost his sense of wonder; but then McGinty had not been in Sicily, he had been in Augusta; he did not go to Montreal but Dorval, to Yundum not to West Africa, to Gander not to Newfoundland. When he went to Cairo he went to Almaza, to Dum Dum not to Calcutta.

He was happiest when he was at home taking the cylinder head off his motor-bike or on Sunday mornings on the Great West Road passing Tom, his friend, and knowing that Eunice's ankles were prettier than the ankles of Tom's Betty; he liked to know that. He had always gone one better than Tom. He was happy when he was flying, listening as carefully as any nurse to the sound of his engines, looking at the rev-counter, watching the pressure gauges, knowing, in each change, what there would be to do when they came down.

Here, on the island, there was nothing for him to do. When he was not working McGinty looked to be entertained. The island entertainments, what he had seen of them, shocked him to the marrow; he did not know which were worse, the moonlight picnics that seemed to him wanton—"Necking parties," said McGinty angrily— or the blood sports, the cockfights like the one to which
128

Filipino, thinking to amuse him, had invited him and that did not seem to him sport but downright indecent cruelty. McGinty liked films or midget-car racing or, if there were nothing else on, turning on the radio and sitting by the fire. He liked dancing and taking Eunice out for an afternoon's shop gazing. On the island there were no films, no cars, no radio, no shops, no dance floors. McGinty liked ice cream better than beer or rum: there was no ice cream on the island. He did not care for books; at home he read newspapers morning and evening: there were no newspapers on the island. There were no cigarettes that he could smoke; he had tried an island green one and nearly choked himself. "Enjoy it! What is there to enjoy?" he asked Valentine bitterly.

"Get to know the people," suggested Valentine. "Their customs and their food and their songs. I mean it," said Valentine. "I am going to do it myself." McGinty stared. He had not thought of the islanders as people. "I am going fishing with the boatman Luck. Come too," said Valentine. "I want Filipino to take me up to their temple on the hill. I want to go round the villages with Niu. You should do that too," said Valentine. "Get Filipino to take you, or any of the men. If they ask you to one of their picnics, for instance, go."

McGinty did not answer. To Valentine's surprise he blushed.

The island girls would have liked to have seen more of McGinty. A young white man was something new for them. They knew that Valentine was for Charis; they acquiesced in that as right and fitting, but no one seemed to have claims on the other Tsula. "And he isn't white, he's pink!" said Flora Annie, laughing with delight.

There were plenty of girls. The island abounded with girls, all plump and sweet and laughing, with big eyes and tiny teeth, but McGinty was quite firmly and thoughtlessly faithful to Eunice, his own Eunice Robinson, who lived with her father and mother in Hounslow and worked as a typist in the Gillette razor-blade factory on the Great West Road. To him the girls were islanders, bints, and he did not look at them; but last night, after dinner, when he went for a short walk, he had met a procession winding in the fields.

It was a very innocent procession, if he had only known it, part of the customary island arrangement for courtship during the full moon of this spring courtship month; all these young men and women would, in a night or two, be united in marriage or the island concubinage; that is to say, as soon as they had settled on each other the man would take the woman to his home and house-keeping would begin; nor was there any change; there was no divorce on the island, husband and wife were husband and wife till they died; nor could a man change or exchange his concubines, though he was allowed as many of these as he could properly support and satisfy, and they all lived in concord together.

This was the courtship time, and the young men and women walked down in groups to the beaches, waving sugar canes, which presently they would eat, and carrying flowers to garland one another and hollow two-foot bamboos that held arrack; they would drink it from one cup that was passed round and round. With them was a drummer, and some of the men had flutes; in front of them, dancing backwards, was a figure in a full red flowered skirt and anklets of bells, its chest buried in garlands of chema flowers and a handkerchief on its head; to the beat of the drum and the melancholy skipping rhythms of the pipe it held out its skirts and danced. It was the island dancer, a boy McGinty saw with disgust, not knowing that here all dancers had to be boys. It was most improper in the island for women and girls to dance, but McGinty would not have believed the islanders could think anything improper.

He stood on the path, revolted, as the picnickers passed; whether they were sorry for his loneliness, or whether they wanted to tease him, standing upright and disapproving by the path, he never knew but he found himself swept along with them. He was in a wave of laughing, of waving fronds, of soft hands touching him, the drum beating in his ears, the dancer whirling in front of him as they came down to the beach onto a bay of white sand by the sea.

The men sat down in a circle with the drum and Mc-Ginty sat with them. "I could see myself sitting there," he said afterwards. "A nice fool I must have looked!"

130

The men began to sing. They sang each a verse of a song that McGinty felt was probably obscene and was addressed to one of the women. The women sat apart where the palm leaves made patterns of shadows in the moonlight on the shore; the colours of their clothes were strained away by the moonlight, only the clinking sound of jewellery or a puff of cigar smoke showed where they sat, until one of them rose, delighted, holding her scarf across her face and sang an answer back, demure or saucy, that moved the men to fresh laughter and fresh sallies.

The arrack from the bamboos was passed round in a coconut bowl; it tasted raw and burning to McGinty, and they kept giving him little stubs of green cigars that he refused to smoke. Then the women drew nearer, and suddenly, behind him on the sand, he felt someone warm and soft sit close against his back and a hand, small and warm, came round his chest and slid, with a soft movement, inside his shirt and laid its palm on his right breast. Eunice! thought McGinty and pulled it out of his shirt and shook it away as if it had been a snake. He was outraged. From behind him came a little laugh; but it was not altogether a forgiving little laugh and, on the lobe of his ear, suddenly, he felt a sting of excruciating pain. He leaped to his feet, the men leaped with him, the women were scattered on the sand. McGinty lost control of himself. "You . . . You . . ." he shouted in the moonlight. He could not think of anything to call them. "You . . ." he shouted again. They all stared at him, the smeared painted face of the dancing boy looked up at him inquiringly; then the noise of his shout was lost in the waves along the shore; the stars looked down, the fireflies twinkled along the grass verges, and the drummer softly began to beat the drum again. "I go home," said McGinty with what dignity he could and walked away. When he had gone he heard them laughing. That soft laughter followed him all the way up the beach.

"The little bitch, she bit me," said McGinty. Tears of mortification and homesickness were in his eyes. She had drawn blood. Now, the evening after, his ear still showed an angry small red mark.

He had been given a room at the back of the house that looked over the servants' courtyard. After Valentine

131

had gone and he was idly lying on his bed he saw Flora Annie (named for *Flora Annie Steel's Cookery and Household Management*) come out to pick flowers for the dressing tables; her curves, as she reached up to the sprays of flowering creeper, were far more luscious than any known to Eunice, her eyes were black and laughing, and her lips, which were mischievous, were red, but it was someone very like Flora Annie who had bitten McGinty on the picnic and he refused to look at her. The sound of that laughter was in him still. All at once he felt he could not bear the place for another minute.

Valentine had promised not to try to get off the island, not to send a message to the outside world. "He promised for me, I didn't promise," said McGinty.

In some ways Mr. van Loomis had overestimated McGinty; in the matter of the transmitter, for instance. He had read stories of prison camps and, though he had no idea how a transmitter was made, he told the islanders to keep a watch for McGinty's collecting of any likely things such as tins or wire. "Though why wire for a wireless, I don't know," said Mr. van Loomis. In any case there were only one or two tins and very little wire on the whole island. In other ways Mr. van Loomis underestimated McGinty. If this were war, Mr. van Loomis had no idea how total and unremitting modern warfare was; his war was like the Germanic wars that ceased by treaty in wintertime; he was vigilant of McGinty but he took it for granted that they could eat and sleep in peace, that there would be a truce at siesta time, for instance, and for coffee and cigars after dinner.

When McGinty excused himself from dinner, saying that it gave him indigestion and that he had a headache, Mr. von Loomis believed him. "He looked miserable enough," said Mr. van Loomis afterwards. "Of course that sort of boy, when he looks miserable, looks ill conditioned, but he looked ill. He might have had a headache."

In a way McGinty had; he had a problem and he always said of a problem, "That's a headache." But Mr. van Loomis was not to know that.

When they were all on the veranda with their drinks, the servants busy and gossiping in the courtyard, Mc-

Ginty came out of his room and made his way down to the beach.

Lamps were lit in the house behind him; savoury smells and the sounds of that perpetual singing drifted from the servants' quarters, spiced by the smell of Niu's waterpipe that he smoked before serving dinner. McGinty could see Valentine on the veranda, drinking and talking to Charis. Charis made him think of Eunice; with a lump in his throat and an empty stomach McGinty went proudly down to the beach. He despised Valentine.

He walked along the beach, picking his way among the boats; when an islander wanted to take his boat in, he lifted it and put it on the beach, but Mr. van Loomis's heavy canoe had to be brought up on rollers; McGinty stubbed his toe on one of these and swore. Once or twice, in the fading light, he found his face in a fishing net, stretched emphemeral from post to post; it seemed to him that all the island was trying to catch him and thwart him, but at last he found what he was looking for, the rubber dinghy.

He knew a fishing boat would be safer and lighter and easier to manage but he preferred his rubber dinghy. He tested it and picked it up and carried it to the sea edge. When he saw that it floated well, he lowered himself into it; the paddles were in it, where he and Valentine had left them. He began to paddle out to sea.

His dinghy was small and lonely on the stretch of water between the mainland and the lighthouse where Mr. van Loomis's canoe had swept so proudly that morning. McGinty felt small and lonely too; the beam of the lamp shone out to sea, but it seemed to him he came no nearer to it. The moon was not yet up; outside the beam the dark was very dark, and he seemed to be paddling in it without moving. His arms ached and his empty stomach ached and his eyes felt hot and tearful; then, with the noise of a soft slur, the dinghy grounded on a shoal of sand, below the rocks at the back of the light. He stepped out and picked his way across, slipping on the rocks and stumbling into pools.

Now that he was near to it he could see how the beam of the lamp splayed out from the rocks in a wide luminous ray that was humming with insects; he wondered where they came from on the barren heap of rocks, and if the light had brought them from the mainland, flying on their small wings all the way he had paddled so slowly. There was a whirring noise and a small blow on his chin that made him jump; a cockchafer had hit him in the face. McGinty shuddered and shook it off. Then he saw a dark shape on the rocks ahead of him: it was Mario, still fishing.

When the islanders fished by night they went in twos; one held a torch which he shone into the water, the other balanced on the prow of the boat to spear the fish. Mario was not skilful enough to spear; in any case he had no companion, and he had always to fish from the shore with a line. He had made himself a new line that had taken him days to get ready; he had traded watching the light with Jéo for the string, but, as before, he had baited it too heavily and he had caught nothing. He was feeling injured, doubly so because Jéo had gone again to the mainland, leaving him to watch the light. When he heard McGinty he thought it was Jéo come back and he scowled.

McGinty saw the dark bunched shape and the big heavy head that turned round towards him, the eyes shining under the matted hair, and he knew that this was someone who was what McGinty called "not all there." Ten years ago he and his gang would have tormented Mario, but now McGinty had grown up. He became inordinately gentle. "Hello," said McGinty gently.

To his immense surprise it answered in English, a kind of English. "Whadda want?" it said.

McGinty came up. "You the chap in charge of the light?" he asked. In the moonlight, which was beginning now to sift down over the sea and the reflected light of the lamp, Mario looked a monster; a word came to McGinty that must have dropped from Valentine when he talked aloud in poetry. "Moon calf" came into McGinty's mind; Mario did look like a moon calf, clumsy, childish, with his thick low forehead and mat of hair and shining dark eyes. There seemed no one else on the lighthouse. "You the chap in charge?" asked McGinty again.

No one had ever called Mario a chap before. He did not know what it was, but it did not sound unfriendly. He knew McGinty must be one of the strangers of whom Jéo

134

had told him. He could see McGinty in the reflection of the light. "Red as Loomis," muttered Mario to himself. "Speaks like Loomis but not like Loomis speaks. He speak as if he don't . . . hate me," said Mario.

"Any objection to me having a look see?" asked McGinty.

Mario gathered he was asking his permission. No one had ever asked Mario's permission for anything before, and it made him feel shy. He turned his head away and said gruffly, "Look."

The lighthouse itself was simply a round pillbox of cement in which the kerosene for the lamp was stored and in which Jéo and his father or Mario lived while they were at the light. In one corner was a string bed, Jéo's hat on a peg, a few gourd and earthenware utensils, and some stores. Jéo's clothes were two cloths of cotton, his possessions were an oil saucer lamp, a palm-leaf fan, and a knacker board. From the pillbox iron steps led to the lamp that stood railed under a corrugated roof; the lenses, shining with warmth, were crawled over by myriad insects; the noise of their wings almost drowned the noise of the sea. McGinty felt them crawling in his clothes and in his hair and stepped quickly back. There was nothing on the platform but a stool and the lamp and, lying on the floor beside it, a canvas cover. He went back down the steps, shaking himself and beating off the insects with both hands.

Down below, in the room, he shone his torch round again and saw in the corner an old iron safe. It was open. In it were some signal flags and cords, a few papers, and a rough log clipped with rusty clips to a board. The only log Jéo could keep was to make a division for each moon and then make, in each, small marks for each ship, with a horizontal line for a steamer and a vertical one for a sailing ship. When the ketch came the Inspector read the marks and then made up the log. McGinty could not read Jéo's log but he guessed it was the counting of ships. There were not many marks in each moon. "Then they do pass here, not often, sometimes," said McGinty. "I thought they must," and he looked round again and once more went up to the platform. There he picked up the lamp cover and looked at it, and he began to think.

The cover fitted over the lamp and its flaps laced up; if McGinty put it on with the opening turned towards the sea the beam was hidden except for a narrow slit; if he turned the edges of the cover slightly back, they left a larger aperture like a narrow panel, and a narrow but just as powerful ray shone out to sea. Hastily, looking back at the mainland, he slipped the cover off again; then he thought of how Mr. van Loomis lingered talking at the table after dinner, of how, in the servants' quarters and the villages, they would sit round, eating and smoking and talking; the moon was up, Jéo's picnic would have begun. McGinty began to think he need not hurry. He put the cover on again and arranged his panel; he worried a little about the cover scorching and catching fire with the heat of the lamp; if he soaked it in sea water the glass would crack. "Have to risk it," said McGinty. "If I keep it on only five minutes at a time it ought to do; then take it off and cool it. Now, what can I use as a shutter?"

He remembered, down below, that Jéo had a playing board. He had seen the islanders playing a species of draughts on those boards, but flicking the wooden draughtsmen with their fingers. He ran down to the store-room and fetched it. It was exactly right, about two feet square, made in one piece of light wood and inlaid with the island veneer of chequered dark and pale wood. McGinty began to arrange the flaps, and he was almost happy; he was doing something positive again. As he worked he whistled.

His whistle reached Mario where he sat lapsed back into his misery on the rocks. It seemed, to Mario, to call him. It was quite unlike the vague minor-keyed plaintive island music; it was clear and positive. Island music was languorous: this was invigorating. Soon Mario stood up and shambled over to the lighthouse. He was in the door-way before McGinty heard him. Mario saw the knacker board. "That-a-Jéo's," he said.

"Jéo only uses it to play with," said McGinty severely. "I want it for work."

He had planned for five minutes at a time; he thought the cover would not heat as quickly as that. He thought he would send out the most simple signal possible and, after a great deal of cogitation, he decided to signal

S.O.S. followed by V.A.L. "They ought to get that," said McGinty. "All the papers all over the world must be ringing with us, and it will be plain sending. After all, Val's a somebody." He had a wave of homesickness as he thought of the boys calling in Piccadilly; he saw the evening papers, papers with the coppers thrown on them while the old man went round the corner; papers read in buses, on platforms, over the teatable at home. "Paper! Paper! Valentine Doubleday found! S.O.S. V.A.L. S.O.S. V.A.L!" He saw the cables flowing, the far-off paragraphs, the headlines. He set his teeth. "I'm going to do it," said McGinty. "I'm bloody well going to get it through."

He began, standing to the right of the light, working the board as a shutter, . . . — — —. . . . . . —. —. —. . .
He would not have believed he could be as clumsy as he was; his arms and wrists ached, he was unbelievably slow, but he felt that it was plain. "If I can do it every night this Jéo goes ashore, someone ought to see it," said McGinty.

"What-a you-a do?" asked Mario.

"Talking," said McGinty.

"Talking?"

"Yep. Talking."

Talking! Mario felt as heady as if he had drunk a two-foot bamboo of arrack. His poor senses were swimming. He came nearer to McGinty and looked into his face. "Who-a you are?" asked Mario.

"The man in the moon," said McGinty, going on with his signalling.

"Charis show-a me the man in the moon," said Mario. "He-a not real. You-a real. I not-a see anyone like-a you before; so-a pretty," said Mario adoringly.

"Pretty!" said McGinty. "What the hell . . ." Then he saw that when he was angry Mario shrank. "Don't talk cock," said McGinty more gently.

"I do anything for-a you, anything," said Mario. "I show-a you the island. I show-a where the coffee berries are, and raspberries that Loomis let-a no one touch. I show-a you where he keeps the wine and girls. I show-a you girls . . ."

"No girls," said McGinty and, seeing that Mario did not understand, he translated into what he thought was

137

Mario's jargon. "Me no wanting any bints. Now," said McGinty, standing upright and stretching his back and taking off the cover and folding it back on the floor, "you take this board and put it back, and you be quiet about it, see? No-a tell. No-a tell!" said McGinty.

"I cut-a my tongue out," said Mario.

"Needn't do that," said McGinty. "Just don't talk, see?" And he went down the steps with Mario after him and started to find his way back to the dinghy. He had forgotten he was hungry and forgotten he was tired. He was still whistling.

"You-a come back?" Mario asked him, almost running after him.

"You bet I'll come back. Look. Will the keeper, Jéo or whatever his name is, go away tomorrow night?" He saw Mario look puzzled and tried again. "Jéo—gone—tomorrow?"

Mario nodded his head violently. "Moon-time, picnic-time on island," he said. "Jéo gone tomorrow." To be reminded of this would have made him morose; Mario liked the island picnics as much as McGinty disapproved of them, and he was never invited, but now he did not mind. "I tell-a Jéo. Go. Go. Mario, watch-a light. He go," said Mario cheerfully. "You-a come?"

"I come," said McGinty.

"You-a come. I take-a you everywhere. I show-a you Loomis stores. I show-a you Loomis pearls. I take-a you up the mountain." And he asked fervently, piteously, "You take-a Mario away from here?"

"I'll take you," said McGinty easily, and Mario knelt down in front of him and kissed his foot.

"Here! Here! For Christ's sake!" said McGinty and he felt himself go scarlet to his ears. "God Almighty! You mustn't do that or I'll not come back, ever."

"You-a come back," said Mario happily and confidently. "You-a better than Loomis. I glad and proud of you. I-a worship you," said Mario.

CHAPTER XIII

McGINTY practised signalling in his room. The word "possesses' possesses more s's than any other word possesses, practised McGinty. He was getting faster and smoother. It had become accepted now that he did not come in for late dinner, and every evening, while the others were on the veranda, he slipped out in his dinghy across to the light.

For the rest he lived as far as possible to himself and he found it bitterly lonely. McGinty was not used to being cast on his own resources; without his engines and newspapers and radio he found he had no resources. The hours seemed long and empty; he had nothing to do. He lay on his bed or played Patience with an old pack of cards, and defiantly he went out in the siesta time and bathed or sat on the sands under the palms, shying pebbles at a coconut he had set up as a target on a rock. That was the most secret time on the island, everyone was asleep and, often, he paddled across to the lighthouse and fetched Mario. Mario, though it was hard, kept awake for him. Sometimes at night, after the signalling, and McGinty only signalled for half an hour, they would go ashore together again. "Mario Fernandes *is* half a Tsula," said the islanders and shrugged.

Mario showed McGinty the island. He showed him, not Mr. van Loomis's island, but his, Mario's, and this was like a child's, as opposed to a grown-up's, more secret, more guarded, more minute, and far more wonderful. Charis, as a child, had been too sheltered and too conspicuous to know it; the islanders were peasant in their attitude towards it, not old, not young, but ageless; its full magic was only Mario's: No one noticed Mario; he went where he liked, with a child's incognito, and, like

139

Charis with the red seeds and the pearls, he could not distinguish in the grown-up way; some of what he showed to McGinty was, to McGinty, nonsense.

He showed McGinty the weaver-birds' nests that Charis loved and showed him how the nests were made; he showed him the great skeleton of a shark on the shore and an inland sea creek that the animals used as a salt lick; McGinty lay there with Mario one night and saw a mountain cat come down in the moonlight, the white fur in its stripes gleaming with the milky lustre of pearls, and after it had licked with a wet red tongue and noises of guzzling, it had made water and then, like any domestic cat, tidied over the wet place in the sand with its paw. As he had shown the wild cat in an unguarded moment so that they pried on her, Mario showed McGinty where the girls bathed, when they had woken from sleep, to refresh themselves in the heat of the afternoon. The marriageable girls bathed separately from the boys and younger girls; they bathed naked, their rose and brown bodies flashing in the surf, rising, sprinkled with drops, as they stood up and laughed. Mario laughed too and rubbed his thighs, but McGinty felt his ears tingling and hastily called Mario away.

Mario showed him the island temple far up on the hill, an earth-built house, dark with smoke inside from open fires, with old ritual masks and feather shields along the walls, and as strong a smell of incense as any Roman Catholic church. The island was full of rainbows that came from some infraction of the light; they were in the surf all round the island, in the drops that fell as the fishermen lifted and recast their dripping nets, in the spray of the waterfall; now Mario showed McGinty the feather scarf in rainbow colours that was used in the dances, and, on the roof of the temple, an arch that was painted in crude rainbow colours. In the temple, too, he showed him aphrodisiac made of a root and the poison in which the arrows were still dipped and, once every few years, those wicked little darts that Mr. van Loomis had seen.

Mario showed McGinty many things he did not know he had shown. McGinty did not know a great deal himself but even he could see the wealth Mr. van Loomis had built up on the island. Mario showed him the fishing industries round the coast, the pearls, the coral, the fresh and dried fish; he showed him the fields and the Indian corn, tobacco, ground-nuts, and cotton; the coffee and tea, the timber, the vineyards, and the orchards high up on the hill; he showed him the gold washing in the upper streams and the little silver mine.

"What does he *do* with all this? Doesn't he do *anything?*"

Mario shook his head.

"What couldn't he do!" said McGinty. "All this, belonging to one man. It's fantastic. It's not right."

Mario nodded his head violently.

Filipino would have said it was not fair for one man to own more than another; McGinty was not as naïve as that; he knew the size of men was various, but he had not visualized a size as large as this. "He ought not to keep it," said McGinty. "It ought to be used. It ought to trade, go into towns and shops and houses. It would make money, a lot of money. The island would be different then," said McGinty. "It would be more like a place!" He looked round on its sun and balminess. "It might be quite a decent place," he said. "There's room for an airport here. It might get to be a tourist centre like Honolulu; it's pretty enough in its way. The people might be educated and given a chance. Yet one man can sit on it all and keep it like this." McGinty's sense of justice was outraged. "It's not right!" said McGinty.

"Not-a right!" said Mario, nodding violently, and he began to pour out to McGinty his garbled distorted story. McGinty could not understand Mario's English or the long passionate interruptions in Spanish, but he gathered that it was something to do with Mario's mother and Mr. van Loomis. Mr. van Loomis's name came into it again and again.

"Did he take it?" asked McGinty. "He *says* he bought it."

"No-a! No-a!" said Mario passionately, beating his chest. "He-a take it." He came close to McGinty. "You help-a Mario? You-a help?" He laid his hand on McGinty's arm; he was shaking. "You-a help Mario? Please-a! Please! Please!"

McGinty was embarrassed, but he knew that one

should not distress or cross the Marios of this world more than one need. "All right!" said McGinty. He said it to soothe Mario; he did not know that, like Filipino with print, Mario took each word of his as gospel.

"You-a *kill* Loomis," cried Mario fiercely.

"I'll knock him down," said McGinty.

To his horror he saw Mario begin to cry; the tears overflowed and ran down Mario's cheeks. Even though Mario was Mario he was a grown man and his tears offended McGinty. "Here! For the love of Christ!" said McGinty.

Mario dropped down on his knees. "I thank-a God for you! Le doy gracias a Dios por haberte traido. Madre de Dios!" Mario's face was transformed. "I-a follow you all-a my life. You-a beat Loomis. You-a be chief! Jesús sent-a you to-a me! Estoy a tus órdenes!"

"Aw! Shut up!" said McGinty.

CHAPTER XIV

WHEN Charis came onto the veranda for breakfast next morning and kissed her father and took her place, Valentine's chair was empty. "Isn't he up yet?" she asked.

"Long ago," said Mr. van Loomis. "I sent him logging."

Charis stopped with the coffee pot in her hand, the cup half filled. "You sent him—*what?*"

"Logging," said Mr. van Loomis. "May I have my coffee, please?"

"But, Father—"

"My coffee."

Charis's hand shook as she poured it out and passed it to him. "But—you don't mean . . ."

"I do. Why not?" said Mr. van Loomis. "Why should I keep those lazy young scamps on the island doing noth-

142

ing?" He was delighted to see Charis's dismay. "I work. Why shouldn't they?"

"But Father, Valentine is *Valentine Doubleday!*"

"I don't care who he is. He has two hands like the rest of us and a stomach that has to be filled. Why should I fill it for him? What would have happened to me if I had stopped to think who I was when I came here—or to you?"

"But . . . *Valentine!*" cried Charis in misery.

Mr. van Loomis was pleased. He had thought that Charis had cooled; as Valentine grew warmer, she withdrew. Mr. van Loomis thought this annoying but it was natural. Charis too had seen Valentine change and had begun to know that presently she might have something serious to consider; she was considering, but Mr. van Loomis thought she had cooled and he had resolved to blow on the fire.

"But he is our guest, Father."

"He is not! Guests are invited," said Mr. van Loomis. "I sent for them both yesterday and told them they would have to do something for their keep. If someone doesn't go up there the men take days to get the logs down, and why should I go when Doubleday is here doing nothing? Why shouldn't he work?"

"It isn't his work," said Charis in growing consternation. "You know it isn't. He isn't used to it."

"He soon will be," said Mr. van Loomis unperturbed. "In the end it will do him good. He looked stale, as if he didn't get enough exercise. This will exercise him. I sent McGinty to start taking the census. I had thought of sending him to make the inquiry into the cockfighting, it makes me unpopular, but, do you know, really, that young fool barely knows a cock from a hen. I have always wanted to take a census of the island. He must at least know a man from a woman."

"He would hate that," said Charis. "He doesn't want to have anything to do with the island. I wonder why?"

"I didn't do it to please him. There is work to be done."

Charis was not interested in McGinty. "But Valentine logging!" she said. "Oh, I'm *ashamed.*" Mr. van Loomis

143

was glad to see that there were tears in her eyes and that she could not eat any breakfast.

She has it badly, thought Mr. van Loomis. Poor little worm!

〜〜〜〜〜 Meanwhile Valentine was up on the hill. The trees had been felled in the forest and cut into lengths. In Mr. van Loomis's early days the islanders used to carry the logs laboriously down the hill, but he had soon evolved a way of getting them down on the island's solitary river that had its source in a spring almost at the mountain's top, a sacred spring where the islanders used to come up from the villages to see the bubbling water and drink it directly from the earth. Other springs fed the river underground, and by the time it reached the small pool where it widened out before tumbling over the island's only waterfall, the fall that was visible out to sea, it was quite a large river. The fall fell into a pool below where, opening in rapids, the river swirled down into the valley and ran into the sea. At the brink of the waterfall, on the edge of the top pool, Mr. van Loomis had built his sluice gates.

All sluice gates that Valentine had seen, and he had seen them in the Great Lakes and the Maine forests, had been enormous and enormously heavy of heavy wood, raised on wheels by man or steam power. Mr. van Loomis's gates were of necessity nothing like that; they were meant to hold the water back for a short while, perhaps for half an hour, until the pool was full enough to bring the logs down with it in its first rush over the fall. In any case the islanders could not have made heavy gates; they had not tools enough. Mr. van Loomis's gates were simply slats of several thicknesses of bamboo, woven together like the bamboo-hut walls and the house window slats; the thicknesses were laid together, lashed around the edges, and heavily soaked with oil; they gave just enough impediment to the water to dam it for the short while needed.

Standing on the bank, Valentine thought at first that the work went perfectly without him; men dragged or

144

carried logs from the forest and tipped them into the pool where they floated, eddying as the water came down. Two heavy tree trunks ran out from either bank of the pool to the gates; on these, men stood with poles to keep the logs from crushing into the gates. Valentine went up and stood beside them. Logs and water gathered in the pool, which rose higher and higher until there was a shout, the men on the trunks sprang back: the moment had come when the gates could hold no longer. Two teams of men pulled on the ropes that raised the gates in a rough frame (even bamboo, sodden, was heavy), the gates came up, and water and cut logs swirled together over the verge and down the fall, each hitting the pool below with a heavy splash and the thumping reverberating sound of wood hitting wood as they fell and whirled in the white water of the pool. Here were more men with poles, watching warily above to see no log leaped the pool, and running back into the forest when they heard the warning shout in case logs leaped, as they had been known to do, from the fall itself. Afterwards they poled the logs from the bottom pool to the rapids before the rush of water was lost. The logs did not jam, they were cut too short, they slid down easily to the valley; there a great tree had been dragged by bullocks across the stream, making a bar against which the logs would lie, without rotting in the water, until Mr. van Loomis had need of them.

The only thing Valentine actively did was to blow his whistle, then leap from the tree trunk to the bank, and that only when he was warned by the shout, but he began to see, with Mr. van Loomis, that his presence was important, if it were important to get the logs down at all. Left to themselves, the islanders would have left the logs standing as trees and contented themselves with the easily cut and worked bamboo; for themselves they would have gone without jetties and waded ashore from their boats carrying their goods on their heads, as they had always done; they did not want wooden floors in their houses, and they would have gone without chests and kept their belongings in a square of cotton or a banana leaf, as they went without tables and chairs and sat on the ground or, at best, on grass woven mats; in any case they did not sit, they squatted. They did not object to work; they enjoyed the excitement of bringing down the logs and they shouted and laughed as they rolled them or wielded their long poles, but, left to themselves, they would presently have squatted down on their heels for a smoke or to play marbles with pebbles. One of them, a very young one, might have produced the racing grasshoppers the herd boys pitted against one another; or they might have wandered away into the forest and found a dry place and lain down and gone to sleep. Valentine and his whistle kept their energy alert.

It was a long time since Valentine had been made to work; he had worked, and worked hard, but not under orders, as in the army and at school. Mr. van Loomis had given him no choice but to obey his orders, and that gave Valentine a sense of rest. It was a long time too since he had been up so early in the morning. It made him feel sharply alive.

Up here, on the hill, the forest smelled of dried grass and dew and flowers. It had none of the damp leaf-mould earth smell of temperate forests. From where he stood Valentine could see orchids—this is where they get them for the window sills—and, down the narrow glades between the trees, in shafts of sunlight, he saw butterflies, brilliant swallowtails, and bushes of wild coffee flowers. Except for the butterflies, all small life had been frightened away by the log-rolling. There were few animals left on the island, only deer and foxes, a few wild cats higher up the hill, but there were many birds, from the great fishing eagles to the tiny weaver birds and flycatchers. On the way up he had seen monkeys, parakeets, and a swarm of wild bees. Though it was cool, it was unmistakably a tropical forest, but, this morning, he felt part of it, merged into it as if his skin were eating the air and sun as Pheasant said it needed to do. He had woken that morning, feeling the quick of the island as he had felt it even before he landed on it. He could not speak to these islanders, or they to him, but he felt at one with them, understanding and friendly. They worked naked, except for a cloth tied tightly round their waist and passing between their legs; he was only in shorts, and his skin was beginning to tan; if I stay here, I shall soon be as brown as they are, he thought. They had often to wade into the

146

river, and the water was cold; they came out shivering and slapped their chests and flanks to warm themselves and, under the brown, a red blush came up. Valentine, standing, grew chilled too and beat his chest and back; he too had the same red blush. One of the men cut his hand and blood came on the log he was handling; he plunged his hand in the river, and the water, clear green-white, was reddened. They all looked at it as if they liked to see it; it matched their sharp world of spears and cockfights and arrows and drums; at the quick of life there was blood; was that why men had that strange blood-thirsty thrill to see it?

As Valentine stood on the tree trunk by the sluice gates he could feel the trunk trembling under his feet; presently, with the first pull on the gates, he would feel the water stir; only its length behind it on the bank made the trunk safe from being swept down. The logs pounded in the pool, their cut ends lifting, pale against their dark bark or brightly red. Below, on the other side of his stand, was the fall, its huge plume disappearing out of sight into the pool; he could feel the spray on his cheeks and on his shoulders and on his hair; its noise shut out the sea. This was the first time on the island that he had been without the sound of the surf in his ears; he felt as if he had reached a secret place that, before, had been locked to him; now it was opened; it was as if, in joining the island's work, he had been given its freedom.

I should like to stay here, thought Valentine, if I didn't have to go back. Immediately the question came, "Why go back?" "I have to," said Valentine slowly. "I must."

He thought of that going back: of landing; of the examining of passports and health certificates and money and baggage. He thought of Tuggie coming to meet him, and his man Joe, and Wallace his secretary. They would all have news for him, and part of it would inevitably be news of difficulties, upsets, cuts, gaps, quarrels, decisions. Joe would have his ration book, driving licence, petrol coupons; there would be the going through with Tuggie of applications, licenses, and regulations, plans; there would be dictating of letters, signing of cheques; Wallace would have an accumulation of letters, and next morning Joe would bring in more letters and newspapers lying folded on the salver, and the telephone would ring. "Your mother, Mr. Valentine, to say 'Good morning.'" Suppose he did not want to say "Good morning." "Miss Wayne, Mr. Valentine." "Val, darling! At the end of my song in Act Two, you know, where Tony comes in . . ." "Mr. Marks, sir." "My God! Val, Stringer has got in ahead of us and . . ." In that quiet place in the forest it seemed to him unbearable. Why go back, thought Valentine.

"To live."

"That isn't life," said Valentine aloud. He felt the spray on his skin again, the trunk tingling under his feet, and heard the happy shouting. "This is life," said Valentine. It seemed to him that it was life direct; the people, the island, work.

"It's not your work."

I can't flatter myself, thought Valentine bitterly, that my work is important, and, as he thought that, he knew it was important for him and the more he denied it, the more important it would become; and you are alone with your work, said Valentine to himself; it's you who have to face it, who carry it round with you, and the more of it that remains undone the heavier it becomes. You are a freak with a canker; if you don't exercise it, it will eat you up. No it's not a canker, said Valentine, contradicting himself; it's a heart, and if you take the heart out of a body the body can't live. The theatre is the heart of my mind, said Valentine. It's inseparable from me, and that is the truth, and he immediately thought, Nonsense! It's a habit that's all; an excuse like all the excuses that keep people in prison. I want to be free. I need to be free, cried Valentine, and the sound of the river, the cool spray, the lifting logs, the trees, the shafts of light, the glades where the sun fell, the orchids and the butterflies, all seemed to answer, reasonably, "Why not?"

Then, pell-mell, into this man's world, came Charis.

Valentine had been thinking a great deal about Charis. He wondered why he had accepted her at once. Real live people, thought Valentine, ask themselves about other people, ask if they are in love. Why haven't I? Is it because I have been dreaming? But he knew quite well he was not dreaming. This was real. A quiet certainty had grown in him; Charis, this cool slim stranger, had walked

148

easily into a place that no one had been in before, a place that Valentine had instinctively defended and kept empty. He knew, without conceit, that it could have been filled again and again, Ellen . . . poor little Ellen, thought Valentine, dear little idiot, but it could never have been Ellen; even Ellen herself knew that. Now, unmistakably, Charis was there. How had it happened? It's her peculiar faculty for getting under chinks, thought Valentine with irritation; the irritation was not worrying but stimulating; it pricked him into life; and she isn't sweet, thought Valentine as if that were a great virtue, and then he remembered how sweet Charis could be; but not cloying, thought Valentine, sweet and sour, well arranged. That was a strange thing to commend in a woman, but what an important part of a woman it was. Charis was young but Valentine had complete confidence in her, a confidence he needed. Yes, I am in danger of falling in love, thought Valentine, or I am near its safety. He did not know yet which to say. If any string is pulled it will decide it, felt Valentine. I only need a jerking . . . and Charis came riding Dominion full tilt out of the forest.

She came so fast partly because of her own indignation and partly because, with Valentine's advent, she had neglected her riding and Dominion had not been out for days; the white pony, coming out of the green of the forest into a shaft of sun, was dazzling. Charis's cheeks were flaming, her eyes wider, more darkly green than Valentine had seen them. The island had no way of making breeches or riding skirts, and Charis rode in the grass skirt that the women used for road work or harvesting or fishing. The strands of the skirt divided on the saddle and hung flickeringly across her legs, showing them bare from the thigh downwards; they looked slim and beautiful to Valentine. Her bodice was the usual island scarf, tied across her breasts, leaving her waist bare, too, and she wore a straw hat, its brim large and turned back, its crown tied under her chin with cords. Because she was indignant with her father she had lost her paleness and reserve; Charis was Scottish born but island bred; when she was really angry and moved, she showed she was angry and moved; now she was alight with anger and pity.

"Valentine!" she cried, flinging herself off Dominion

before he had stopped. "Oh, Valentine!" Valentine jumped down from the log and caught her and steadied her. "Oh, Valentine! Oh, Valentine!" sobbed Charis.

"What *is* the matter, Charis?"

"Father, Father," sobbed Charis incoherently. "What is he *dreaming* of? How dare he do this to you?"

"Do what?"

"Make you work . . . f-for us. As if we . . . we . . . I'm so *ashamed!*"

"But I like it," said Valentine. "I'm happy. I'm enjoying it."

Her anger turned on him. "Then you oughtn't to enjoy it. You oughtn't to be happy. You should know it isn't *fit!*" said Charis like a wild cat.

Valentine had kept his hands on her elbows. The noise of the fall and the river made it necessary for him to bend down to hear what she said. Her elbows were warm and slim in his hands, he liked the hardness of their small knit bones, the soft flesh over them; his face was close to hers, the shadows of the trees and the light behind them made small dancing sunspots on her skin, and the green of the trees made her wet eyes greener still; her lips were open and trembling. Valentine kissed her on the mouth.

The forest seemed to swing away from Charis; the river sounded loudly in her ears; she was giddy. He kissed her again.

There was a warning shout behind them. Valentine was too late to blow his whistle; he pushed Charis back, and the bank shuddered under them as the ropes strained; the gates came up and another twenty or thirty logs rode and spun over the fall. When they had gone and all the shouting was below, he turned back to Charis. "You shouldn't interrupt when I'm at work," he said, annoyed.

"I'm sorry," said Charis meekly, but she did not look sorry.

After a moment he came and stood beside her, but he did not touch her; he seemed to be thinking. Charis saw how different his face looked from that first day: it looked untormented and at rest. Then he spoke. "Charis," he said gravely, "I suppose you know that I have met and been friends with many women and girls."

"I didn't suppose anything else," said Charis coldly,

but her heart began to beat so fast that it hurt her. What is he going to tell me? she thought. That he is sorry he kissed me because . . . ? She felt hot with shame; she thought it was singularly tasteless of Valentine to boast at this moment.

"I'm not boasting," said Valentine as if he answered her. "There were very many." He said it simply. "I have known them and thought about them and listened to them and planned for them. Some I liked very much, some I loved, some loved me. Some I thought beautiful, like Ellen—you will see her one day, said Valentine abtractedly, his eyes on Charis's face.

There was silence. Charis raised her chin.

"But with one thing and another," said Valentine, apparently with not the least idea that he was affronting her, "with one thing and another, I was lucky enough not to be tied in any way, to any of them."

"Why lucky?" asked Charis, trying to speak lightly and hating Valentine. "Why lucky, if you loved them?"

"Because now I have found you," said Valentine.

Charis's heart gave a jolt that made her catch her breath. Her lids came down on her eyes under the look in his. He asked her, "Charis, you love me, don't you?"

It was some moments before she answered. "How do I know?" said Charis. "I have never seen another woman, except Pheasant and the islanders of course. I had never seen a white man, except my father, till you came, but I can't imagine anyone else who would be like you." She broke off. "I shouldn't talk to you like this. Father would be angry."

"He shouldn't be angry," said Valentine. "I have been very patient with him. Good God! Did he think I should put up with him for one moment but for you? Though I didn't think I should turn into a river hog for you."

Charis did not laugh. She looked at him steadily and the green seemed to burn in her eyes. "Perhaps I love you," she said. "But how do I know? And do you love me? You haven't told me."

"Yes," said Valentine. It was a considered "yes." He bent and kissed her again.

Mr. van Loomis, who had just come up the track and was standing mopping his forehead under a tree, saw them and was glad. "Splendid," said Mr. van Loomis, and before he put his hat on again he said, "God bless them!"

"But why are you crying?" Valentine asked Charis.

"Because . . . I'm . . ." said Charis, and a despair came over her. "Who am I? Nobody beside you. How can I ever learn enough? How can I hope to keep up with you? How can I expect what I want from you?" Then she checked herself. "But that's nonsense," said Charis firmly. "I refuse to talk like that; but please, Valentine, I want to say it plainly and then I shall never say it again; I will be anything, do anything, go anywhere, if I can be near you."

"Hush," said Valentine. "It's I who should say that to you."

"Do you feel *that?*" asked Charis, dazzled. "Then perhaps it *is* love."

"Of course," said Valentine, and to him also it seemed a satisfying and peaceful fact. "I love you," he repeated.

"As a husband?" asked Charis shrewdly.

Valentine was taken aback. Here, on the island, it had not been necessary to envisage himself as a husband with Charis as a wife. Husband, wife, thought Valentine. He thought suddenly of Charis meeting Tuggie, Joe, his mother, Jos, Ellen—Ellen would mind, thought Valentine. He thought of Carlotta; he thought that Carlotta would approve of Charis, they would like each other. Carlotta had been afraid that he would marry Ellen. Carlotta would approve of Charis, and Charis, he felt, would be good with his mother, defend him from her without letting her know he was defended. Charis would answer the telephone, and he thought of the cool calmness she had already; it would not be easy to get past Charis on the telephone. He saw Charis in London, New York, Paris, and, he thought suddenly, there would be a smooth path where there had never been smoothness before; he thought of finding her in the flat when he came in tired and ruffled; but we shouldn't have a flat, thought Valentine, we should find a house, an unmistakable house of our own. No matter where he saw her, he saw her with him, with him but still Charis, still herself, still true. It's not just "Blue Lagoon," thought Valentine. She is true, I know that, and he said firmly, "As a husband."

"A husband is a status," Charis reminded him. "A husband has to be something as well as do it."

"Yes, my dear one, and a wife too," said Valentine. He drew her closer and put his hand under her chin. "I have kissed you, Charis. You have not kissed me. Kiss me," said Valentine, and Charis kissed him.

"Splendid!" said Mr. van Loomis.

CHAPTER XV

As HE came down from the mountain Mr. van Loomis walked more and more slowly. An inextricable sadness was beginning to be mixed with his triumph. He felt old and chilled. "My feet must be wet," said Mr. van Loomis. "It's the dew on the hill," but his feet had often been wet before. "I must be getting old," said Mr. van Loomis. That depressed him more. He sent for Filipino to rub his feet with a towel and bring dry sandals, but when his feet were dry and warm he still felt chilled.

"Everything is going splendidly, splendidly," said Mr. van Loomis aloud to buoy himself up. "Everything is turning out well." Then why should he be filled with this strange depression? He told himself he was unreasonably depressed. He went into his study and sat down in his revolving chair and drummed his fingers on the desk. Time passes and children grow up, thought Mr. van Loomis. One should not be so attached. No sensible parent is attached. No matter how reasonably he said it, Mr. van Loomis felt unreasonably attached; all he could think of was, Charis is gone—gone!

"She isn't gone. Nonsense!" said Mr. van Loomis, and he said it aloud to make it more firm. "She isn't gone. She is still here, and Valentine, I believe, is settling. Given a little while longer he might even . . ." He broke off. Did he mean to keep Valentine here? That was a question Mr. van Loomis had been evading in his mind since Valentine came. If he had been challenged he would have said, "I am quite neutral. It all depends. We must see how things turn out. It is for Valentine . . ." Now that uneasy Scottish conscience stirred and raised its head. "Are you sure you are quite neutral?" it said. "You didn't put out a signal, and when they asked you if you had you didn't tell a lie, that is true, but you gave the impression of a lie." Mr. van Loomis combed his beard through with angry fingers and then drummed on the desk again. He returned to Charis. Already she took Valentine's part against her father. That is all the thanks I get, thought Mr. van Loomis; to be a parent is a thankless task! After all these years I am thrown on one side. He will be her mentor, her companion, her first love. Already she quotes his opinions, Charis whom I brought up to think for herself! My part is done, thought Mr. van Loomis bitterly. He thought of how he had brought her up, taught her, guided her, and then he saw again the ball for his coming of age; he saw the lights shining down on the velvet coats, the well-brushed heads, the tartans, the white shoulders; now he remembered a tartan sash across a girl's white satin dress; he had no idea who the girl was, indeed he had a strange idea that she was Charis; she should have been Charis, a ball should have been given for Charis, it should have culminated in that; she could have worn her pearls . . . and known they were pearls.

Instead of a ball, tomorrow night he would take her up to the temple for the full moon rainbow dances. What have I done? thought Mr. van Loomis. She has grown up without society or state or church. Have I robbed her? Then he looked out and saw his island garden where Charis had grown, his quiet lawns and fragrant trees and the sea shimmering beyond it, and it seemed to him, as it had always done, quiet, healthy, beautiful and good; it was a shelter from the world. Charis had never known displeasure or punishment or fear or darkness or distress; Mr. van Loomis's brow lightened, then it darkened again; she had not known her birthright either.

He thought of some of his dear early friends: the Castle shepherd; Duthie, the foreman at the middle works; Tam, the West Lodge keeper. Was there much difference to a child, thought Mr. van Loomis between Tam and, for instance, Charis's devoted slave Luck, the head boatman? The small Charis had loved Luck as much as he had loved Tam, but yes, there was a difference; he and Tam were out of the same soil. Here, on the island, Charis had been grafted, and a graft is never as strong as a root.

All round him the morning was filled with the activities he had made; they had been his world, but now they seemed to him superficial and unimportant, as if the meaning had gone out of them. They seemed irrelevant, and he wondered suddenly if that was how they appeared to the islanders. Am I irrelevant? he asked himself suddenly, and he felt as humble as he had that moment in the study on the day he had hidden the Water Star. "But the people need me," he said, and the answer seemed to come from that truthful conscience, "They need nobody." "But I rescued them from Mario's mother," and inexorably it said, "Mario's mother would have passed away."

From where he sat he could hear the sounds of water and air and fire and earth that made the island pulse, a pulse as strong and inexorable as creation, that would go on beating through time. "You come or you go," it said to Mr. van Loomis. "A few little scratches that may remain or may be wiped out," and it seemed to reprove him and say, "You have been strangely puffed up."

Mr. van Loomis was indignant. "I have worked as hard and honestly as any man."

"When you worked as a *man* it was permissible," it said. "But that conjuring, that monkeying about with the plane and that about the stars . . . If you usurp . . ." Mr. van Loomis felt suddenly afraid, usurp was an unpleasant word. "If you start something, you may not be able to stop it," it went on unpleasantly. "You don't know what you may raise. This is a terror-striking world, blind and huge. If you usurp . . ."

Usurp. No that was not a pleasant word. Mr. van Loomis tried to think of something else and, thinking of usurping, he thought suddenly and, it seemed to him inconsequently, of McGinty. All his pent-up feeling flooded

155

out in anger against him. "If anyone upsets my plans it will be McGinty!" he said.

Immediately the unpleasant voice came, "Then you have plans?"

"Phaugh!" said Mr. van Loomis, thoroughly upset.

He had set the islanders to watch McGinty. They watched McGinty. They saw him go out to the lighthouse, but that was to play knacker with Mario Fernandes. Sometimes, they all knew, instead of playing knacker, McGinty Tsula made a shadow play in front of the light, but that seemed to them harmless, if mad. They might have reported it, but Jéo was afraid that, if they did, Mr. van Loomis would take Mario off the light, and Jéo was courting a tall girl with springing lines and a high held head and eyes of a warm promise that had several of the island men after her; she made Jéo wild with jealousy and longing; and he could think of nothing else. The courtship moon was nearing its full, and everyone had important matters to attend to. To the islanders Mario and McGinty were not important; what they did on the light harmed no one. "The people always grow careless in the courtship month," said Mr. van Loomis. "They think of nothing but getting wives or else they have daughters to settle." There was no one to tell him that with a daughter to settle he had grown a little careless himself.

Mr. van Loomis did not care to think about McGinty; but McGinty was persistent. "Persistent, puny, and impudent," said Mr. van Loomis; now, suddenly, without warning, that was what he seemed to be himself. "Am *I* a McGinty?" asked Mr. van Loomis. It seemed to him that in truth he was. "Everyman is every man," he had once said to Charis sententiously (he saw now he had often been sententious); but it was not merely sententious, it was true. "We are all brothers," said Mr. van Loomis in disgust. He did not want to be McGinty's brother, or brother to the thick slow simple bestial Mario with his lusts, but he had to admit he was. Yes, I am lustful, thought Mr. van Loomis gloomily. He was brother to the quick visionary in Filipino, even kin to Niu whom he could not fathom. Once again he had the thought that Niu was the island, and now he saw that for these twenty years Niu had not been his servant, but he Niu's.

He did not know when he had spent such an unpleasant half-hour. "I don't know. I don't know," said Mr. van Loomis, and he upset a little pile of notebooks labelled 1, 1a, 2, 2a, 3, 3a, and thoughtfully mixed them up and did not put them in order again. All his carefully thought out, well-organized world seemed meaningless. He knew only that already the island seemed strangely empty, and he was reminded, with the feeling of a pit opening in his stomach, of the day Charis's mother had died at Spey; an empty hollow echoing castle; an empty echoing island.

A sound at his elbow made him turn. It was Filipino with his tray of mid-morning rum and milk. Mr. van Loomis took it and drank it. He felt he needed it.

"Tsula," said Filipino.

"Go away," said Mr. van Loomis, but Filipino lingered.

"Tsula, when you go away with Tsula Valentine, what happen to us then?"

Mr. van Loomis spun his chair round to look at Filipino. "Go *away*? Why should I go away?"

"Won't you go away, Tsula?" asked Filipino.

"Don't talk nonsense," said Mr. van Loomis. "Why should I go away?" His eye fell on the mail bags where they had been thrown down on the day McGinty brought them in. "You stop talking and bring me those," said Mr. van Loomis severely to Filipino.

~~~~~~~~ When Mr. van Loomis had read the first letter of the pile of papers and letters he had sorted on his desk after Filipino had emptied them out of the bags, he sat very quietly in his chair. He drummed his fingers on the desk, on his knees, on the desk. He felt as if they were drumming in his ears.

Presently he took up his pen and absent-mindedly began to trace words on the pad in front of him. He wrote the same word over and over again. Presently he looked down at what he had written; over and over again he had written "Spey." "Spey!" said Mr. van Loomis. He had written it like a signature; it was a long time since he had signed himself that. He stared down at it and a ripple of ominous cold seemed to go over him. Must I go back to being that? thought Mr. van Loomis. Could I go back?

Over and above the steady pulse he seemed to hear the sound of clicking. It was a clicking of typewriters and tape-machines and countless heels on busy pavements; a click of machinery and engines and clocks, of dictaphones and phonographs, cash registers and duplicators, and of clacking, interminable tongues telling, counting, checking, adding. The clicking grew louder, it overlaid and drowned the pulse so that he lost it in a roar. "Mumbo-jumbo!" said Mr. van Loomis. "Abracadabra!" He knew nothing of Valentine's world of forms and coupons, but his governed world of wonders was much the same, and to him, even more than to Valentine, it seemed dreadful; he dreaded it as he dreaded kings and politicians, politics and policies, intrigues and calculations. It seemed it had come after him now. He remembered how once an empty whisky bottle, one of his own firms', had been washed up on the shore. Darkest Africa! thought Mr. van Loomis; soon there will be nowhere dark and mysterious left under the moon. Now the roar of clicking sounded close, in his ears. "No!" cried Mr. van Loomis sharply aloud. "No. I can't go back. I can't."

"Tsula! Tsula!"

He lifted his head. For the last few minutes a sound had been steadily growing, not in the room, but outside in the air. It grew to a near roaring drone as Filipino came rushing in, panting and glowing. "Tsula! Tsula! It's come. It's come!" Mr. van Loomis could hear the servants running through the house and out from the kitchen, as they would be running from villages. He could hear the excited cries in the garden. He sat still.

"Tsula! Tsula!"

Mr. van Loomis bent his head over his desk and pretended to be writing.

"Tsula!"

"Go away."

"Tsula!" said Filipino firmly. "Tsula!"

And Mr. van Loomis had to look.

They could see the plane now out of the window. It was flying high over the sea. Mr. van Loomis made quick calculations: Valentine was in the forest; even if he heard

158

the plane there over the sound of the river it would take him a long time to come out on any place where he could signal. Valentine was safe. But McGinty? Mr. van Loomis did not know where McGinty was; he had sent him out into the villages, but if McGinty were in a village on the hill or on the shore he could very well make a signal; he could light a fire as a beacon, wave a white cloth if the plane came near. Sweat broke out on Mr. van Loomis's neck. He sat tensely, his hands pressed on the desk, waiting, as still as if he were frozen there, but Filipino was eager and ever helpful.

"Are you thinking what to do?" asked Filipino. "Give me your keys, Tsula. I will get your gun. You can fire the gun, Tsula, and make the plane come here." Mr. van Loomis kept his gun locked away; he had not known that Filipino knew he had a gun, or indeed what a gun was. Now Filipino was saying impatiently, "Give me your keys." Mr. van Loomis had the feeling that Filipino would not have hesitated to fire off the gun himself. "Tsula, the keys!" It was almost peremptory, but Mr. van Loomis only said, "Not yet."

"But if it's not yet the plane will go away," cried Filipino.

"It's . . . too soon," said Mr. van Loomis. If Valentine goes now all this may stop, thought Mr. van Loomis. He has not spoken to me yet. Nothing is arranged. Valentine could forget Charis. Pride rose in him, and he thought, Well, Charis could forget Valentine, but he knew that Charis would not; with these reserved cool girls life went deep; they did not forget, and Mr. van Loomis's resolution hardened. "Be quiet, monkey!" he said angrily.

"Tsula. I get your gun."

"No."

"No?" cried Filipino again. He could not believe his ears.

"No!" said Mr. van Loomis fiercely. He did not wish to explain, but Filipino's eager eyes were on him and Filipino's lips were parted to argue with him. This boy is becoming a nuisance! thought Mr. van Loomis. He is getting to be familiar, much too familiar! He glared at Filipino so fiercely that Filipino was intimidated and became sulkily silent.

The plane did not come near the island. Why should it? It was looking for the Water Star or the wreckage of the Water Star. It dipped over the bay, turned south, circled again over the Hat, and flew away out to sea. Filipino gave a little wail. Mr. van Loomis lifted his hands from the desk with a long sigh. Where they had lain were two wet patches on the wood.

A typewritten page of the letter caught his eye. "We must also tell you," it said, "that your brother, the late Earl, was about to make a gift of the Castle to the nation; we were actually negotiating with the National Trust at the time of his death. He intended to keep the south rooms and tower for the perpetual use of the family. If you should want us to continue . . ." What should I do now with a castle? thought Mr. van Loomis. All I am fit for is a cell. He looked again at the letter and remembered that the turret room was in the south tower. "My little room!" said Mr. van Loomis aloud.

⁓⁓⁓⁓ Deep in the morning of log-rolling and discovery with Charis, Valentine had not even heard the plane. He and Charis knew nothing about it until they came down and met the first islanders running up from the beach.

McGinty did not hear it in time. Mario had been showing him a hive. It was a hive of wild bees in a loop of wax and honey on a tree; the humming from it rim filled all the little glade where they had found it at the back of one of the villages that McGinty had to visit along the shore. "Of all the damn bits of luck," he said to Valentine afterwards. "With those bees raising hell, I didn't notice anything till too late."

"What's that?" he had said suddenly, raising his head. He had shaken Mario's arm to quieten him, then he had turned and run down to the beach as if all the bees were after him. Mario ran behind him, but, by the time he had lumbered through the village, scattering children and baskets and chickens, McGinty had stopped running. He was lying face downwards on the sand under the palms.

For a moment Mario did not understand; then he too

heard that other humming and, looking, bobbing his great head at the sky, at last he saw the speck that was the aeroplane flying away over the Hat.

McGinty was lying still except that every now and again his shoulders heaved. Mario watched him. McGinty looked oddly small lying there. Was he crying? Mario moved forward and, putting his hands on his knees, bent down to look at him.

"M—McGinty? Sir?" he said. McGinty liked Mario to call him "sir," but now, "Go to hell!" said McGinty's muffled voice.

Mario waited, puzzled and dismayed and hurt, until McGinty sat up and pushed his hair back into its crest and wiped the sand off his cheek and chin with his hand; but there were tear marks on his face where the sand had stuck. Yes, he had been crying. Mario averted his head. There was a long silence.

"Cheer up, old cock," said McGinty, but Mario did not look up. McGinty stood up and brushed his clothes, then gave Mario a pat on the shoulder. "It's all right. I'm not angry with you," he said. "It was just bad luck. Forget it! I'll get out somehow."

He patted Mario's shoulder again. Mario wanted to be reassured, and McGinty's hand on his shoulder made him tremble with gratitude. Together they went up the beach back to the village again.

In the study Mr. van Loomis was having a passage of arms with Filipino. The tears were running down Filipino's cheeks.

"It's gone. You let it go!" cried Filipino.

Damn the boy! thought Mr. van Loomis. He will go and tell all this. He saw that he must deal firmly with Filipino and he said witheringly as he had often said to Charis, "When you are grown up and know some of the things you don't know now, you will know that most men have a reason for everything they do."

"And if the reason is against other men's reasons?" Filipino flung back.

Mr. van Loomis thought for a moment of slapping him; for a moment he thought he would vent on Filipino all his anger and nostalgia and feeling of inadequacy and grief. Then he felt curiously weak and he said, "Hush."

161

"Hush!" cried Filipino. "I not hush!" He shook back his hair and ran out of the door. Mr. van Loomis sat thoughtfully on at his desk, drumming with his fingers. Events were growing too strong for him. He, Mr. van Loomis, was gradually being outmanœuvred. He shut his eyes. He longed for peace.

It was nearly mid-day. The island, under the full sun, was hot and growing more languorous each moment, but Mr. van Loomis suddenly shivered. He stood up, pushing his chair back so sharply that it rocked and almost fell. He could have sworn he felt, on his cheek, the chill revivifying dampness of a Scottish mist.

CHAPTER XVI

<hr>

FILIPINO was very cast down when the plane went away; he had had a taste of the world and he was avid for more. That morning, when he had been in Valentine's bedroom cleaning the English shoes that seemed immensely precious to Filipino (though Valentine had at once taken to the comfortable island grass sandals), he had seen two magazines in Valentine's dispatch case, which was open. Filipino neatly slipped them out; they were a copy of *Vanity Fair* that had an article in it about Valentine and a copy of the American magazine *Life*. "Then it will be about life," said Filipino reverently, and he discarded Valentine's shoes, leaving them half cleaned on the floor, and carried the magazines quickly away to his hut on the beach, where he read them on his bed. He read the one called *Life* first, and, as he read, his eyes dilated more and more widely and he breathed quickly through his beautifully shaped nostrils. He had not imagined that life could be anything like this.

"The time has come to remake Europe," read Filipino, rapt. (He had thought Europe was made, long ago.)

"What the subcommittees of the Paris conferences must now do is to take their rump of Europe and make the best of it. . . . As they worked on their tasks," read Filipino, "a dream also burned in the hearts of some. That dream, dating from the days of Charlemagne (picture on next page) is that they might eventually unite into something like a United States of Europe." Filipino did not understand about the rump or the significance of the United States of Europe, but he had heard of Charlemagne; he turned to the next page and looked at his picture. If dreams had burned in men's hearts ever since Charlemagne, he, Filipino, was linked with them; dreams did nothing else but burn in his heart. Filipino had his first living taste of history.

"Marian congress at Ottawa," read Filipino; "250,000 Catholics assemble to honor Virgin Mary. Against the night sky," he read, "the Virgin made her most dazzling appearance in giant fireworks, standing in the new moon, wearing a crown of flashing stars." "Like our dances, only better," said Filipino. He knew of the Virgin Mary through reading and also through Pheasant; Pheasant had a small statue of her in her hut, Mary, in a blue cloak with a crown of painted gilt; that had always been wonderful to the islanders, but this was far more wonderful. Nothing could have brought home to Filipino more vividly the place of Mary as Queen of Heaven than the description of the fireworks; he had felt the glow of religion at moments in the rainbow dances, but this seemed to be not of earth but of heaven; but then, so is the rainbow, heaven too, thought Filipino, and a strange thought came into his mind that this idea of the Queen of Heaven and the island idea of the rainbow were the same. But two hundred and fifty thousand people! thought Filipino, dazzled.

"Camera explodes on New York," he read, wide-eyed. "This remarkable aerial picture looks as if some smokeless bomb has just burst on the town of Manhattan . . . Actually no devastating bomb has exploded, and the apparent collapse of the buildings is merely the photographically distorted result of a low-altitude wide-angle picture." This was Greek to Filipino, but he saw that, lower down, it said, "To get an approximate idea of what the
163

mid-town area of Manhattan really looks like at 3,440 feet, hold the pages on a plane parallel with the floor and place chin on the words, 'New York.' " Earnestly Filipino placed his chin on the words "New York" and looked. "Is that a *town?*" asked Filipino. It looked, rather, like a formation of coral to him. He decided he must go up to the house and look up some of these new words in the dictionary (much in use by him and Charis at this time), but he met Niu, who had discovered Valentine's shoes thrown down. Niu was still scolding when they heard the aeroplane.

When Filipino met Charis that afternoon they were both of them brimful of news, but it was characteristic that Charis did not tell hers (in any case it would not have been news to Filipino; the whole island knew it), while Filipino's words tumbled over themselves in his haste to get them out. He asked Charis to come into the garden, and he had the magazines in his hands and spread them out before her.

"They are not written like the other newspapers, are they? It isn't like our talk, is it?" he asked. That made them all the more exciting to him, but they seemed to depress Charis.

"It isn't our talk," said Charis despondently.

"But it can be. We can learn it," said the eager Filipino, but she shook her head.

"We could never catch up," she said.

More than at the articles, they looked at the advertisements. If the advertisements in the English papers had puzzled and depressed Charis, these terrified her. Looking at *Vanity Fair,* she felt she had been taken into the temple bedroom of some strange, terrifying priestess woman who was initiating her into a cult of strange and binding rites. Are women like that? thought Charis, frightened. Do I have to be like that? She felt inept and clumsy and as ignorant as a child.

She picked up *Vanity Fair* and looked hopelessly at the photograph of Valentine. *". . . at thirty he is author, actor, producer, and film director. He has a strong sense of reality, a satirical wit and a sensitive eye that goes deep. . . ."* Charis sighed. She had said she would not

164

speak or think self-pityingly, but how, how could he ever have patience with me?

She turned to a picture of a coat. *"Drenia builds an Empire coat,"* she read. *"Fullness flung far far back, slim front tapered to a high, buttoned top, shoulders smooth. . . ."*

"Black magic in soft suede," she read, getting more and more frightened. *"Your first thought for the last word in handbags . . ."*

"It's very cleverly written, isn't it?" said Filipino.

"Yes," said Charis with distaste.

"Do all the women you know wear stockings all the time?" she asked Valentine.

"Not all the time," said Valentine cautiously. "But usually, yes."

"Do they all have handbags?"

Valentine said that, yes, he thought they all had handbags.

"All the time?"

"Yes, all the time."

And underclothes? What in the world were underclothes? If you had clothes, why did you need other clothes to go under them? On the island you wore your cloth and scarf; if you were cold, you put a shawl over them, but *under*-clothes? It was a long time before Charis identified these with Pheasant's petticoats, which she had always thought Pheasant wore to make her skirts rustle, and with a large capacious garment that Pheasant called her chemise.

"Oh, dear!" said Charis, and she said it in despair. "How shall I ever be a woman like that?"

"Women are only people," said Valentine.

Charis shook her head. If women were people, that made her less of a person, someone near to an echo or a ghost. I shall never catch up, she thought hopelessly. I shall always be a stranger, the one who is outside. Her ignorance seemed to pierce her through and through and her loneliness appalled her. "You had better not marry me, Valentine," she said. "I should only disgrace you. How should I understand women like that? How shall I ever understand? I don't know *anything*."

"I think you do," said Valentine, but she shook her

head again. He put out his hand for *Vanity Fair*. "Let's look at it and find out what you don't understand."

"I understand the articles," said Charis as Valentine turned the pages, and she said it less timidly. "I could . . . almost . . . have written that one about you, not in those smart words, of course, but in my words. And in the tapestry one," said Charis more cheerfully. "Father and I once traced the history of tapestries, though I have never seen any of course. The one about Rabelais, I could follow that—"

"And you could read the letter in French and the Spanish sonnet without translation," said Valentine gravely, but his eyes were beginning to twinkle. "For someone who doesn't know anything, Charis, you seem to understand a good deal."

"With you to guide me, I . . ."

He put his arm round her. "I am here to guide you," he said, and happiness flooded her again. Then her eyes came back to the photograph of black magic in soft suede. "But the clothes!"

"My dear love," said Valentine gently. "You can buy clothes!"

Charis was comforted. In Valentine she had a star to steer by, but Filipino was going round and round, rudderless.

"There are so many things," said Filipino. He catechized Valentine and McGinty. McGinty was more interested in the magazines than Valentine; he liked the advertisements. "That's a nice gadget," he would say, stopping Filipino at a page every now and then. "We have one of those at home."

"One of *those?* In *your* home?" Filipino turned to look at McGinty with eyes of wonder. He looked at the photograph again. It seemed to bring him almost too close.

"Yes. On the kitchen mantelpiece," said McGinty easily.

"A-aah!" said Filipino dizzily. "Please, what is a mantelpiece?"

He looked up "gadget" in the dictionary but could find only *"Gadge: an instrument of torture."* "Does gadget come from that, do you think?" he asked Charis. "Perhaps because it's so hard to think of one?"

166

"It's a modern word," said Charis. "You should look in the supplement."

"*Gadget: any small ingenious device, a what-d'ye-call-it,*" read Filipino in the supplement. That delighted him. He looked up with his eyes shining. "Is a coffee machine a gadget?"

"Of course," said Charis.

"Then I have invented a small ingenious device; I have invented a what-d'ye-call-it," said Filipino, and he looked through the pages feeling he was at one with the inventors of lawn mowers and foot-warmers and expanding suitcases. "How clever men are!" said Filipino, but now he did not say it with longing but with pride. How far he had come from the days when he and Charis used to stare at Pheasant's sewing machine!

In spite of the disappointment over the rescue plane and Mr. van Loomis's inexplicable behaviour, the day passed in flashes of wonder. Filipino even went up to the kitchen courtyard before dinner to tell the servants about it, and a whole conclave of people had gathered and was listening. "Think," said Filipino, and he stretched his arms high. "Think of tall houses, a house on a house on a house. Twenty, thirty, fifty houses, one on top of another. Twenty, thirty, fifty, a hundred houses—"

"Not a hundred houses," said Niu.

"Tsula Valentine has told me. In New York *more* than a hundred houses. Some of the houses there are made of stone cut as smooth as the palm of your hand." They all looked at the palms of their hands.

"Stone is not meant to be cut," said Niu disagreeably. "It is too hard."

"Out there, nothing is too hard," said Filipino. "They could teach us to cut stones. I shall go there," said Filipino, hugging his knees as he sat folded down on his heels. "I shall go and come back, and then *I* shall teach you."

"Wah!" said all the young men, but Niu, smoking his waterpipe, took the mouthpiece from his lips and looked coldly at Filipino. "Pah!" said Niu and spat.

⁓⁓⁓ That evening Mr. van Loomis called for Filipino to take a message up to the priest in the temple. No one was quicker than Filipino with a message; he took it by word of mouth and brought the answer back and never made a mistake, but now, Mr. van Loomis saw, he barely listened.

"Do you hear me?" asked Mr. van Loomis. "No, you don't hear me," and he asked, "What has got into the boy?"

"Sir," said Filipino, his lips moist with longing, his eyes gazing far beyond Mr. van Loomis. "Sir, if we had a telephone you could tell this to the temple by telephone. You would lift the telephone receiver," said Filipino reverently, "and, far off from you, your voice would speak. How wonderful!" said Filipino. "Sir, why shouldn't we have telephone on the island? Why shouldn't we have electricity? Tsula McGinty says we could make electricity from the waterfall. Light from water! Have you seen electricity? Did you have it in England? Did you have a lawn mower? Did you read the world's Forty Best Books all in one set? Do you know which they are? I do," said Filipino. "Did you ever fly K.L.M.? Have you seen an air hostess? Sir, we could have cars. We have good roads now on the island. Tsula, did you ever have a car? Oh, did you, Tsula?"

"Yes," said Mr. van Loomis shortly.

"*Yes?* What kind of car?"

"Well, the last car I had was an Hispano—"

"You didn't have a three-and-half-litre Packard super-eight," interrupted Filipino. "McGinty Tsula says that is a wizard car! A Packard super-eight one-forty-five hp.," repeated Filipino; he had to be careful or he forgot its order. "What is a super-eight?" asked Filipino.

CHAPTER XVII

To McGINTY, the taking of the census proved to be only a little less boring than sitting in his room playing cards and practising his signalling and trying not to look at Flora Annie.

When he had first heard of it he had come to Valentine with an offended face. "Send me to take a census! To count the people, the children, and the number each family has of cattle and pigs and goats! Go round to every stinking village! Why the hell should I?" said McGinty, aggrieved.

To his surprise Valentine did not sympathize. "Why shouldn't you?" asked Valentine.

McGinty did not like Valentine's tone and he said again more sulkily, "Why should I?"

Valentine was impatient. McGinty's continual chafing spoilt the island. "Oh, don't be so *stupid!*" said Valentine. McGinty stared at him in surprise. "Can't you give way to anything?" asked Valentine.

"I like that!" said McGinty, trembling with indignation. "Give way! I like that from you! You give way all the time. When we left Rose Bay no one wanted to get home more than you; you were full of the play and seeing Mr. Marks and everything. *Then* you were *someone*. Now look at you," said McGinty. "You amounted to something, but now!— You haven't the guts of a bloody louse. He says, 'Wait'—and you wait! 'Go there'—and you go! 'Do this'—and you do it! Who are you? Are you nobody? You make me sick!"

"Don't be a fool," said Valentine. "While we are here we have to give in. Then why not give in with a decent grace? What is the good of kicking all the time? It's a friendly island."

"Friendly!" said McGinty and felt the little scab of dried blood on his ear.

"Yes, if you let it be," said Valentine, though he felt he was wasting his time. "It's a pity to rebuff it. To rebuff anything or anyone hurts you."

"Hurts *me?*" McGinty was astonished. "How could it? What could it do to me?"

"I don't know," said Valentine, and he said slowly. "If you belittle things, they have a way of growing big; if you underestimate them, it's then they strike you."

"Wind and piss," said McGinty rudely.

He had to take the census. On foot or by boat, he went from village to village. They all looked the same to him, though those on the shore had their houses built on stilts and those on the hill were enclosed by a ring fence to keep the foxes or an occasional wild cat from the chickens; in every house he found, monotonously, the same few things: the string bed, the wooden tub like a giant mortar and the wooden pestle for threshing the grain; the same wicker scoops for sifting it and the two flat round stones that made the handmill for grinding; there were the same cocks and hens and pigs, the same gourds coming now into yellow flowers, the same babies crawling among the cocks and hens. Inside the houses, though McGinty never went into them but did his duty by peering in through the door, was the same dim shadowed light from the bamboo walls and slatted windows, and, in it, an occasional gleam of dark eyes or the glint of an anklet or an earring. There was the same smell of cotton steeping in dyes, of native cigars, of wood smoke and oil. None of it, to McGinty, was interesting; he brought out his red book and, going from house to house, Mario called out the Terrequenese Mãnoese words that Mr. van Loomis had tried to teach McGinty, who had not been able to remember them for five minutes.

"I must have someone with me who speaks English," he had said.

"Send Filipino," Niu had suggested, but Mr. van Loomis shook his head. Filipino was troublesome enough already without being encouraged to talk to McGinty; then, "But there is no one else," said Mr. van Loomis.

170

"There is Mario Fernandes. He speaks English," said Niu.

"Yes," said Mr. van Loomis and pondered. He found that most of the sting had gone out of the thought of Mario. Valentine had exorcised it. Mario could no longer trouble Charis. Mr. van Loomis's anger seemed to have died out on the air. "Yes," he decided. "Take McGinty Tsula to Mario Fernandes. Let them get to know each other." No one told him that they knew one another already.

McGinty did the counting while Mario called out the words: "Men?" and Mario would hold up his finger, usually only one finger. "Women?" perhaps one or two, or three, occasionally four. "Children, male, female?" any amount, and any amount of pigs and goats; there were few cattle; a bullock or a cow was really precious. McGinty would go through it as quickly as he could and then stride away again.

The people were astounded at his lack of manners. There was none of the talking and badinage and laughing they knew as courtesy; McGinty was quick, terse, and impatient. They knew what he came for, but it was a new idea for them; they had to get used to it, and there was, naturally, some confusion about the number of pigs and children and, sometimes, of women.

"Do they have more than one wife then?" he asked Charis, not because he was interested but because he had to write "wife" in his book and did not know how to designate the others.

"Write the first woman as 'wife,'" said Charis. "The rest are the concubines." She saw McGinty looked surprised and said, "Of course you don't have concubines in England, do you?"

"Here on the island," said Mr. van Loomis, "we have more women than men. That is so everywhere, I believe, except, perhaps, Tibet. Charis, you remember I told you about Tibet? I told you about England too," he said disapprovingly. "In Tibet a woman marries all her husband's brothers that are younger than he, and it is her business to initiate the young ones into sex. There are, I believe, no prostitutes there; the system does away with the need for prostitutes; there are no prostitutes here either, but that is owing to our system of concubinage. You are thinking we are immoral," said Mr. van Loomis.

McGinty was; he could not have imagined talking calmly and approvingly in this way of such things to Eunice, and Charis was younger than Eunice. He blushed to the tips of his ears.

"We are not immoral," said Mr. van Loomis. "On the contrary, we are far more moral than most countries. Concubinage doesn't make marriage light; here it's something added to marriage. Here, when a man takes a wife, it is indissolvable. Even death cannot divide their partnership; in spirit and flesh they are one, and if one dies the other cannot take another husband or another wife. Nor can a man change his concubines."

"Doesn't the wife resent them?" asked Valentine.

"Not at all; having entered into her husband's flesh, she recognized the need for them."

"Christ almighty!" said McGinty.

"How could a woman, a young woman, be expected to enter into a man's flesh?" asked Valentine. "An experienced, older man?"

"Couldn't she—by faith," asked Charis uncertainly.

"Oh, faith," said Valentine as if that were nothing.

"Charis is right," said Mr. van Loomis. "More right than she knows. If husband and wife are one, what he feels he needs, she feels he needs."

"Even other women?"

"Yes," said Mr. van Loomis firmly.

Charis's lips trembled.

"That would be too utopian," said Valentine. If this were island training he was not sure he was pleased. "It would be too easy," said Valentine to Charis. "A man looks to his wife to have a standard."

"But he may not be able to keep to it," said Charis.

"H'm," said Valentine. Charis had a way, without meaning it, of neatly turning the tables on him.

McGinty was really shocked. "It's not her fault," said McGinty. "Poor little kid. That's what she has been taught. How could she help it, brought up here away from everything? This island makes you soft, that's what it does," said McGinty, but, passing the island young men working on the road or going up the mountain with their

172

bows and arrows or watching a fisherman stand naked, straight as a column, on the tip of his boat, his spear ready in his hand, McGinty could not say there seemed anything soft in them; he looked at their skins, firm and smooth, golden brown; at their lean hips and broad shoulders, the strength of their backs and the swelling muscles on their arms and legs, and was puzzled and sighed. There were certainly ways in the world that Eunice had not dreamed of, but, McGinty thought, that was disloyal, and he shut his mind again. The census remained a whim of Mr. van Loomis, the people were "natives," not to be counted as people, and the island was a prison that kept him out of life.

"Oh, God! I wish I had a smoke," said McGinty. The lack of cigarettes made him more restless and irritable. The island green rolled ones were still horrible to him. Then he thought if he had had a cigarette now he could not have smoked it.

For two days now McGinty had had a never-ceasing headache; he felt sick, and his skin, even his bones, felt tender; he had noticed how pale he looked, with dark marks under his eyes. "It's this native food," he said. "It's upset my stomach." Running down the beach in the sun to try and catch the plane had made the headache worse; now he could hardly see the figures in his book; the people were tiresome; they were excited and could not attend or stop chattering, for some dances they talked about as happening that night. In the afternoon, taking Mario back to the lighthouse, he stopped paddling and dipped his handkerchief in the sea and put it on his head, so that the ends dripped coolness down his neck. Mario watched him with interest, but in a few minutes the handkerchief was dry. The sun was very hot; the shallows of the sea struck brilliant points of light into McGinty's eyes; the pain grew worse and, when they reached the light, he felt too sick to go back to the house and paddle out, as he always did, later, when the lamp was lit. There was no shade except for the shadow, growing longer as the afternoon lengthened, of the pillbox on the sand. McGinty lay down in it and shut his eyes. Mario looked at him in surprise.

"Give me some water," said McGinty.

Mario brought his water bottle and McGinty drank,

173

but the water was warm. He would have given anything for a cool drink. He was burningly hot. "When I get a little cooler I'll have a bathe," said McGinty, but he did not get cooler.

He was acutely uncomfortable. The sand was gritty and the rock was hard under his aching head. Round the corner, on a fire of dung and driftwood, Jéo was cooking the evening meal which he and Mario would eat before he went to the mainland; it was rice and fish, boiling in sea water, and seasoned with garlic. The smell came in waves to McGinty; it would have offended him at any time, now it made him feel more sick. He wished Jéo would finish and eat and then light the lamp and go. "Sir, you-a hungry?" asked Mario. "I give-a you food." McGinty shuddered.

Mario squatted down not far from him and watched him, puzzled; he did not take his eyes off him. McGinty wished he too would go away. Presently the sun dipped down to the sea and the sky grew red. McGinty opened his eyes and sat up. "You-a better?" asked Mario.

"Bloody!" said McGinty. He was still hot but he thought he might as well bathe; he longed for the cool water to close round him; he stood up and found he was giddy. Mario had jumped up too, and now he had to put out his hand and steady him. McGinty recoiled. He did not want Mario to touch him, and then he found the hand was trembling, and, for a moment, he had a glimpse of the depth of feeling he had roused in Mario. "Poor . . . sod," said McGinty, and for that moment he felt strangely humbled; then the pain in his head and his nausea drove all thought of Mario away. He shook off Mario's arm without knowing what he was doing and went swaying a little down to the sea and stripped and plunged in. At first it was better in the water; he floated on his back, looking at the darkening shape of the island where points of light were beginning to appear; sometimes he felt he was floating in the island, sometimes with it, sometimes they were both floating in the sea; then the pain became too bad to be borne in the water, and he found that he was shivering; he swam out and dressed but he was shivering still. That was strange because now he was hotter than ever; he burned and shivered at the same time,

174

and there was a twanging in his ears that might have been the insects in the light, but as it was not yet lit there were no insects. Have I got fever? thought McGinty. He tried to feel his pulse, but his pulse had disappeared, and, in any case, he was shivering too violently to feel it. "It's a chill," said McGinty, and he said to Mario who still stood uneasily by, "Give me a drink." Mario brought him his water bottle. "No! Drink. Drink. Wine, stingo, arrack," said McGinty.

Mario would not have dared to have asked for himself, but now, without a word, he went in and asked Jéo. Jéo shook his head. Mario growled something at Jéo and clenched his fists and scowled, and unwillingly, from a bamboo that he was about to take ashore. Jéo poured a little arrack into a gourd bowl. His two hands round it to prevent it spilling a drop, Mario brought it to McGinty. McGinty drank it, though it felt like raw fire to him; he felt it burning through him. Then he lay down in the sand again and shut his eyes. In a few moments he was sick.

Mario sat puzzled and dismayed. That was what he did himself when he was drunk, but what he did and what McGinty did were surely different things? Surely one small drink could not make his young god drunk? Mario sat down again on the rocks by McGinty and stared at him, the question going round and round in his poor muddled head.

CHAPTER XVIII

"THE moon is full tonight," said Mr. van Loomis. "It's the night of the ritual dances up in the temple. All the people will go in celebration of the marriages. It's the end of the courtship month. I think you two should go with me."

Valentine had just broken to Mr. van Loomis what he already knew.

"You don't want to part with her I know," said Valentine.

"I do," Mr. van Loomis could have said, but it was not altogether true. This was what he wished, but he did not want it. He was still unreasonably depressed. He sent for Charis and kissed her on the forehead. He could not kiss her properly, his doubts and depressions of the morning were not gone. "I am delighted," he said, but he could not feel delighted. "It was what I hoped." That was true, but as he said it he felt "hoped" was an understatement. He caught Valentine's eye and, for a young man, Valentine's eye was stern. "We shall have to go into things," he murmured to Valentine.

"What things?" said Valentine compellingly, but Mr. van Loomis waving his hand and said, "Later. Later." Honesty forced him to add, "There is perhaps a good deal . . ."

"To be cleared up," Valentine finished it for him quite smoothly. "I agree." And he said, "I heard about the rescue plane. You didn't stop it."

"No," said Mr. van Loomis. "It didn't stop."

It was on Valentine's tongue to revert to the matter of the signal. "Did you put out a signal?" "You have asked me that twenty times" had been Mr. van Loomis's testy answer, which, of course, did not say "yes" or "no." Then the matter of the Water Star. Yes! thought Valentine grimly. There are several things! Then he looked away over the veranda rails across the garden to the sea. He saw the points of lights, the fireflies, lanterns, stars; the spaces of the garden and the thickets of shadows from bushes and trees; he smelled the flowers and wood smoke, faint smells of dinner, smells of dew; the drums were beating softly from the temple on the mountain where they were getting ready for the dances; he heard laughter and voices and singing, Pheasant's singing; the sound of insects, of the waves. He looked across at Charis, and she looked back at him and smiled. "Ah, well! Never mind," said Valentine. He felt he forgave Mr. van Loomis.

"I treated you badly, Valentine," said Mr. van Loomis.

176

"But I wanted to find out what you were made of, and I was gratified, gratified. Don't think," he said severely to Charis, "that the outside world is peopled with Valentines."

"Nor McDugdales of McDugdale," said Charis. Mr. van Loomis looked at her sharply, but Charis was perfectly demure.

"The world today is peopled with McGintys," said Mr. van Loomis. At his tone Filipino, standing beside him with a tray of drinks, opened his lips to say, "Is there anything wrong with Mr. McGinty?" but Mr. van Loomis went on, "McGinty is the mob. The image of the crowd."

"There has to be a mob," said Valentine. "Someone has to be the crowd."

"Phaugh!" said Mr. van Loomis. "Well, let me forget McGinty for tonight. I don't want to spoil it. We shall drink to your happiness."

"And then," said Charis to Valentine, "shall we stay here or shall we ask Father to give us a hut and go to it now? It's getting late," said Charis.

"How was I to know?" she asked Pheasant tearfully later. "Father was angry."

"Should jest think he was! Massa Vala'tine *will* think we's brought you up a nice no' count chile," said Pheasant bitterly. "Ah's 'shamed!"

"No one on the island is married except like that and we are on the island. How was I to know that it mattered?" said Charis rebelliously.

At the moment she wished very much that her mother were alive. "If she had been here she would have . . . foreseen," said Charis, and she thought, resentfully, that fathers made very bad mothers. "If she had been here I should have known," said Charis.

She still thought it did not matter and that the island way was best. There was a new small hut built on a promontory high above the sea; it was empty, clean, and waiting, with palm trees and a small chema tree in the garden; a path ran down onto the beach and a stream came past it so that water was handy; it had an outhouse of bamboo that would have done for Dominion and a fence covered with quisqualis all round the garden so that it was private. The islanders did not like it because it stood alone and high, and she had immediately thought of it for Valentine and herself. She still thought it fitting and more honest, altogether better, that they, having declared themselves, should have asked for some quilts and cloths, some pots and pans, and gone there to set up house until they left.

Father could have given us all we need, thought Charis. He is the richest man on the island, and all the girls are given things when they go to their new homes. I should have had cows and goats as well as Dominion. She thought of herself and Valentine with their own little herd boy . . . but no, not even servants, thought Charis. I could do all there was to be done; we could come down here when we were hungry; we would want to be alone. The thought of being alone with Valentine made her blood beat. There, she and Valentine would have been alone with the moonlight and the scent of the chema tree and the sound of the sea. Her head reeled a little as she thought of it, but . . . "You are not an islander," Mr. van Loomis had said to her severely when he called her into the study. "I am," Charis might have said. "What do you expect me to be?" Instead she had stood with hot cheeks, burning with shame, as Mr. van Loomis explained to her coldly and clearly what she had said and Pheasant expostulated. "Shame! Shame!" said Pheasant. Charis looked at her; she had never felt this shame before. Now they were talking of things like marriage settlements and special licenses and church weddings, strange cold things as if this were a contract.

"Marriage is a contract," said Valentine.

"You are not an islander," said Mr. van Loomis.

To Charis everything Valentine did was wonderful, but she could not help the feeling that their love was being spoilt. In a way she could not explain she did not like this talking and arrangement. She wanted a more simple love. Valentine saw she was not happy and talked to her. "We don't want a love like that," he said. "Flash-in-the-pan love."

"It needn't be flash-in-the-pan."

"Not with simple people, but we are complicated," said Valentine, and again he said. "We don't want a love like

178

that. Ours can be tested," and he laughed and said, "We want a good one that will last."

He was not altogether laughing; he was strangely serious for flippant Valentine, but it still seemed to Charis that they were living in a curious and false state that was not sense; she was contracted to Valentine; they could kiss and talk and be left alone together, and all the while they had to pretend to ignore this other trembling that had grown up between them. Valentine felt the strain of it too, she could feel it when he kissed her, when he held her tightly and put her quickly away from him.

"We shall have to wait for a ship," said Valentine.

"It will be a long time to wait," said Charis. Pheasant, who overheard, told her no lady would talk like that.

"How should I know? I have never seen a lady," said Charis.

~~~~~ They started up the path to the temple after dinner. Walking by Charis on Dominion, Valentine had the same sense of music that he had had before, on his first day. Drums had been beating all evening from the hill, but now music seemed to rise again from the island verges as if the sea itself, with its coral and its sand, its rocks and caves, were music. In the forest, as they went up, the evening insects sang, the cicadas suddenly drowning everything else, then as suddenly ceasing. But it was more than that; it was music rising from the whole island, and Valentine felt it in his bones.

In it he was aware of Charis's silence as she rode, sitting still in the saddle with her head bent. Charis still felt out of place in this world of talking, of contracts and settlements and traditional rings. "I have a ring of my grandmother's," Valentine had said. "I should like to give it to Charis; my grandfather gave it to my grandmother as an engagement ring, a diamond set in diamonds." Charis had never seen a diamond, she longed to see one, but she felt there was much in this that Valentine forgot. It was all strange and new and outside her horizon, a horizon that, when a ship came, she knew she must break, but, even so . . . The feeling between her and Valentine was warm

179

and strong and sweet, this sensible life by arrangement felt cold. Do we have to have it? asked Charis, though, in a way, she wanted it herself. Which was the most important? Valentine said that one should enclose the other, but could it? She was frightened that one might destroy the other. "I am such a stranger," said Charis.

Valentine walked with his hand on the pommel of her saddle. Now the moon was coming up and its first light touched the tops of the trees. Valentine could feel something trembling in him as if he were its sheath; he was grateful to Charis for not speaking. Mr. van Loomis walked ahead of them, and accompanying them, catching them up and passing them, were islanders, soft-footed, some carrying torches, all climbing the hill.

The drum beats came down to meet them and the ground, to Valentine, seemed to vibrate under his feet. The air in the forest was tense, and the lights of the torches flickered and threw shadows; the trunks of the trees and the ground were reddened with light as they passed. Presently they heard the river and walked with the sound of it until they came round a bend in the path to the wide ford, with the water tumbling silver in the moonlight, deafening the noise of the drums. They forded it, Dominion splashing through, Valentine walking on the stepping-stones, and its spray blew on their faces. On the far edge Dominion stopped to drink, and Valentine stood waiting while the pony sucked in the water and then lifted his white head and blew out his nostrils. There were fireflies all along the banks and one, flying, caught in Dominion's mane. Valentine captured it and held it in his hand, and it illuminated his whole palm; when Dominion was ready he let it fly away. Still Charis did not speak.

Now they left the river and climbed higher than Valentine had been before and coolness met them. There was a new feeling in the air: it felt no longer tropical but light and cool and filled with the dampness of mist. Here were Mr. van Loomis's apples and peaches and plums. They came in sight of a building round which all the torches on the island seemed to be gathered, and beyond it was a stretch of beaten earth that made a courtyard like a shelf on the hill. Here there was a fire, from which the sparks flew up, and tall torches alight with their ends driven into the ground. At the far end, away from the building, seats had been made covered with deer skins for Mr. van Loomis and Charis and Valentine; around them and on each side of the space the islanders squatted or stood; in front of the temple three men, their faces covered with masks, sat cross-legged; beside them, standing in the moonlight and the torchlight, were the drummers, their faces painted white and vermilion, as Charis remembered them. The music was loud; Valentine could see boys with cymbals, and he could see a gong hung between two posts.

Charis had slipped off Dominion before he could help her; she seemed not to want him to touch her, and she went forward with her father and sat down on the stool between him and Valentine's seat. Valentine felt dizzied by the noise and the lights in the crowd; then he felt a cool hand in his, friendly and slim. "Come, I take you," said Filipino.

He led Valentine to his place and squatted down beside him. Valentine could see Filipino's skin gleaming cool where the moonlight touched it, gold where the torchlight fell on it; he could smell his hair oil and, once again, the fragrance of the flower behind his ear.

"You must tell me what it means," said Valentine to him.

"Ohé," said Filipino abstractly.

Valentine believed that Filipino, like all of them, was waiting for the dances, that they were empty and would presently be filled. But Filipino was anything but empty; his mind was a shimmering maze of American advertisements, than which nothing can more subtly fill the mind; it was a maze of typewriters and newsprint, of race horses and refrigerators; gasoline and brown and white shoes; he had cut out as many of the things as he could and pasted them on the walls of his peaceful little hut, where he meant to learn them off by heart. He had shown them to Resurrection, who had looked at them and smiled and was not shaken; Filipino felt shaken to his depths. Now, sitting by Valentine, he had a sudden thought: all the things that you see you take into you, thought Filipino. If you like these things very much you take them deep into you. I like them very much, but if I take them all in, thought Filipino in alarm, what will be left of me? There will be no room for me. I shall be gone. For a moment he thought of tearing down all the pictures and throwing them in the sea, of going back to be Filipino as Resurrection was Resurrection, but, if he did that, he would still remember them. "No, the only thing is to learn them," decided Filipino.

The dances began.

Into the circle, on the floor of beaten earth, came a boy dressed with a scarf of feathers in bands of colour with sleeves so that they formed an arc when he held his arms out. The music changed to a cadence that Valentine recognized as having heard continuously all over the island since he came. Then he remembered it was Filipino's song, the song he had sung that first day. The boy's dance was a posturing, a walk and a stamping, beating first with his heels and then with his toes on flexible small feet; he held his arms wide, flexing his hands, and stooped, laying his palm flat to the earth and then holding it over his head; round his wrists and ankles were bells and shells; his face was quite expressionless; he only breathed quickly through his nose, and Valentine could see his eyes turning and shining. "He rainbow," said Filipino. "He touch earth. He shine. He bring earth to heaven."

"These people worship the elements," said Mr. van Loomis over Charis's head to Valentine. "They worship their manifestations, sun, moon, rain, earth, and they live by the phases of the moon."

"I see," said Valentine politely; he had seen long before that.

Now came smaller boys with banners on bamboo poles; they wore cat skins round their waists and necklaces of shells and tufted cotton; and after them came the goddess Earth; she was a thickset man, his body oiled so that it glistened and shone, his skirt pleated so that it swung in a circle as he spun and danced; he had four shields that the boys carried in, and they had curious feather devices that Valentine could not make out, but the goddess opposed them one after the other to the four corners of the court as he sang; Valentine thought they were the winds. To Valentine, the man's deep voice and rolling movements seemed to be seriously of the earth, and he was glad he was not seeing this as a tourist, or even as a writer, or as most white people see primitive dances as something neo-childish or grotesque or humorous; he saw this as fundamental, as something the islanders needed, as seriously symbolical and significant, as it was meant to be. He seemed to have put off his sophistication and to see it as an islander; this was the island earth that turned life back to earth, and again from earth to life, on which the sun beat and the rain; the powerful, slow, cruel, all-healing, all-giving, all-taking, inexorable earth. He felt Filipino fidget beside him. Mr. van Loomis had said everything went in the shape of a circle; Filipino the islander, touched by a few books, a little talk, and two American magazines, was growing away from his native simplicity: the sophisticated Valentine was coming back to it again.

Earth circled with his or her feather shields, and now the sun came on; the sun on the island was as fierce and as harmful as it was beneficent; the sun in the dances was a great snake, its mouth stretched on bamboos, a forked cotton tongue wriggling out from its mouth at the end of a brown arm, and its body mounted on several men whose legs rushed and ran under it. "Aaaah!" came in a breath from the islanders.

To Mr. van Loomis, the dances, as they always did, brought a sense of rest, but now he had no feeling of joining in them; he felt locked away, as if he looked down at them from a great way, almost as if in memory, and he thought again of that small room high up in the South tower. Although he treated the dances lightly, each time he saw them he seemed to find himself again; now he found himself in his small tower room. "Odd," said Mr. van Loomis. Charis had been a little nervous that Valentine might laugh at the dances; she had a regard for them and would have felt it if he had laughed. She looked at him and saw a response in his face that surprised and pleased her. "Then . . . you like them as much as that?" He did not answer. He took her hand and held it on his knee, pressing her fingers to tell her to be quiet. He needed to be quiet. Something was struggling to find life in Valentine, and he remembered how, the first morning he

183

had come to the island, he had felt as if it were the morning of a new world, that morning light its first light.

When the Water Star disappeared he had felt the first crack in his certainty; it had left him open and defenceless, and, since he had landed on the island, life had come into him in a way it had not done for years and he was freshened. It may be purely physical, thought Valentine. I was tired, I needed rest, but it seemed to him to be more than that. Charis, of course, had had her effect, but this, though it had to do with Charis, was something apart from her; this was something in Valentine alone. What was wrong with me before? thought Valentine. Why was I drying up? And he thought that perhaps Charis had been right and he had forgotten how to live. He pressed her fingers again as they lay under his hand on his knee, and she looked sideways at him and smiled.

Now the sun was devouring the shields of earth, shield after shield. "He take all wind away," said Filipino. "Burn up all harvest, all fruits and corn." He himself found it boring but, as Valentine had asked him, courtesy made him explain. In the nick of time the rain came, a giant green frog who moved in front of earth and battled with the snake. The drums beat frantically, the pipes shrilled, the gong clanged with the drums, and the people drummed too with their heels and slapped their thighs and shouted until the rain and the sun were embroiled together and sank each side of earth in legs and arms and cotton coils and the rainbow stepped over them and held out his arms and shone. "He friend to both," said Filipino. "He join rain and sun, he join heaven and earth. On the island we believe we related to the rainbow."

Related to the rainbow; to air and earth and fire and water; strange, thought Valentine, how we forget that we are made of clay and go back to dust, and it came to him that for years he had lived in a fifth, a false, element; for years he had touched nothing, seen nothing, heard and tasted and smelled nothing that was not made by man. I had forgotten who I am, thought Valentine, and he remembered how, once, he used to say, "I want my head in the clouds but my feet on the ground." I did not know what I was saying, thought Valentine, but I was right. Then into his mind came a thought that had nothing to do

184

with the elements or the island or the night or Charis; it was a title. Utterly incongruous, it came into his mind and stayed plainly there. "What has it to do with all this? Good God! What in the world makes me think of that now?" asked Valentine. "A slick title like that?" The title was "Whisky in December."

"How do you get your ideas?" People often asked Valentine that, and he always said, truthfully, "I don't know." He did not know. Sometimes it was a few words, a sentence, a happening; sometimes an incident he had seen or remembered; anything could set him off. "I can't write a play from a title," he objected now. "I have no idea . . ." But immediately it had started off: it begins in Lossiemouth. "Why Lossiemouth of all places? I don't even know where Lossiemouth is," objected Valentine. "I don't know anything about Lossiemouth. Why Lossiemouth?" But he had met that objecting Valentine before and knew that his function was that of the opposition party in politics; he considered him and swept him aside as the play began to shape itself in his mind.

He looked up and saw how the light from the torches and fire went up into the night, and he felt the stool he sat on vibrate with the dancing and the drumming, and he felt as if the dances had invaded earth and sky and were passing through him. He felt a peculiar response: he was tingling with life, and then he ceased to think of himself; the life of force at this particular moment was rushing into this idea that was scarcely born and that was to begin in Lossiemouth. "Yes, Lossiemouth," said Valentine firmly. "Though really it doesn't matter where it is. 'Whisky in December.' It's a good title," said Valentine. "I must go home." Then he saw he could not go yet; he had to discipline himself as he had once been disciplined by his grandmother and would yet be disciplined by Charis; he had to wait.

Dancers and priests and boys carrying garlands had come up to them. "They make your marriage speech," said Filipino and rose to his feet. Scarves and garlands were put round their necks, and Valentine noticed how politely the priest lifted Mr. van Loomis's beard to allow for the jasmine flowers. There was a speech from the priest, echoed with running murmurs from the crowd, and

185

Charis stood up, holding out her hand to Valentine, who rose beside her. He could feel her hand quivering in his, and he realized, all at once, that in the island eyes this was their marriage. He tightened his hand on Charis's hand and felt her fingers immediately respond. Hand in hand they stood, like king and queen, in a dream of clouds and music and torches and beaming brown faces. Valentine felt he would need or wish no other ceremony; he felt a tide of life and response in this, and it felt to him auspicious. Then Charis spoke; though he did not understand a word she said, he approved her clear, quiet way of speaking; she was speaking for him as well as for herself, and it came to him that she would often do that. They sat down, and there was a running murmur from the islanders of unmistakable warmth and pleasure.

"Now I shall speak," said Mr. van Loomis. He felt expansive and benign; he smoothed his beard and stood up, high above them all, and held up his hand for silence. Then he put his hands on Charis's and Valentine's heads. "My people," he began, and his voice rang down the mountain. "My people, I . . ."

His hands stiffened on their heads. "God's breath!" said Mr. van Loomis. He was looking far over their heads down to the sea.

He released them abruptly. A ripple of sound went round the courtyard as the people whispered and jostled and craned and stood on tiptoe trying to see what Mr. van Loomis saw. Mr. van Loomis stood, glaring down at something far over their heads. Valentine and Charis stood up, and the resourceful Filipino stepped up on the seats they had left. "There. Down there. From the light!" cried Filipino. Now they could all see, and, at once, the meaning of McGinty's shadow play dawned on even the most simple of the islanders. They saw the beam of the lighthouse shine steadily and then break into flashes as McGinty's patient message was flashed across the sea: "S.O.S. V.A.L. S.O.S. V.A.L." spelled Valentine, and he cried out, "It's McGinty!"

There was a pause, and from the far horizon a pinpoint of light began to wink back.

"Wé!" cried Filipino.

"Wé!" cried all the islanders, but their eyes rolled sideways to look at Mr. van Loomis. He towered above them and he did not say a word.

"It's an answer," cried Charis, startled.

"They are answering him," said Valentine, and he shouted, "Good man, McGinty! Stout man!" Charis saw, with a pang, how his eyes were bright and how excited he looked; involuntarily her hand went out to him, and Valentine paused. Charis? thought Valentine. The island? I had meant to stay here longer. "Whisky in December?" I have to write that now. He hovered, he felt, between two worlds. "Oh, *bother* McGinty!" said Valentine.

The far light went out and the beam of the lighthouse shone steadily and unbroken. The people stirred and blinked. They could not believe they had seen what they had seen until they looked at Mr. van Loomis. Mr. van Loomis stood towering, he had not moved.

"Father."

"They have played a trick on me," said Mr. van Loomis, and his lips trembled. "A trick!" he said. He was outraged. He seemed to swell and his eyes glazed. "By God, I shall skin them alive for this! How dare they?"

"Father!"

"McGinty and Mario!" said Mr. van Loomis through his teeth. "An oaf and an oaf!" If McGinty were an oaf that was a strangely lucid message to be sent across the sea.

"You have to hand it to them," said Valentine.

Mr. van Loomis snorted and glared at Valentine. "You take Charis home," he said. He jerked Filipino off the seat to the ground. "Go through the crowd and find Jéo and Luck and a crew for the canoe," he ordered Filipino. "Go down to the beach and get it ready, and don't bring me anyone who is drunk. I want to go fast."

"Ohé," said Filipino.

Mr. van Loomis held up his hand, the ring flashed in the torchlight, but it was only to tell the drummers to begin again for the next dance.

The drums obediently began to throb, the people obediently sank down, but all the heads turned to follow Mr. van Loomis as he strode out from the courtyard. The drums beat intermittently, the dancers looked over their shoulders, the people whispered and stood up again as he

187

had gone. "Wé! What will he do to the young Tsula? The young Tsula is a very foolish young Tsula. Tsula Loomis is angry! What will he do? What will he do to Jéo? To Mario Fernandes? But it is the young Tsula who made the light to talk. What will Tsula Loomis do?"

Almost unnoticed, Valentine and Charis walked out among the whispers and found themselves on the quiet road. Filipino had taken Dominion with him.

Behind them the fitful drumming grew steadier, and the priest, perhaps to calm the people, had started the rainbow song.

As Valentine and Charis walked away from the music, the whole island seemed to quieten, but they heard the insects again, the noise of the river, and, as they came nearer, the sound of the sea. The path ran in moonlight where it was open to the sky and disappeared into shadows under the trees. The air grew warmer; the cool cloud air was gone, but a breeze came up from the sea to meet them. They came down into the valley, walking hand in hand, Valentine peaceful, his mind busy; even with Mc-Ginty's signal and its answer and all that the answer meant, he was still busy thinking on "Whisky in December." "Whisky in December," he said aloud.

"What did you say?" asked Charis.

"Nothing . . . yet," said Valentine.

All at once Charis stopped, pulling at his hand.

She had stopped at a hut that lay just off the path, so that, through the open door, they could see the four walls turned to a deep glow by the light of an oil-wick lamp that stood on the floor. It was not Charis's hut—this was inhabited. On a string bed lay three children asleep. As Charis and Valentine watched, the mother came in with a saucer light and took it to the door, shading it from the breeze with her hand, looking up the road where the flickering shine of the lamp prevented her from seeing Charis and Valentine. "She is waiting for her man," whispered Charis. "He would be with the others up at the temple."

The woman went to the children and stood looking down at them. "I had thought of children," said Charis softly. "Children, but not of our children. Our children," she said, listening to the sound of it. "If you have children," she said, but to herself, not Valentine, "you won't be strange to them, at least it isn't likely, nor will they be strange to you."

They watched as the light from the moving saucer lamp fell on the man's bow and arrows set down against the wall, on a basket of grain and a hen tethered by its legs to a bamboo pole of the door; all the while a small pot bubbled on the fire with a savoury smell. The woman set down the light and pulled a quilt out from the bed and covered the three children. Then she took the light up again and stood and watched while the children slept and the drums beat far away up on the mountain.

Charis's hand tightened on Valentine's, his hand tightened on hers. "That is what I mean," said Charis. "It doesn't matter where we are or what we are; that is what I mean."

"It is what I mean too," said Valentine.

CHAPTER XIX

McGINTY had been lying for a long while on Jéo's bed. That was, in itself, surprising. Even Mario had noticed how he would never touch anything native, nor go into the huts or touch the children or drink from their cups. Now he lay on Jéo's bed, his eyes shut, his head moving restlessly, and occasionally a sound that was not a word but a groan burst from his lips. Mario had not seen anyone ill before, and he did not like it. Timidly he laid two of his fingers on McGinty's forehead; it was dry and burning hot. No one, Mario thought, should be as hot as that. Mario's instinct was to go as far away as possible and leave McGinty alone, but he hesitated; a feeling that he did not understand held him to McGinty. He wanted to do something for him; he remembered that McGinty had soaked his handkerchief and put it on his head to cool himself; now he cautiously pulled the handkerchief out and took it down to the sea.

It was dusk, and on the mainland he could see lights and more and more lights moving up the mountain to the temple, which showed as a small blaze of red light on the mountainside. All at once Mario felt miserable; every other man on the island had gone to the dances; if he were with McGinty, Mario did not mind being shut out, but now there was this uneasy McGinty who frightened Mario. He shook his head miserably and dipped the handkerchief in a pool and carried it to McGinty and put it on his head.

As if that had started an idea, McGinty called for water. Mario tilted the water bottle. It was empty. "No more-a water."

"Water. Water."

"You got-a no water. You not-a drink our water."

"Water. Water."

He did not seem to understand what was said to him. Mario peered into McGinty's face and shook his head again and timidly offered McGinty some of their own water in a bowl; to his relief McGinty drank it eagerly, but in a moment or two he began again, as if he had never had it, "Water. Water." Mario grew more and more disturbed.

He sat down on the foot of McGinty's bed and leaned his elbows on his knees, his matted head on his great fists, and wished Jéo would come back. When it was dark he lit the small saucer lamp, though the storehouse was lit already from the reflection of the great light that, as the dusk deepened, shone more and more strongly. To Mario, the little light was companionable. He felt the handkerchief that now lay askew on McGinty's head; it had dried, but Mario did not dare to take it down to the sea; that evening Mario was afraid of spirits.

Then McGinty suddenly sat up and called out, "Christ! What's the time?"

"Night-a time," said Mario.

"You bastard! Why didn't you wake me?" said McGinty savagely. Mario drew back, and his eyes, looking at McGinty, shone with slow tears. He turned his head away and squeezed his hands between his knees. McGinty took

190

no notice of him; he heaved himself from the bed and staggered because the pain in his head almost blinded him.

"Lie-a down. Lie-a down," said Mario, jumping up.

McGinty lay down again helplessly. On the rough string bed, if he lay still, the pain ebbed away and was bearable. If he lay still, he seemed to be lulled by the sound of the surf beating on the rocks outside. It told him to lie still and presently he would be healed; anything that troubled him was far away; he had only to lie still, to let himself drift. He closed his eyes; he could feel sleep or unconsciousness mercifully stealing over him, but, with a new effort, he struggled up, braving the pain that came as he moved. He sat up dizzily and struggled over the edge of his bed and stood up, the pain shooting in his head and back.

"Lie-a down. Lie-a down," pleaded Mario again, but McGinty was stubborn. "Must signal," he croaked and shook his head blunderingly; it was a movement very like Mario's familiar one. McGinty turned round to the doorway. "Christ!" he said and held his head, but still he did not sit down; blindly, feeling with his fingers against the wall, he found the steps and, leaning on the rail, went up to the light. Mario could hear him fumbling and then he called angrily to Mario to bring the knacker board. Mario wiped his eyes and nose on the back of his hand and took the board up, and McGinty began his evening's signalling. Painfully, his hands jerking, his face burning, but, oddly, not sweating, his breath coming in a curious loud gasping that he could not help, he went on. "Got to get it . . . through," said McGinty. "Must. If it's . . . last thing I ever do. Got to get it through."

How long he stood there he did not know. The lamp seemed to swell and dwindle in front of his eyes; sometimes he could scarcely find the cover, to put it on and off; his hands slipped and fumbled. In the pauses the sound of the drums came from the island and across the sea to them; to McGinty it was beating in his ear. His throat and tongue felt dry, and twice he sent Mario for water and did not seem to notice how much he drank or that he was drinking it from a native bowl. He had lost sight of everything but this one thing, that the signal must be sent and he must send it; he had forgotten to whom and why.

In the next pause he thought suddenly of Eunice; he thought her hand was on his arm; he felt her hand vividly, and he wanted to do something he had never done with Eunice's hand, press it to his eyes, press his hot lids against it, feel its coolness with his lips; then he found he was holding Mario's hand where Mario had stolen up to stand beside him, and he cast it away with such venom that Mario was sent reeling and he himself fell against the light, scorching his shoulder and chest; the burning pain made him think there was another hand, a hot brown snake of a hand, in his shirt, and he thought the throbbing came from his ear and that the bite had festered and spread all through him, but when he put up his hand to his ear all he could feel was the last dry skin of the scab. "I don't know," said McGinty and dropped to the stool near the rail and leaned his head on it, looking out with eyes through which the pain was shooting across the sea that rolled in quiet moonlight.

The moon track glimmered in a wide gold band; near the lighthouse, as they hit the rocks, the waves were lit with phosphorescence in the spray; McGinty's eyes hurt and he turned them away, back out to sea, and far out, on the horizon, he saw something stab and shine and disappear, stab and shine and disappear. It was a full minute before he understood that it was a signal answering his own.

He leaped for his board and began to signal back; he tried desperately to be clear. He waited, but he was too dizzy with pain to read the signal, nor could he think now of anything to send back to acknowledge it but his own, and he went on, painstakingly, S.O.S. V.A.L. S.O.S. V.A.L., while the light winked back and presently went out, leaving only moonlight. He dropped the board and sank back on the stool, his breath coming in such loud gasps that Mario thought he was crying. "They . . . got it . . ." said McGinty. "It . . . got through." Then he was sick again over the rail.

"You-a sick! Sick!" cried Mario frantically.

"No. Better now I puked," said McGinty. For a moment his skin felt cold and clammy and he shivered; he

192

felt wetness on his cheeks; not, surely, tears? His head was eased by the sickness; he felt weak and very tired. He had done what he could and had an answer. His task was finished. Perhaps, soon, he would be on his way home. Home and Eunice.

Thinking of Eunice made more tears run down his cheeks and, for the first time, he gave in and sobbed on the rail. It was silly, it brought the burning back and all the pain, but he could not help it. "Must have a flaming bad chill!" he said.

Then he felt Mario stiffen beside him, and across the water, clearly, came the sound of many paddles and a chanting. "Hé, hé, hé."

"Loomis," breathed Mario, and he began to pull at McGinty. "Come-a down," cried Mario frantically. "Que voy a hacer si te encuentra aquí? Baja!" McGinty did not move. "Por amor de Dios!" begged Mario. "Baja! Baja! Hide! Hide! Hide!" begged Mario.

McGinty shook him off. "I'm not going to hide. Let him come. Let them all, the whole damn boilin' of them, come."

Mario was still with a sudden stillness. He had remembered that he was with McGinty; he remembered what McGinty had said. "You-a not afraid," he breathed. "Dios mío, no tienes miedo! You-a knock Loomis down. You-a more than anyone!" cried Mario, and he seized McGinty's hand and covered it with kisses.

"God almighty!" McGinty snatched his hand away and rubbed it on his trousers. "I hate you slobbering all over me. Now go. Go away. Do you hear? Bugger off. Scram."

Mario did not go but stood there, lowering in his surprise. He could not understand why McGinty did not want his adoration. For the first time he wavered; he did not like this sickness in his god. "You-a sick," he said as if it were an excuse. McGinty did not answer but turned his head away on the rail.

That was how Mr. van Loomis saw him, crumpled and forlorn, his head against the rail, framed by the light, his hair tumbled. It looked a boy's rough head, and, for a moment, Mr. van Loomis's anger was stayed. He landed and crossed the rocks by the light of Jéo's lantern and climbed the stair with Jéo and Luck and Filipino and the

193

boatmen crowding after him. Mario shrank into the shadows but McGinty did not move. Mr. van Loomis stood and looked down on him as he sat huddled on the stool by the rail, and when Mr. van Loomis spoke he spoke far more gently than he would have believed possible when he had seen the signal from the temple. "What have you been doing?" he asked as he might have asked a schoolboy.

"That's my sodding business," said McGinty.

Mr. van Loomis's anger glazed again. "You have no business here," he said. "Here or on the island. You have broken your word."

"Didn't give you . . . any word."

"It was understood," thundered Mr. van Loomis. "You took advantage of it. You have had my hospitality."

"Didn't want your . . . bloody hospitality," said McGinty wearily.

"I could have you deported for this."

McGinty's eyes flew open, bright in his strange-looking face. "Deported! You'll have us deported all right, *and* sooner than you think. Then you'll lose your precious Valentine. He'll come to his senses then. You didn't see—"

"I saw," said Mr. van Loomis.

"They'll send a boat or a plane," boasted McGinty, his breath coming faster. It was odd what a noise his breathing made; it came in long, loud breaths, interrupting him. "Val's a V.I.P. even if you treat him like dirt. He's news! They'll be after him at once. They'll have been looking for him. They'll be here any time tomorrow I should think."

"That is unlikely," said Mr. van Loomis. "You had an answer, yes, but she may be a small ship without wireless, probably a fishing boat, in which case she will fish all night, perhaps for two nights, before she goes in, or she may have been a route steamer, in which case she may wireless but more likely will wait till she makes port. Valentine's name will mean nothing to them. There will be plenty of time for me to deal with you first. I confined you to the island—"

"Confined nothing!" said McGinty. "Just because the dumb clucks here think you're God don't kid your-
194

self . . ." He did not think he could go on with this talking; the words seemed to explode like signals, like rockets, in front of his eyes. Jéo had come on the platform and examined his light as if McGinty had stolen it and then picked up his knacker board with a look of reproach; and Luck and Mario and the boatmen kept their eyes on Mr. van Loomis but Filipino kept his on McGinty. He thought McGinty looked extremely strange and wondered that Mr. van Loomis did not notice it; McGinty's skin, even in the yellow light, was too yellow, his eyes were dark-ringed as if they were bruised, his lips were cracked, and he looked as if his skin might crack too, but now he began to hurl abuse at Mr. van Loomis, and Mr. van Loomis stopped and looked at him sharply. It was incoherent abuse, mixed up with obscenities and strange sobbing breaths; even Mario could tell it meant nothing. He went round, behind the lamp, to McGinty and pulled his sleeve. "No-a! No-a!" whispered Mario. "That no-a *good!*"

McGinty shook him off and stood up swaying. "Who do you think you are?" he hurled at Mr. van Loomis. "You think you're God. You're not God, you old impostor, you God squatter! You can't keep me off the light, you don't own the light. You can't keep me off the sea, you don't own the sea. You don't own anything. You can't push everyone around, we're not all a pack of bloody sheep." Mr. van Loomis seemed to swell in front of his eyes into a monstrous size and he put up his hands to ward him off and screamed. "God almighty! You're not God. You great turd!"

In the beam of the light, insects spattering harmlessly against him, with his height, his white clothes and white beard and fine white head, to Mario, Jéo, Luck, Filipino, and the boatmen, Mr. van Loomis did indeed look a god, the incarnation of the wrath of God. Mario pulled McGinty's sleeve more urgently. Mr. van Loomis's eyes flashed with anger and he lifted his hand; his ring flashed. Mario quailed and hid his eyes, and Filipino cried out, "*Tsula!* What you do?" But Mr. van Loomis did not hit McGinty. Instead he took him firmly by the shoulder and lowered him onto the stool and laid his other hand over McGinty's eyes, across his forehead. "You must be

195

quiet," said Mr. van Loomis to McGinty. "You are very ill."

At the touch of that firm, authoritative hand McGinty crumpled. His body sagged and tears ran down his face and he shuddered from head to foot. He made one more effort to get up but he could not find the rail, or his own feet; pain ran up his back to his head and he screamed; he felt hands grip him and tried to fight them off, but they held him on the stool; he tried to speak but his sickness choked him; he retched and shuddered, and the effort of retching hurt him so that he screamed again. Mr. van Loomis held him and he began to sob. "Take me home," sobbed McGinty. Please take me home. I want to go back. I want to go home."

Mr. van Loomis jerked his head for Luck and Jéo to come. "Take him to the boat." But before Jéo or Luck could touch McGinty, Mario gave a sudden cry. "No-a!" bellowed Mario. "No-a!" He had stood dumbly watching; now he leaped past Mr. van Loomis at McGinty. "You-a said. You-a promised!" They thought he would tear McGinty off the stool; Filipino and a boatman caught his arms, but he beat them off like flies. "He-a said!" sobbed Mario. "Ayúdame, Virgen santa! Madre de Dios, ampárame! Now-a what I do? What I do?"

He stood, stricken, while he saw Luck and Jéo pick McGinty up from the stool and carry him off the platform and down the steps and over the rocks to the canoe as if he had been a child.

CHAPTER XX

MR. VAN LOOMIS sat at his desk and he was, once more, terribly uneasy; "terribly" was the right word; he had a feeling of guilt that almost amounted to terror. He heard words like an echo of something he had heard before.

Where? He was afraid it was in that impediment, his conscience. "Ridiculous!" said Mr. van Loomis. "I have not let it worry me before. Why now? And in any case I had nothing to do with this. Nothing!" That was true, but the feeling remained.

He tried to think of gentle, peaceful things: he thought of peaceful voices rising from the shore, of picnic laughter, of girls coiling up their blue-black hair with flowers, of necklaces of shells; he thought of the fishing nets glittering in the sun and the sound of wet cloths being slapped on the wash stones in the river; of the games of knacker and smoking in the evening, the sleep at mid-day under the palms, the smell of cooking, the small, carefully husbanded stacks of corn and the basket loads of fruit; of the sleepy babies nodding on their mother's backs and the herd boys singing; but he knew that to think of the island as only like that was to be deliberately wishful; *"charming and innocent and murderously cruel,"* remembered Mr. van Loomis, but what is that to do with me? I warned him we had a tiger sun. He still knew that, to the islanders, he and not the sun had struck McGinty. "But I didn't. I did nothing at all. I am only a man," he said helplessly. They knew otherwise; there were the stars, clearly to be seen, fixed in daylight to mark the triumph of the Water Star. He had even humbled himself to explain how, from that distance down, from any well or deep-sunk shaft stars could always be seen. They smiled. "We saw them. You showed them to us. They were not there before." McGinty had disobeyed Mr. van Loomis. "It's sunstroke," said Mr. van Loomis. The islanders smiled again. "It happened at night," they said. "At night there is no sun." It was terrible not to be believed. "I am more conjured against than conjuring," Mr. van Loomis might have said, and yet there was a grain of truth in it; he remembered how he had said that he abjured magic and had wondered if magic had abjured him.

Last night when he had brought McGinty in, the house had hummed with this last stroke. He remembered Valentine's shocked face.

"I told him to wear a hat," said Mr. van Loomis brusquely, "but he wouldn't be told."

"And there isn't a doctor," said Valentine, appalled.

197

He was white with dismay. "There isn't even a thermometer." He felt a thermometer would have been comforting. Charis could not share this feeling; she had never seen a thermometer, but she could see Valentine felt the island and all of them were inadequate; that hurt her, but still she tried to comfort him. "Pheasant and Niu know what to do," she said.

Pheasant ran her hands over McGinty and shut her lips. "Too much fever," said Pheasant. Niu came and stood at the foot of the bed and watched him for a long time; he too pursed his lips and shook his head. "If there is anything to be done they will do it," said Charis, but her eyes were frightened.

"They can only cool him and cleanse him," said Mr. van Loomis. "No one could do more than that."

It was dreadful to Valentine to see the contained, limited McGinty broken apart like this. McGinty, who had so few words and those only the words of his kind, now used strange ones; he babbled of snakes and rainbows and picnics and fires and drums. He held Charis's hand to his head and his cracked purple lips and then flung it away from him; he counted men and women and children and chickens in the island words that Mr. van Loomis had tried to teach him and that he could not remember before; they were on his tongue now, and then he went back to drums and rainbows and snakes again.

"Will he . . . die?" asked Valentine.

"It will be very bad luck if he does," said Mr. van Loomis. "Leave him to Pheasant and Niu. They know best what to do."

Towards dawn, on the next night, the priest, for whom Niu had sent Filipino, came down with a draught in a horn; it was pungent dark stuff that Charis said was made of a bark and animal urine. Valentine thought it was, in any case, a strange medicine to be administered to McGinty, who trusted in prescriptions in hygienic glass bottles that he bought at a qualified chemist or got from the hospital dispensary. Valentine could not help feeling that he would have been very angry if he could have known, but, after it, he gradually lay more still, and, presently, small drops, like body dew, began to break out on his face and neck and Pheasant quickly pulled off the wet

198

sheets he had been packed in and began to fold him in blankets. "Blankets! For that heat of fever?" asked Valentine. "Fever goin'," said Pheasant shortly; her hands worked quickly. "Danger time, Massa Vala'tine. Him very weak. Help me, Massa Vala'tine." She called to Niu to come, and she and Valentine began to rub McGinty's feet and legs, rubbing upwards while Niu massaged his heart and gave him small sips from a cup that stood by the bed. This time Valentine did not ask what was in it. Imperceptibly McGinty's limbs relaxed and the sweat came more easily. Pheasant sponged him off and brought fresh blankets. Presently Niu brought another draught, and this time McGinty drank it. He opened his eyes and sighed and shut them again. "Soon," said Pheasant, "soon he sleep nat'ral. Thank th' Lawd!"

Valentine stood up, cramped and stiff, his arms aching. He looked down at McGinty and thought his face looked younger than he had ever seen it, wiped clean of all expression; though it looked young and peaceful, something in McGinty's face disturbed Valentine. He called Mr. van Loomis. "Is he all right?" asked Valentine. Mr. van Loomis spoke to Niu, who answered quietly. Valentine could tell it was a noncommittal answer.

"It's too early to tell yet," said Mr. van Loomis. "Niu says he is weak, but we all know that."

"He looks different."

"He is very ill," said Mr. van Loomis.

Pheasant motioned them to go away, and they left the room where Niu was closing the slats to keep the growing daylight out.

Mr. van Loomis went back to his room. Mario padded after him. When they had left the lighthouse Mario had followed Mr. van Loomis into the boat and sat down at his feet. Mr. van Loomis had not sent him back. Mario had not spoken, but slow tears ran down his face. Now his eyes had great red rims and his tears oozed if anyone spoke to him. The servants looked at him and silently offered him a cigar or a drink or an orange, but Mario shook his head at these things he would have prized before and he refused them all; even the boys left him alone. He followed Mr. van Loomis wherever he went, and if Mr. van Loomis went into the study he sat on the

199

floor outside the door. Mr. van Loomis could hear him sniffing and wished he would go away.

"McGinty will get better you know," said Mr. van Loomis.

"I hope he-a die!" said Mario fiercely. More tears came out of his swollen lids and ran down his cheeks. Could any creature have so many tears? thought Mr. van Loomis. "Mario been *fool!*" said Mario and wept.

Mr. van Loomis began his letters. He refused to give time or room to this ridiculous feeling of guilt, but he could not write sense. He tore up the sheet he had written. Niu came to say that breakfast was ready. Mr. van Loomis went to join a silent Valentine and Charis. He drank some coffee; he did not feel like eating, but, when he saw how they all looked at him, even little Webster, he shook his shoulders and smoothed his beard and ate fish and ham and eggs and toast and marmalade and fruit. "I shall not have people staring at me," said Mr. van Loomis. Afterwards he went back and shut himself in the study.

On his desk lay the letters from London. He had not broken their news to Charis or Valentine. There was much to be done, much, as Valentine said, to be made clear, and it was immediate; at any moment the rescue might come. "But I was right; it must have been a fishing boat or they would have been here by now."

He had a curious distaste for the idea of beginning anything, either to settle his affairs in Scotland and England or on the island. I want no more places, thought Mr. van Loomis. Not Spey, nor the island. I can't manage them. I'm tired. I'm getting old. I need a little place in which to end my days. There is no more fight in me. Still, there were these arrangements to be made; arrangements at any rate for Charis, who would have a considerable dowry apart from Spey and the estate; there were the arrangements of Archie's, the affairs of the firms and the administration of the estate. "I shall have to go to London. Phaugh!" said Mr. van Loomis. Suddenly he felt angry with Charis; it was Charis, he felt, who had brought all this on him; but it was not Charis; it was that pulse beating, underneath the busy clicking; it was time, and time was growth. Do I have to grow, even at my age?

groaned Mr. van Loomis. How can I grow? And he had a vision of a small quiet room where there was time for quiet and meditation. "That is how I should grow," said Mr. van Loomis. "If I had my room in the south tower . . ." That is what I want, thought Mr. van Loomis. He thought again and said, "That, now, is the only thing I want." But the little room seemed impossibly far away. To reach it, he remembered, one had to climb up a long, steep, winding stair. That seemed to him fitting; he had all these papers on his desk, all these problems to resolve, all these . . . obscurities, thought Mr. van Loomis (that seemed a good name for them), to be made clear. He drummed his fingers and then, reluctantly, began to work.

When Niu called him for luncheon he found only Charis at the table. "Where is Valentine?" he asked.

"Writing," said Charis. "He mustn't be disturbed." She said it with an air of importance that annoyed Mr. van Loomis.

"He shouldn't be writing now," he said. How hard and indifferent they all are, thought Mr. van Loomis. All bent on their own little schemes. He scowled jealously, but Charis was so absorbed that she did not see him scowl. "There you are," said Mr. van Loomis. "That is gratitude. Pah! I have done with all of you."

He went back to his study and shut himself in. Charis went to sit with McGinty while Pheasant snatched a little sleep. Mr. van Loomis could hear McGinty muttering those tangled words and then he caught Charis's soothing voice and McGinty was quiet. Mario was stretched on the matting by the door, at last and ungracefully asleep, hair tousled, his breathing stertorous.

Perhaps Mr. van Loomis slept a little too in his chair, a troubled sleep of dreams, but Filipino seemed to be suddenly in the room, opening the slats, and on his desk was a tray of tea. Then Pheasant came rustling in, freshly dressed and starched, to tell him that McGinty was in a natural sleep.

"Thank God!" said Mr. van Loomis. He felt as if a weight had slipped off his shoulders. "I thought I had killed him," said Mr. van Loomis and caught himself up. "I thought *it* had killed him. Thank God!"

The house was very quiet while McGinty slept. He slept through a hushed night and through the next morning, past noon. They began to wonder if he would ever wake again.

Mr. van Loomis went and looked at him several times; he still could not get McGinty off his mind, and, as it had surprised Valentine, McGinty's face surprised Mr. van Loomis. McGinty's face looked young and empty, its cocksure look and hardness gone; it was the emptiness that haunted Mr. van Loomis; it was now a curiously innocent face; curiously, thought Mr. van Loomis, no grown-up person has a face like that, and, as he had not wanted anything before, Mr. van Loomis suddenly wanted the haven of that room high up, shut, in the turret of the tower.

He waited, drumming his fingers against his thigh, and then stepped out into the full noon glare of the garden. He found a garden boy under a bush asleep, and, pushing him with his toe, he woke him and sent him to fetch Niu and Filipino.

~~~~~ "On the island we have rainbows," said Mr. van Loomis to Niu and Filipino. Why he began like this he did not know, except that in his tiredness and general heartache he saw ideas as rainbows, phantoms of colour, ephemeral, that were flung up and glittered and dissolved away. "Yes, rainbows," said Mr. van Loomis.

"Between earth and heaven like a bridge," said Filipino glibly. "I wrote a song about it once," he said. "I called it 'Rainbow Bridge.' It would have been a beautiful song, only the lines didn't come right and I couldn't think of the music." He and Niu waited. After a few minutes, though they both stood politely, Niu moved his feet in his slippers and coughed and Filipino curled his bare toes on the matting and hid a little yawn. Mr. van Loomis had sent for them in siesta time; they had thought he must have something important to tell them; instead he talked of rainbows.

Niu was tired. He had been up for two nights and he had been asleep when the garden boy had woken him; he was old to be woken like that and he felt shaken. Filipino had not been sleeping; lately he had not slept well; he was worrying because he found it too hard to learn the names of all the myriad things in the magazines. "I shall know what they are when I use them," said Filipino firmly (he firmly believed he would come to use them). "Then I shall know them; a child knows them then, but now . . . That is electric razor," said Filipino. "That is potato masher." The worry came back. "How dreadful if I should say, 'That is potato masher,' and it is a telephone." He saw now that he was far from understanding the magazines, and suddenly he regretted the days when his hut was empty and he lay on his bed unencumbered, free to dream and think of his songs. Then he thought of what McGinty had told him about driving a car and took heart again.

"Could I drive a car?" he had asked dizzily.

"Why not?" McGinty had said. "Plenty of native boys do, and you are eighteen."

"Am I?" Filipino hardly knew how old he was.

"Of course you could drive a car, if there was a car," said McGinty. That dazzling thought chased all others from Filipino's mind. I should be the first driver on the island, thought Filipino in ecstasy.

Meanwhile Mr. van Loomis had begun again. "Very soon now," said Mr. van Loomis, "a rescue ship or a wind-machine will come."

"Plane," rapped out Filipino. "Last one was a Catalina, flying boat. Mr. McGinty told me."

Mr. van Loomis ignored him. "They will bring petrol, and we shall get Tsula Valentine's plane out of the cave and he will go away. Tsuli Charis will go with him, and McGinty Tsula if he is well enough. Pheasant shall go if she wishes and . . . I shall go with them," said Mr. van Loomis with a sharp breath. He had decided now.

"You, Tsula!" Niu breathed. His eyes flickered. "But . . . you will come back?"

"No," said Mr. van Loomis. It was in his mind before, but now he had crystallized it and he had crystallized something else. "I shall not come back and I shall leave the island to you."

"Wé!" said Filipino, but for a moment Niu did not un-

203

derstand. He was old and he had been woken suddenly. He stared at Mr. van Loomis and said nothing. Filipino jerked his arm. *"Listen!"* said Filipino. "Don't you hear what Tsula says?" Niu hissed at him and moved his arm away, and Filipino began a long explanation. Slowly Niu's eyes came round to Mr. van Loomis and he looked at him as if his eyes would pierce him. "Tsula will leave the island to *us!"* finished Filipino triumphantly.

"How, Tsula?" asked Niu.

"That is what I wanted to ask you," said Mr. van Loomis. "The island should belong to its own people, its own spirits. Your father was chief, your grandfather, all your line, but if I go, can you rule it? Or will you let someone, like Mario's mother, take it from you again?"

The muscles in Niu's throat worked and his hands clenched on his cloth. "Tsula is speaking to you," said Filipino shrilly. "You must answer him. Answer."

"Where are your manners?" said Mr. van Loomis to Filipino sharply. "You must not interrupt your grandfather like that."

Filipino fell back, chafing and impatient.

Niu's eyes had been smouldering with anger, but, as he looked at Mr. van Loomis, they grew clear and glowed. After a few moments he spoke. "Tsula, now I know you are a great man," said Niu.

That was the true island courtesy, thought Mr. van Loomis, to think of the other person even when you are alight with your own happenings. He hoped Filipino, in the background, had marked it, but Filipino was busy trying to spur Niu on.

"You have been a great man to us," said Niu. "Now you are a greater man," and he gave Mr. van Loomis the island obeisance, his hands joined together in front of his face, his head bowed.

Mr. van Loomis had not seen Niu make it before. Filipino fidgeted. "We are chiefs," said Niu in his slow, sepulchral voice. "I am a chief. For twenty-five years we have been servants and children." Niu's eyes flashed. "We shall not let anyone take it again."

"But you understand, I shall be gone. There will be no one to protect you. If you are chief, you will be alone."

"Ohé," said Niu.

But he has forgotten what that means, thought Mr. van Loomis. "You are not afraid?" asked Mr. van Loomis.

"Tsula was not afraid."

"I wish I had been," said Mr. van Loomis, and he felt the weight of all he had done dragging on him still. He began to explain the plans he had tentatively made. As he talked, Filipino drew nearer, almost pushing Niu out of the way in his excitement. Mr. van Loomis spoke of the transferring of the island rights, the transport of Charis's dowry, his own goods, his books, of what he proposed to leave behind. He spoke of the arranging of a magistrate to help Niu, of internal government; "I leave you a better island than I found it," said Mr. van Loomis.

"And we shall make it more better," said Filipino. Niu made a movement as if he would slap him, but Filipino edged past him. His face was kindled with enthusiasm. "We shall make it *much* more better," he cried. "Look!" And from his waist knot he untied something small and round and held it out on his palm. It was the Australian sixpence McGinty had given him. "It's *money!*" said Filipino.

Niu looked at it and from it to Mr. van Loomis. "What does it mean? Money," he said, trying the word. "What is money?" Filipino opened his lips impatiently but Niu checked him.

"*I* shall tell you what it means," said Filipino. "I shall show you. Tsula, when you leave the island to us, will you leave the things that are here? Will the pearls be ours and the gold? And the fishing and the fruit and the wood in the forest?" He sounded as if he were bargaining. "Will we have all the cattle? And the fields and plantations? Will you leave us the house?" Niu began to breathe quickly too, and a further weariness fell on Mr. van Loomis. "Will they all be ours?" bargained Filipino.

"Yes, if you want them," said Mr. van Loomis.

"We want," said Filipino, and his eyes were bright and greedy.

"They will all be yours."

"Then," Filipino drew a deep breath, "*if* we had a steamer to come and get them and we sent them away on the steamer we would get money?"

"You would get money."

"Much money?"

"A great deal of money."

"Wé!" said Filipino in triumph. "That is what Mr. McGinty said." He turned to Niu. "You see. You heard. We shall *trade!*" said Filipino. "I shall go away with the Tsulas, and Tsula van Loomis will send me to college. I shall go to commercial college and agricultural and engineering and mines," boasted Filipino. "I shall go to them all, and then I shall come back and teach you."

Niu shook his head, bewildered.

"Then we shall trade," said Filipino. "We shall have our own trade. You don't know what is trade, but I shall teach you. We shall buy and sell," said Filipino, trembling with excitement. "We shall buy . . . *things!*" said Filipino reverently. He turned to Mr. van Loomis. "Steamers would come, wouldn't they, Tsula?" he pleaded. "People would come? We could have a hotel. Tsula McGinty told me about hotels. Don't you think people would come?"

"They would come," said Mr. van Loomis.

"Mr. McGinty said we could have an airfield. He said ships might come here for pleasure."

"You don't know what people are," said Mr. van Loomis.

Filipino stopped, puzzled.

"People are like McGinty Tsula," said Mr. van Loomis. "Here, on the island, you do not like McGinty."

"But he is clever," said Filipino.

"Clever!"

"Isn't it . . . a good thing to be clever?"

Mr. van Loomis did not answer that. He felt defeated. No matter what he answered, he saw he would not convince Filipino. Filipino had gone beyond him. He did not know how to deal with Filipino. He saw Niu looking at him attentively and he stirred himself again. "If you let people come here—" he began, when Filipino interrupted him.

"Not 'let people come,' Tsula. We *want* that they come. We shall welcome them."

Mr. van Loomis shook his head. He felt Niu's look searching him and saw Niu's hands working on his cloth.

206

"You don't want them," said Mr. van Loomis. "If you let people come, they will bring things . . ."

"That is what I said," said Filipino joyfully.

"That is what you said," Mr. van Loomis agreed gravely. Niu noticed how grave his voice was. "It is true they will bring you things. For instance, they will bring radio."

"Radio?" cried Filipino. He knew now about radio.

"They will bring cars."

"Cars!" Filipino nodded. "I shall be the first on Mānoa, the first Terraquenese, to drive a car. Oh, I want to drive a car!"

"They will bring cinema and shops, shops full of things for sale."

Filipino nodded ecstatically.

"They will bring people to keep the shops, white men and Chinese and Indians. They will keep the shops for money."

"Could I buy a watch?" interrupted Filipino, looking at his sixpence. "Tsula Valentine has a gold watch. I should want that mine is a gold watch too."

"You could buy a watch——"

"With my own money?"

"You can buy anything for money," said Mr. van Loomis, and he said it so gravely that even Filipino this time was struck by his gravity. "You will begin to want things. Your women will begin to want them. You will have to get money to buy them. Soon your lives will be getting and spending."

Filipino did not see anything wrong with that.

"One day," said Mr. van Loomis, "you will sell a little piece of island land—for money."

There was a small hiss. Niu had understood. He withdrew his gaze from Mr. van Loomis. He looked at Filipino as if he had not seen him before and his face hardened.

Mr. van Loomis went on. "Everything will be different. The cars will want roads," said Mr. van Loomis. "Not roads like ours, but hard roads, that will take a hundred men all their lives to keep; the islanders will make the roads for money. The people will want houses, not island houses, but houses of stone and concrete."

"I will explain you 'concrete,'" murmured Filipino aside to Niu.

"Stone and concrete and corrugated iron—"

"What is corrugated iron?"

"Hideous and cheap," said Mr. van Loomis briefly. "Soon the whole look of the island will be changed. They will bring their foreign drink. Ask Pheasant about that drink," he said to Niu. "The men will want girls, not their girls, but yours. You have heard what McGinty Tsula calls them."

"Bints," said Filipino promptly. He did not think it mattered what you called girls, they were still girls, but even he did not much like the sound of it; still, girls were a small part of life to Filipino, and he went on. "We could have electricity," he said, "and telephone service and cars. We should have petrol. Think," said Filipino, "if Tsula Valentine had landed on the island then we should have given him petrol and he could have flown straight away and no trouble. How good!" cried Filipino in admiration.

"Listen to me," said Mr. van Loomis. Filipino raised his head dutifully, but Mr. van Loomis knew he was not hearing what Mr. van Loomis meant him to hear. "Listen," said Mr. van Loomis, speaking desperately. "I could have had all those things. I could have brought them all. Why do you think I didn't? Because I knew what they were," said Mr. van Loomis. "Money and people bring radio and cars—"

"And gadgets," interrupted Filipino reverently. "Gadget" was now his favourite word.

"Yes, gadgets," said Mr. van Loomis as if gadgets were not important. "But they bring other things as well." He was speaking earnestly. "They will bring noise and dirt and disease and unhappiness." He had forgotten he was speaking to Filipino; he was speaking for the island. "Disease. Misery. Squalor." He saw that Niu's eyes were on his face, Niu was trying to pierce out his meaning. "Don't bring them," said Mr. van Loomis. "Be wise. Leave it as it is. Think. Listen. They won't speak your language, you will learn to speak theirs. They won't understand your gods, they will bring theirs. Soon you will have missionary Tsulas teaching you; you don't know missionary Tsulas but you soon will; they will teach you and tell you of their God and you will forget your own, your sun and rain, your rainbow. Ships will come, people will come, and your people will go away. I have told you they will take your girls; the girls will go to them, and soon there will be new islanders, half-islanders, half-breeds." As he said that he had a twinge of guilt; he remembered some fine but blue-eyed islanders; even Charis knew of them. He wavered and went on weakly. "Your villages will be pushed farther and farther away. The beaches will be good for their wharfs and cafés and bathing places. They will take the beaches. The mountain will be cool for their houses, they will take the mountain." Now Niu was looking at Filipino. "You are not listening to me," said Mr. van Loomis, and he said in despair, "You don't understand."

Niu's eyes went from Mr. van Loomis to Filipino, from Filipino to Mr. van Loomis; his face was seamed with lines of worry. Mr. van Loomis felt he could almost see the thoughts whirling in the old man's head, backwards and forwards, up and down like a shuttlecock, round and round. "Niu!" he cried sharply, and Niu's eyes came up to look at him again. Niu stared deeply, and the lines of his face hardened into pain. "It will be their island," said Niu.

But Filipino was looking at the sixpence in his hand. "It will be our money," said Filipino.

CHAPTER XXI

For three days now the house had been keyed to Mc-Ginty, and yet all round him schemes and life had gone on in which he had no part; even Flora Annie, as she carried the sheets he had been wrapped in away to the wash house, had ceased to bother her head about him. She had been chosen by, and had decided to choose, a fine young boatman, grand-nephew of Luck and with some of his prestige; in a day or two she would be going to her new home.

No one really missed McGinty.

"If you found your plane you could fly it without Mr. McGinty, couldn't you?" Filipino asked Valentine.

"Yes, but I should be sorry," said Valentine.

"You could get another Mr. McGinty," Filipino pointed out. That was true; there were other McGintys. There had been something machine-made in McGinty and yet . . . "We and the others, the different ones, are founded on McGintys," said Valentine. "He is good, faithful, reliable, and skilled—isn't that enough?" But it was not enough. It was good, it was excellent, but it was not enough; even in the little tumbling baby, Golden Treasury, playing in the servants' courtyard, it was not enough. "There has to be something else," said Valentine slowly. "There has to be a response."

"Response, Tsula?"

"Yes," said Valentine, "between you and everyone, between you and everyone. You make it and it is life." And he said, "I didn't understand that before."

Filipino did not understand, not even enough to ask Valentine to explain.

Valentine went back to his writing.

Through the shock of McGinty's collapse, through the delirium and nursing and anxiety, through the newness of his relations with Charis, in his own tiredness, the idea of the new play had steadily taken shape. Now he had begun to write it. "I can't help it," he said crossly to Charis when she looked surprised. "It's no use looking at me like that. Perhaps I am heartless, but it always comes at the most inconvenient times; it always will." And he added defensively, "It won't make McGinty better or you happier if I refuse to write."

He wrote while he should have slept. He wrote all morning; Filipino interrupted him with tea, he let the tea get cold; Niu brought him luncheon and clucked to see the untouched tea tray; Valentine ate a few mouthfuls of chicken and rice and let the rest get cold. Charis came in and looked at him and crept out again, but Pheasant waddled in with a sandwich and a glass of hot milk and stood her ground while he ate it. "You kin' eat with one han'," said Pheasant unmoved. Valentine wrote on while the sun climbed and grew hot and everybody slept again; he took off his shirt and threw it on the bed and went on writing; when his elbows grew sticky and his forearms stuck to the table, he cursed and took his bath towel and spread it on the table and wrote on that.

In the afternoon Mr. van Loomis knocked at his door.

Wearily, steadily, with a pain at his heart, Mr. van Loomis had gone on with the settling of his affairs. Now Niu and Filipino had gone and the letters were ready for writing, he had to speak to Valentine. "I shall make a clean breast of it," said Mr. van Loomis. It would not be pleasant but he felt noble; he also felt slightly pressed. He had his eyes and ears and every sense alert for a plane or ship. "Even with a fishing boat, someone must come soon," said Mr. van Loomis. "I must have a settlement with Valentine," and he knocked at Valentine's door. There was no answer. Mr. van Loomis knocked again and opened the door and went in. Valentine was writing and looked up angrily.

"Valentine, I want to speak to you."

"Does it have to be now?" asked Valentine's look, but he said "Yes" dutifully and put down his pen. He looked down at his paper, a word caught his eyes and he picked up the pen and altered the word and started to write.

"I have something to tell you. A great deal to tell you," said Mr. van Loomis.

Valentine sighed and looked up, but in a moment he was reading again. He crossed out a line.

"I don't find it easy to tell you," said Mr. van Loomis.

"Mmmmm?" said Valentine.

"I had better go back to the beginning," said Mr. van Loomis. "I . . ." He cleared his throat. "First the Water Star. I . . . er . . . have to confess I played a trick on you, Valentine."

"Mmmm?" said Valentine.

"If you don't want to hear I won't tell you," said Mr. van Loomis with acerbity.

"Mmmmmmmmmmm?" said Valentine.

Mr. van Loomis went out and shut the door. Valentine

did not know he had gone. *"Act Two. Scene One,"* wrote Valentine. *"Emily's bedroom, the same evening."*

Mr. van Loomis found Mario waiting for him, awake and looking calmer and more kempt. Pheasant had sent him to wash and get a fresh cloth and comb his hair. Now he followed Mr. van Loomis into the study and stood by his desk. "Loomis?"

"Yes?" Mr. van Loomis spoke more gently now than he used to speak to Mario.

"Sir . . ."

Mr. van Loomis wondered who had taught Mario to call him "sir."

"Filipino say you-a go away. Take me with you," said Mario. "Not-a leave me here."

Mr. van Loomis thought for a moment and then he saw that he could not leave Mario, not to Niu, not alone here. Niu in power would be even more cruel than he, Mr. van Loomis, had unwittingly, or wittingly, been. Have I to keep Mario for the rest of my life? thought Mr. van Loomis. He supposed that he had. "I shall take you," he said with a sigh.

"Mario been fool," said Mario bitterly. "Now I-a wise. I-a come with you. Iré con usted y estaré con usted siempre! Gracias! Thank you, sir. Thank you, Loomis." Things were changing. Mario had not been known to thank anyone before.

Mr. van Loomis went back to his letters. He had a great many letters to write, cables to get ready, lists and accounts and plans. He was glad that he had kept the island in such perfect order, kept all his books up to date, books of estimated figures and actual stocks. He told Mario, "Don't let anyone disturb me." But Mario did not know what disturb meant. The first person he let in was Pheasant.

"Sah!"

"Not now," said Mr. van Loomis like Valentine, but Pheasant was insistent and said, "Sah! Please!"

"What *is* it Pheasant?" He saw she had news of McGinty. "Well, has he woken?" asked Mr. van Loomis. "How is he?"

Pheasant drew a deep breath. "He isn'!" she said.

Mr. van Loomis spun round in his chair. "Do you

212

mean he is *dead?*" Sweat broke out on him and he was cold with horror, but Pheasant rolled her eyes and shook her head. "I thought he was better," said Mr. van Loomis.

"He'm body bettah," said Pheasant, "But, sah, his sense done gone. Lawd a'might! Him lakh a chile. He jes' don' remembah."

Mr. van Loomis turned his chair away from her, back to his desk. She was telling him what he had known and did not want to hear. "Nonsense!" he said, and more loudly, "Nonsense." He pushed back his chair and went down the corridor and into McGinty's room. Pheasant hurried after him.

"See," said Pheasant. "Jes' look."

The room was not shaded now, the slats were open and the evening breeze came in; McGinty had been washed and his hair combed; his bed was scrupulously neat. He lay quite still, looking at his finger.

"McGinty."

McGinty looked up at Mr. van Loomis and smiled.

The fronds of the orange creeper stirred gently round the window and tapped and rustled. Pheasant went to the door and took from Niu a steaming bowl of soup. Webster tiptoed behind with a dish of fruit. McGinty smiled at Webster, who smiled back. He seemed lapped in good will and peace, but Mr. van Loomis stood there appalled.

"McGinty," he said sharply, but McGinty only looked up and smiled at him again, much as he had smiled at Webster.

"Are you . . . quite happy?" asked Mr. van Loomis. He did not know why he asked that except that McGinty looked happy.

"Yes, thank you," said McGinty politely and returned to look at his fingers.

"It come back," said Pheasant. "Fo' sho' it don' las'. It don' las', but Lawd-a-mighty!" said Pheasant.

Mr. van Loomis noticed that someone had put a little pot of marigolds by McGinty's bed. He knew the islanders believed that anyone touched with madness was holy and marigolds were sacred flowers. "Take those away," he said sharply to Pheasant.

213

Pheasant took them away, but next time Mr. van Loomis came to see McGinty they were there again.

Mr. van Loomis saw the servants and islanders glance at him and quickly away again when he met them: they scurried out of his way. "I am so potent," said Mr. van Loomis, "that they will be glad to be rid of me." But it did not sound like a joke. He had said it aloud so that Mario stared at him. Mr. van Loomis leaned his head on his hand and wearily shut his eyes. He felt he wanted to hide.

"Tsula."

Mr. van Loomis gave a snort of exasperation and opened his eyes. Niu was standing in front of him. "Is it only Tsula Valentine who must not be disturbed?"

"Tsula."

"What do you *want?*" said Mr. van Loomis irritably. "Is it something for the priest who brought medicine? Give him two pigeons."

"I have given him one pigeon, Tsula."

"Then?"

Niu swallowed, his lips moved silently, and then he said, "I can do everything but one thing," and he broke out, "Tsula, send Filipino to Zambun."

Filipino to Zambun! Mr. van Loomis sat with his pen in his hand, staring at Niu. When he spoke his voice was thin with astonishment. "Filipino? *Filipino!* To Zambun? Are you out of your mind, Niu? *You* ask me to do that?"

"Tsula, you once said . . ."

"I was only trying to frighten him."

"Don't frighten him, Tsula. Do it. Send him." Niu's breast heaved. "Send him away."

"But . . . he is the best boy on the island. There is no one like Filipino!"

"There is no one like Filipino." For the first time there was feeling in Niu's voice, a feeling of passionate alarm. "You heard him, Tsula. How can I stop him?"

"Nothing can stop Filipinos," said Mr. van Loomis. He heard an echo, a slow inexorable beat. "Nothing can stop Filipinos."

"There is Resurrection," pleaded Niu. "That is a good quiet boy. Everybody loves him and trusts him, but Filipino is nothing but trouble. Trouble! Trouble! Trouble!"

214

cried Niu passionately. "No quiet. No rest. Nothing but mischief. He is an uneasy boy, he stir us all up, all the time. To the young men he is like yeast. How can I stop that?"

"I will take him with me," said Mr. van Loomis.

"If you take him, Tsula, he will come back. You heard him. Nobody comes back from Zambun," said Niu.

"But he is your grandson!" said Mr. van Loomis, stupefied. Niu did not answer. Mr. van Loomis said, "You can't be afraid of a boy."

"I am afraid," said Niu calmly. "I am an old man and a boy is strong. You told us, we shall lose the island."

"He is only a boy. He will quieten."

"Resurrection is the quiet one, Tsula."

"But Filipino is a good boy."

"He is good." The admission fluttered from Niu like a sigh. Mr. van Loomis knew what that sigh meant. He had felt it with Filipino himself. He remembered the trousers, he remembered the coffee machine. "He is good but he makes bad," said Niu, and Mr. van Loomis had to agree. "If he goes while you are still here, Tsula . . ."

"I have told you, no!" said Mr. van Loomis. "You must learn to deal with Filipino. It's no good trying to stop him. If you put your hand on a water spring to stop it rising, what happens? It comes up somewhere else. What you ask is wicked, wicked!" said Mr. van Loomis with heat. "I'm not a devil or a witch doctor. Nor are you." Niu did not answer, and Mr. van Loomis said sharply, "You hear me, Niu." Niu nodded but there was no change in the hardness of his face. "You must deal with Filipino in your own way," said Mr. van Loomis, "when I put the island in your hands . . ." And he looked at Niu's hands thin and dark against his white cloth. He remembered with a feeling of coldness how he had thought of them peeling the silk-thin apple skins, rigging those cobweb boats, sending those arrows steadily to their dead-line mark. He saw the cock flapping its wings on the stone and the small dead hand. "Niu!" he said sharply.

"Yes, Tsula."

Don't be absurd, thought Mr. van Loomis, but his spine crept and he began to talk eloquently and earnestly to Niu of how he was to manage Filipino. Niu stood in front of him and said, "Yes, Tsula," "No, Tsula," but his face did not change or relax. The bones stood out under his dark skin and caught the light as if they were polished. He looks like a skull, thought Mr. van Loomis and shuddered.

〜〜〜〜〜 The afternoon had drawn out, the sun began to sink towards the sea, and the fantails flew down in the garden for the evening grain. The gardeners were watering the garden when Valentine stood up and stretched and went down to the beach and bathed. He came in and dressed, went into McGinty's room to look at him, but McGinty seemed to be asleep and Valentine came out on the veranda and called to Charis. "Come and play a game with me. I need something to clear my head. I have worked myself blind."

"I should think so," said Charis. "It poured out, didn't it?"

"I always work like a vomit," said Valentine cheerfully. He stood looking down at her. "I shall finish it now," he said contentedly. "I can see the end. Well, are you pleased with me?"

"How can I tell till I have seen the play?" said Charis, but she could not hide the pleased smile that touched the corners of her mouth.

Valentine bent down and kissed her. "It's a real play, Charis," he said and drew a deep, satisfied breath. "Be a good child and give me a stingo, a strong one, and then come and play with me."

They played chess; they had played every evening with the set in red and white ivory that Mr. van Loomis had brought from Spey. He and her mother, he told Charis, had played with it. Her hands touched these pieces, thought Charis. My mother! She remembered how she had wanted her that morning before Valentine came . . . almost as if I knew he were coming, she thought. She had needed her the night she and Valentine became engaged. I shall always need her, thought Charis. She hoped she herself would not die young. I want my children to have

216

a mother . . . and a father, she thought, looking at the top of Valentine's head as he bent over the board. Her mother could not have felt about her father as she, Charis, felt for Valentine. That was not possible, decided Charis. Poor little Mother married to Father, not married to Valentine! She picked up a knight and held it against her cheek.

"Come along," said Valentine.

Charis's bliss seemed too great for her to hold. She had to make a prick and let it out. "When I play chess with you, you cheat," she said severely.

"My dear love, I don't!"

Charis put her hand on his. "I don't mind if you cheat," she said, and Valentine leaned across the board and kissed her.

Mr. van Loomis, looking at them from the doorway, forgot his worries and heartache. "I don't care," said Mr. van Loomis. "I don't care what happens or what I did or didn't do. It was worth it," said Mr. van Loomis, and he added, like a pat on the back, "Sheer magic!"

~~~~~~~ On his way back from the house, Niu met Filipino. "Where are you going?" asked Niu.

"To swim."

Niu opened his mouth to forbid it and suddenly closed his lips. A spasm went over his face but he said nothing angry. "Go then," he said gently.

When Filipino had gone Niu went into the courtyard and sat down on his heels under the lichee tree and finished his water pipe. He did not speak and there was no expression in his eyes; they were looking on the ground or else past the garden and the house out to the glimpse of sea that could be seen from the courtyard; only once did he raise them, and that was when Resurrection came up from the garden carrying a basket of short-headed jasmine flowers for the evening garlands. Pheasant, tired out by watching McGinty, shocked by what had happened to him, exhilarated and sad at the prospect of parting from the island, was a little drunk on rum; Flora Annie, filled with the tremblings and speculations of a bride, had drunk

217

too; they were laughing and weeping and making a good deal of noise. Pheasant had sent Webster in to sit with McGinty; she laughed and drank at will. Resurrection filled her lap with flowers and waited for her permission to go.

Flora Annie looked at him and wondered if she should change her mind about the young boatman. Resurrection had never courted her but he was old enough to marry.

"When will you get a wife?" asked Flora Annie, and she said softly, "Why not now?" But Resurrection only smiled. He looked tall and strong standing there in his white cloth, his skin gold in the last sun.

"Ask your grandfather," coaxed Flora Annie.

Niu looked appraisingly at his second grandson; as Charis had seen, he saw how like Filipino the younger twin was: Filipino, but quiet, gentle, strong. He could not bear it and told Resurrection to go back to his work so curtly that Flora Annie thought he was angry with her and stopped giggling. Presently Niu put down the mouthpiece of his pipe, coiling it carefully on its holder, and went into his hut. The sun was getting low and the inside of the hut was dim, but Niu did not need a light. He went to the string bed in the corner and pulled a peg of wood out from one of the back posts, where it fitted so evenly that it might have been part of the post. In the hollow it hid was a tube made of bamboo stoppered with grass. He opened it and took out from it a tinier tube and three darts, each infinitesimal as an insect's leg, each feathered, with its end wrapped round in a long thin bamboo leaf. Delicately Niu unwound the leaf from one of them, taking care not to touch its quivering end, and fitted it to the tiny tube. He did not take more than one dart and, holding it like a cigarette, he stepped out of his hut and walked through the courtyard.

"Where are you going?" Pheasant called to him, her voice rollicking, and Golden Treasury stood up unsteadily and held out his arms. But Niu shook his head. "I'm going to call Filipino," he said, and he went down to the beach.

"Did you notice?" said Flora Annie. "Niu was not wearing his slippers."

⁓⁓⁓⁓ Filipino was exhausted with talking and planning and thinking; he was in a maze, a whirl, a heat of thought; if Niu had not let him go down and bathe he felt he would have broken apart. He wanted to lie in the sea and cool himself, to dive and forget with nothing but water in front of his eyes; to tumble and be tumbled and roll and stretch.

He let the great waves sweep over him and beat down on him; he rested on them and was borne in on their crests and plunged under them; he dived and rose and plunged and floated, let himself be swept out and swept in, be soaked and pounded, until his body began to overtake his mind and soothe it with real tiredness. He was glad Valentine was not with him; he felt he needed the whole sea, nothing less; he was filled with prowess and strength and glee. At last he swam in and lay exhausted but still tingling on the sand.

A little later he stood up and went to his hut and rubbed himself down; then he carefully and completely oiled his body and his hair and combed it, standing in front of the polished shell that served him as a mirror; then he put on a clean cloth; presently he would go up and fetch his garland.

In the growing dusk his cut-out pictures on the hut walls were hard to see. He was glad. They were wonderful, but now he was not in the mood for them. I don't want them always, thought Filipino. For some reason he was thinking of the song he had been making long ago when he went to meet Valentine and McGinty . . . but it wasn't long ago, thought Filipino in surprise; it was only a few days ago. What a way he had come since then. He picked his sitar off its peg where it had hung silent all these days and tuned it and gently ran his hand over the strings.

A song about snow did not seem to fit him now. He looked at the sun that was turning red as it neared the margin of the sea. I shall make a song about fire, thought Filipino, but he seemed to have lost his knack; no words would come, no melody, and he sighed. He had to finish dressing; Niu would be calling him to serve dinner, and he laid down the sitar and stepped outside his hut to pick a flower from the chema bush that grew there. The first flower he picked had a long sharp thorn and he threw it away on the sand behind the hut and picked another, putting it behind his ear.

Feeling clean and neat and at peace, the warm sand between his toes and his fresh cloth round his thighs, he sat down on his bed, facing the sea, and lit a cigar, one of the island green rolled ones that smelled pungent and satisfied his nostrils that were used to island smells. He laid his sitar across his knees and ran his hand over the strings. He put his cigar down carefully on the edge of the bed and began to play; words came easily into his mind, then: What is a litre? On the telephone you say, "Hullo. Hullo." The World's Best Books. Do you fly K.L.M.?

Filipino sighed. The song was lost and the sitar was silent. He took up his cigar again but left it smoking in his hand. Gradually peace stole into him again.

Niu heard the music as he came up behind the hut and paused. It was a long time since he had heard the sitar or Filipino singing and he smiled. Then he lifted his head sharply. Through the music came a small noise that was growing familiar on the island now, the insect droning of an aeroplane. His face hardened and he raised the little pipe.

Charis heard the plane too; she had at that moment lifted her queen to take Valentine's bishop; all her life she was to remember the feel of the small embossed carving of the little queen's crown, the smoothness of the head, its red colour against her white hand. She put the queen down. "Listen," she said.

Valentine listened. At first he heard only the sound of the surf; then he heard the sound of the aeroplane in the surf; then he heard the plane distinctly and alone.

McGinty heard it and did not hear it. Webster had run out and left him alone. McGinty lay looking at the vase of marigolds and they seemed to him a pretty colour. He heard the whirring, droning sound and a thought, an uneasy pain, reared itself in his head and he struggled to be clear but his head was too tender and he let it go. Per-

220

haps the noise was from Webster's grasshoppers, his fighting grasshoppers, that he had brought in their cage to show McGinty. Webster had promised McGinty a grasshopper for his own. McGinty lay and waited. Presently he forgot Webster and looked at the marigolds again.

In the courtyard Pheasant was singing, but more loudly than usual.

> *"Swi-ing loah, sweet char-ariot*
> *Comin' foah to carry me ho-oame,"*

sang Pheasant most suitably.

> *"Swing loah . . ."*

She too heard and looked up at the sky and, with a cry to Flora Annie, she jumped from her stool and a whole lapful of flowers showered down over Golden Treasury, who sat up and began to put them in his mouth.

In the study Mr. van Loomis sat upright and still in his chair. He had not yet called for a light and the study, with its shadowed walls and its faint smell of incense from the evening insect-smoking, seemed small, quiet, and sanctified. Outside the noise of the aeroplane filled the sky. Mario crept in and knelt down nervously by Mr. van Loomis's feet. He rolled alarmed eyes at Mr. van Loomis, who did not speak but put out his left hand without looking and patted Mario reassuringly on the shoulder, as McGinty had once patted him. Then he felt something touch his foot: Mario had bent and laid his great forehead on Mr. van Loomis's shoe.

Down on the beach Niu knew that he must hurry. At any moment Filipino might cease playing and hear the plane. Standing in the shadow of the hut, he lifted the blowpipe to his lips and filled his cheeks.

The droning of the plane grew louder. The sunset rays were far across the sky, and now they caught the brightness of a speck that shone silver and grew larger every second as it neared the island and took the shape of an aeroplane. But Filipino still had not heard it. He was absorbed in his music; he seemed to have passed these tormenting objects by and his song was growing in his head.

221

Perhaps, after all, thought Filipino, I shall write songs . . .

The shape of Filipino seemed to swell in front of Niu's eyes as he held his breath. "You can't stop Filipinos." He heard Mr. van Loomis say it, and he shifted his feet in the sand to stand more firmly and trod on the flower Filipino had thrown down and the thorn went into his slipperless feet. "Ouch!" said Niu, stung. A ping sounded in the air, and he stood looking down at the little dart, upright and quivering, fixed harmlessly in the sand.

The music of the sitar had stopped. Filipino raised his head. The air all round him was filled with the sound of the aeroplane's great hum as she circled round the bay, her huge wings shining. "A Catalina flying boat!" cried Filipino and dropped the sitar and sped for his canoe.

Niu let him go. He stood and looked at the spent dart and a thought quivered in his mind that was tense and hurt with the thing he had tried to do. He did not know what the thought was, but he had failed to kill Filipino, and he looked at the dart with puzzled eyes. It was the first time he had missed; he did not understand it. The thought quivered in his mind: on the island they believed that a spirit was more potent when it was dead; in that case, was it better not to have killed Filipino? Should he have killed Resurrection? I don't know, thought Niu. Perhaps I shall not live long enough to know; perhaps I shall see it before I die. Baffled, he nodded his head, which meant, in the island way, that he did not know. What will happen now? he thought. The breeze blew in the palms and the scent of the chema flowers filled the breeze. What will happen will happen, thought Niu. He bent and picked up the dart.

A sound behind him made him turn. It was Resurrection who had come after him with his slippers. A great irritation filled Niu. "Who told you to come down here?" he said. "Who said you could leave your work? Lazy, tiresome boy!" He slipped the dart back into the blowpipe for safety; having been blown, it was out of true and could never be used again. He had wasted it for nothing. Filipino's flying figure had reached the sea. Muttering to himself, Niu put the pipe away into his sleeve and looked sharply at Resurrection. He could not tell what Resurrection had seen; the boy did not speak but knelt down and submissively but firmly fitted the slippers onto Niu's feet. In spite of himself, Niu felt soothed. He stood, resting his knuckles on Resurrection's shoulder, and together they watched the flying boat circle to the sea.

"Serendipity asks for you," said Resurrection. "He says, what shall he do?"

"We must get the welcome ready," said Niu, but he did not move. He stayed leaning on the broad young shoulder; then he gave Resurrection a sharp kick. "Get up. Why are you kneeling there like an owl?" he said. "Tell Serendipity to blow up the fires. Tell Orange Flower to open the rooms. Pheasant and Flora Annie must see to the beds and towels; you must bring flowers. There are the fish I was keeping for tomorrow in the kitchen pool; catch them and clean them. Three chickens will do," said Niu, considering. "Jéo is having a feast; he will have a stuffed kid at least. Send one of the boys to Jéo. Webster must go for fresh curd. We must have fruit. Wait! I shall come. Wait! Send Filipino . . ."

He checked himself and Resurrection waited. "No. Leave Filipino," said Niu.

CHAPTER XXII

THE Catalina came down on the sea, sending up a shower of water; the drops shone red in the sunset light as they fell, and, as the plane with her great wings rocked on the sea, she was stained too, from nose to tail.

In the study Mr. van Loomis stood up and went to the window. After a moment he said to Mario, "Go down to the jetty and bring the new Tsulas to me."

He could make out dots of men on the flying boat and could see the island boats putting out to her. A hubbub of excited voices came to him from the shore, and once again the servants were running the forbidden way through the garden. He heard Niu scolding and calling and knew that rooms would be prepared, the cooking fires blaze up, and that there would be a fit dinner for the guests.

He saw Mario go lumbering past the morning glory to the steps. Am I, thought Mr. van Loomis, to exchange my quick light messenger for this poor shambling creature? He sighed and supposed he was. "But I shall not need Filipino," said Mr. van Loomis aloud. "I have nothing to order now. Nothing to create." He went back to his desk and fetched his glasses, and he saw Charis and Valentine walking arm in arm along the jetty, waiting to greet the strangers from the plane. Charis, he thought with satisfaction, is almost experienced now. Through his glasses he could see the first canoe reach the flying boat and a man climb down from her to meet it. He put the glasses on the table.

"It is over," said Mr. van Loomis. "This is where I put down my little stick."